THE TRAVELER'S STONE

CORINNE AARSEN

978-1-9993810-7-3 (mobi)
978-1-9993810-2-8 (e-pub)
978-1-9993810-3-5 (paperback)

This novel is dedicated to my three brothers,
Richard, Jan, and Brian.
As kids, you didn't always treat your little sister
as well as she thought she deserved,
but I sure love you all now.

PROLOGUE

*J*once believed the confrontation between my sixteen-year-old niece Kimberly and my sister Marilyn on the day of our brother's funeral was the sole catalyst for launching Kimberly and I into a world of intrigue and betrayal for which we were woefully unprepared. If Marilyn hadn't said what she had, if Kimberly hadn't stormed out of the house when she did, or if I had not followed my niece into the woods, then maybe what followed wouldn't have happened.

Now, looking back, I realize the bizarre circumstances that unfolded that day had little to do with my actions or those of my niece and sister; rather, the true catalyst was a meeting twenty-two years before when three captivating children appeared unexpectedly in my life—and vanished just as abruptly.

And now I write, not because anyone will read these words—they are solely for my eyes—but because doing so breathes life into my memories, *breathes life into Kimberly*. Indeed, the ink is not even dry; yet, my words are lifting off the page and fashioning themselves into the moving images of those astonishing events that irrevocably changed our lives. As I scratch ink onto the page, I feel as if Kimberly is peering over my shoulder just as I once

1

hovered over hers on that long-ago day when the Diviner's vision gave ease to my troubled heart. Her irrepressible vitality is stirring the air around me. And her nearness, shadowy and ethereal though it may be, allows me to fuel the hope that she is indeed alive, and that one day—*one day soon, I pray to the gods*—we will reunite.

PART I

REPRIEVE

CHAPTER 1

*I*n my world, I'd never sought out a psychic. I wasn't sure if I believed anyone even had extrasensory abilities. But here in the Lands of Vendome in a world I couldn't name, I desperately wanted to believe the Diviner Julitha had the ability to see into my world. More than anything, I needed to know if my niece was safe at home and if I would soon join her.

"Can you truly see whether Kimberly is back in my world?" I asked Julitha. We were sitting in the shade of a giant oak tree in the beautiful gardens that surrounded the Diviner's small cottage. I'd been in her company for barely an hour but already my misery over Lox's devastating betrayal had begun to lift. "And can you tell me more about how you saw me getting home? That was true, wasn't it? You didn't make that up?" Now that the seed of hope had been planted, I couldn't bear for it to be extinguished.

Julitha spoke in a gentle, reassuring tone. "Be assured, Meredith. You *will* return to your world. Here, give me your hands."

I wiped my fingers, sticky from the delicious honeyed bun I'd consumed, on my napkin before allowing the Diviner to clasp my hands in hers. She tilted her head slightly as she gazed intently at me. I'd expected her to speak, but she remained silent.

When she finally released my hands and sat back in her chair, I demanded, "Well?" She didn't appear offended by my severe tone, and instead regarded me with concentrated interest.

"When I look for the thread that leads to your niece, I am blocked by your anxiety, anger, and resentment. These emotions make you resistant to my...presence. But do not fret," she added hastily, briefly resting her cool fingertips on my forearm. "We will be successful later, when you are calmer and thus conducive to allowing me to follow the connections beyond yourself. I promise you."

I bit back the words of dissatisfaction I wanted to fling at Julitha, reminding myself that she wasn't accountable for my current unwanted circumstances. Being stranded in this alternate world was all on Lox. Julitha wasn't to blame. She'd given me a gift. Her first words to me—*you will return to your own world*—were beads threaded on a lifeline of hope. I was clutching this gift with both hands.

"Share with me what you have experienced so far in these Lands," she encouraged as she topped up my glass of chilled tea.

In the end, Julitha's sympathetic ear and inherent kindness caused me to divulge my tale in far more detail and emotional depth than I'd intended. I told her everything, including the events that led up to my brother's tragic death and the circumstances that placed Kimberly and me in the woods behind my sister's home. By the time I finished, I'd consumed three glasses of tea and regained my appetite. I did not hesitate to reach for another bun.

I knew my tone was peevish when I spoke. "Lox had no right to pull me from my world, especially with no way to send me home. It's not fair. I didn't ask for any of this."

Given her sympathetic ear, I expected Julitha to share my condemnation of Lox. Instead, she looked at me as if debating whether to respond, then turned the conversation in an unexpected direction.

"Have you not been suffering from melancholy since long before your brother's death? And did you not tell me you have been yearning to be free of a life that did not satisfy you? Well, here you are." Julitha waved her hand, palm up, in a graceful gesture. "An escape, of a sort. Or, at the very least, an opportunity to gain clarity about what path you will deliberately set yourself upon as you move toward your future."

I scowled as I dribbled honey on my bun. "That's absurd! I might have been wishing for life to be different, yes. But believe you me, this is not what I had in mind."

"Were you specific with what you did have in mind?"

"But how... I didn't...no, I wasn't specific."

"Failing to define *and focus* on your specific desires and how achieving them will make you feel only allows events to occur in your life by default rather than by intention. But no matter," Julitha reassured. "All is well. You said yourself that your niece had begun healing during her time here in a way that could not have happened so quickly had she remained in your world."

"That's true," I conceded, biting into the bun, distracted momentarily by the delectable flavours in the honey. Julitha had earlier shared that she and her bees had a special understanding. Whatever it was, it made for scrumptious honey.

Julitha smiled encouragement. "And you have reason to feel optimistic about what your future holds, yes? A new path has opened up? One filled with hope, and one that promises deep personal satisfaction and fulfillment?"

"On condition I make it home, yes."

"You *shall* return. Have no fear in that regard, Meredith."

I savored my mouthful of food as I contemplated her words. After consuming the last morsel on my plate, leaned back in my chair and admitted, "I do feel hopeful, Julitha. Thanks to you. But what about Kimberly?" My worry would never fade until I could see for myself that my niece was safe and well. "Are you sure you will be able to 'see' her? Should we try again? Oh! This is hers." I

7

retrieved the shirt I'd draped over the back of the chair next to me and held it out, thinking of what Lox had told me about using my scrapbook and polaroid to add to the power of his 'call'. "Would it help?"

"Very likely, yes," she said, without taking the shirt. "But we shall make the attempt later. Please trust me in this, Meredith," she added when she saw I was about to argue. "We will delay only a little longer. And we *will* be successful, I promise you. Now, tell me again what Hiltha divined about you."

I laid the shirt on my lap as I thought of the old crone Kimberly and me had encountered in Conraz's hunting lodge on the day of our arrival in these Lands. So much had happened since then, yet it wasn't difficult to recall her words, which I shared with Julitha. "She said the one who called me was not the one who found me. Obviously Lox performed the calling and Fredryk found me, or rather abducted me." I added in a disgruntled tone. "Or perhaps Conraz is the one who found us. Or maybe even Jazper. That part hardly matters now. She also said the Dust of those who came before opened a path for my destiny, whatever that means. But what she said about another Traveler is the intriguing part. Her exact words were, *you must find the Traveler. He shares your path and is more than what he seems.* She also cautioned me to 'beware' as if there was some kind of danger in all this."

I'd been staring down and fiddling with Kimberly's shirt, but now stilled my hands and lifted my eyes to meet Julitha's rapt gaze. "Do you think what Hiltha said is reliable? Or was she a crazy old crone like Conraz claimed?"

"Of course she is reliable." For the first time, Julitha's tone was severe. "One is not granted the title of Diviner if one's Gift is anything less than accurate and reliable, although it often takes time to gain clarity from our visions. You have already been told that, among Diviners, there is a great variety of Gifts, but I shall explain further. We all See in different ways and access our Gift through different means. No one of us is alike. Here, give me your hands again." Julitha rested her forearms on the table, her palms facing up. "You are much more relaxed now. And, although it is still premature for me to look for the thread that leads to your beloved niece, perhaps I can Divine more details of your path while you remain in these Lands."

It was a completely different experience this time. As soon as I placed my hands in hers, I was enthralled, so much so that had a snarling tiger appeared from behind her chair I do not think I would have wavered from the intensity of her gaze.

Julitha remained silent for an extended moment. When she did speak, she enunciated her words with great deliberation as if that would puzzle out their meaning.

"The one you despise will unlock the final door to your heart; yet, this one cannot be trusted."

Despite the shivers her words sent down my spine and my inability to withdraw my gaze from hers, I dismissed her comment as irrelevant. She was referring to Lox. He had broken my heart and shattered my trust. I did not need a fortune teller to warn me against him.

She inhaled deeply through her nose before continuing. "The Traveler in West Scapah…he…his back is turned. I cannot *See* him clearly; yet, he *is* the means of your return."

I tingled with anticipation at the thought of meeting this other Traveler and finally going home. I didn't want to interrupt Julitha, but I made a mental note to tell her later that Lox had tricked me into believing the Traveler in West Scapah was an imposter.

"The heart of the one who loves you is true," Julitha continued, gripping my hands tighter. *"The fineness in his being shines like a beacon through the cracks of his broken soul."*

Julitha had been looking at me in a far-sighted way while she 'divined'. On these last words, she dropped her gaze and released my hands.

I wanted to ask the meaning of her last statement, but I was distracted by her sudden gaunt look. Dark circles had appeared under her eyes where none had been a few minutes before. Her perfect, creamy complexion had lost its glow. "Julitha, are you okay?"

"Oh-kay?"

"Oh, sorry. That means, 'are you fine' or 'are you feeling alright'. It's a catch-all kind of word that we use a lot in my world."

"Ah. Then yes, I am oh-kay. It is simply that intense Divining such as I just performed is draining. If I look a little pale, it is normal. I shall soon recover. Have you had enough to eat and drink?" she asked, nodding at the food and refreshments on the table.

"Yes, thank you. Did you see anything of Kimberly's whereabouts?"

"No, but neither did I look. My dear Meredith, do not let that concern you," she said with a tinge of impatience in response to my frown. "I promise you, I will See her. I shall prepare a potent mixture of herbs for myself that will enhance my Sight. And I shall make use of her item of clothing as a talisman of sorts. But, for now, let us take respite. I will set up the hipbath so that you can soak away your cares. We shall both indulge in a nap and wake refreshed and rejuvenated. Then I will take you to the beach. The sea air never fails to ease one's troubles."

"The *beach?* You mean we're close to the ocean?" Even as I spoke, I realized the air felt and smelled different. I'd been too distracted to contemplate why. I now recognized the tangible freshness that signified salt air.

"Yes. An element of my craft is creating and selling amulets and wind chimes blessed with healing charms, whether for emotional, spiritual, or physical ills. Most of these I assemble from shells I collect on the beach."

"I saw wind chimes hanging by your front entrance. You made those?"

"No. Those were made by my mother and grandmother, also

Diviners. They are infused with soothing comfort so all who enter Spring Willow Cottage are granted at least a modicum of relief from their troubles."

The dark cloud of despair that had enveloped me since Lox's devastating news had indeed dispersed as if snatched by a passing ocean breeze. I was far less troubled now than when I'd first arrived. But I was certain my improved spirits had more to do with Julitha's insistence of my eventual return—and her warmth and kindness—than with her wind chimes. I said nothing to dispute her claim, though.

We both stood and began stacking the used dishes on the tray. "I would love a bath. Thank you, Julitha. And clean clothes." Then added under my breath, "Deodorant would be a bonus."

CHAPTER 2

*A*fter a bath in a small copper tub and a nap in a cozy bedroom in the attic, I woke feeling surprisingly light-hearted. Julitha's insistence that I would return home had ignited a flare of hope at the core of my being. Perhaps I was naive to put faith in Julitha's assurances; regardless, I chose to cling to the lifeline she offered. At the very least, my renewed sense of optimism would give me the strength to cope with journeying to West Scapah in the company of Lox and Fredryk, men I'd hoped never to see again. No more than two moons, Julitha had said. I could put up with my undesirable traveling companions for two months. After all, I had put up with my unpleasant ex-husband for far longer.

I dressed in the clothes Julitha provided. They were as pretty as she'd promised and of exceptional quality. The silk chemise under my shirt felt lovely against my skin, although it was decidedly odd to be without my modern, underwired bra, which Julitha had taken away to soak. Over this chemise I wore a printed cotton tunic in coral and ivory around which I wrapped a wide leather alabaster belt that was as soft as butter. The taupe skirt was made from a fine damask linen with a jacquard print. Despite the fact that Julitha was taller and slimmer than me, the clothes fit much better than those Aster had provided, although I had to leave the top button of the skirt unfastened and, had I not slipped on my boots with their square heels, the hem of the skirt would've dragged on the floor.

As I wound my way down the narrow, wooden staircase carrying Kimberly's shirt, I heard Julitha call out to me and made my way toward the sound of her voice. I found her at the back of the cottage in a sunroom seated at an expansive workstation. Its surface was covered in thousands of shells, small and large, sorted by the subtlest of hues.

Seeing her in the midst of her creative endeavor and wearing her beautiful clothes caused a flood of longing to wash through me. It had been years since I'd nurtured my own creativity. When I got home—and it was when, not if, thank god—I would leave my unfulfilling job and pursue a new career in textile manufacture and design. And I would not allow my well-intentioned but over-bearing sister to deter me.

I was relieved to see that Julitha seemed to have recovered her health. She stood up when I entered the room, smiling in delight as she took in my altered appearance. I let her take one of my hands in hers, surprised to find myself easily returning her smile. Spending a few days with the open-hearted Diviner would not be a hardship.

"You look much restored, Meredith. And lovely clothes can make all the difference, do you not agree?"

"Julitha," I exclaimed as a wonderful idea occurred to me. "Why don't you come with us to West Scapah?"

But she'd begun shaking her head before I even finished voicing my question. "I could be away from those to whom I provide care for an extended time, yes, but not without significant preparation first. Your journey to West Scapah will take weeks.

My dear Traveler, there is no need to look so worried," she added when I pulled a face. "I am certain, after you have had a few days to rest, you will find the prospect of spending time in Lord Loxley's company much less daunting than you do now."

I had to make a concerted effort not to sound churlish as I responded, "I highly doubt that."

"Come. Put aside your troubles," Julitha instructed in a matter-of-fact tone. "Shall we stroll on the beach?"

"Okay. But shouldn't we try to see something of Kimberly's whereabouts first?"

She shook her head as she released my hand and took Kimberly's shirt from me, although she merely draped it over the back of a chair before retrieving a heavy canvas sack. "We will have a much better chance of success later. Do not fret, Meredith."

Although I did not understand what would be different later, I allowed myself be comforted by her unwavering reassurance.

Once out of the cottage, Julitha linked her free arm in the crook of my elbow, a gesture I was unused to but one that seemed so natural for her. We made our way along a wide graveled path through her back garden and into a sloping copse of tall evergreen trees. Soon after we entered the woods, I glimpsed the sea through the branches and heard the rhythmic sound of the surf. When the path descended sharply into a narrow, hairpin turn, Julitha released my arm and took the lead.

The panoramic beauty that greeted us when we stepped out of the trees momentarily took my breath away. I stopped in my tracks and filled my lungs with the invigorating sea air, feasting my eyes on the magnificent beauty before me. A white beach swathed in early afternoon sunlight stretched ahead of us in a long and gentle arc. The tide was out but, being a prairie girl, I had no capacity to determine whether it was still retreating or if it was on its way back in. Sea birds big and small, some with long narrow beaks and others like the gulls of my world, were either floating on the breeze or feeding in tidal pools. On the surface of the water past a line of breaking waves about half a mile from shore were a handful of small boats in which the occupants appeared to be fishing.

"What a beautiful spot, Julitha. You must love it here."

"I do, indeed," she chimed, handing me an empty cloth sack. "For whatever treasures you spot," she added.

As we ambled forward I realized we were walking on layer upon layer of shells. The crunching sound of our footfalls reminded me of the day Kimberly had stormed out of my sister's kitchen, broken china crunching unpleasantly under her heavy soles. Had that really only been a week ago?

"Collect any that take your fancy," Julitha instructed. "I mostly incorporate whole shells in my designs, but some of the broken pieces have unusual hues. I will be elated with whatever specimens catch your eye. Knowing they were collected by a Traveler will only enhance their capacity to provide healing."

I wanted to correct Julitha's misplaced assumption that, regardless of what Travelers of Old were renown for, this particular Traveler had no such power.

When Julitha asked me to recount the childhood adventures I'd shared with Rikka, Jaybex, and Lox, I didn't hesitate. While I shared my tale, I kept my eyes on the ground, stooping and picking up any shell that caught my attention. After distractedly examining it, I would either place it in my bag or discard it. The Diviner did the same.

"Julitha, is the Traveler in West Scapah really able to send me home?" I asked after relaying my tale. Hope was good, but belief was better, and I so badly wanted to believe.

"Yes," she answered simply. "Next you will ask me how. And that, my dear Traveler, I cannot answer. However, I do know that the *how* of it shall be revealed to you in due time. It always is, is it not? Is that not how life is presented to each and every one of us?"

Julitha noticed my frown and chuckled. "Be at ease, Meredith, for I am not speaking in riddles. Allow me to expand in the hope that you understand a little more about my craft and thus establish firm faith about what I See in regards to your path.

"The purpose of the Diviners' craft in these Lands is to blur the lines between our physically manifested world and our non-physical spiritual world; in so doing, I attempt to See—and I say 'see' but 'feel' would be more accurate when describing my Gift—from the broader perspective of my higher spiritual self. From this vantage point, I am given a sense of your potential paths, somewhat like a detailed map." The Diviner tilted her head as she gazed unfocused at the shell in her hand. "It's as if I am above a forest and, despite the canopy of leaves, I am able to see all the paths, large and small, that wind through the trees." She rested her gaze on me and gave a nod, as if satisfied with the image her words had created. "Your most logical route to what you desire most is illuminated for me as if by a string of lanterns. But unlike permanent paths and roads in a forest, each choice you make each moment of each day revises your potential pathways, but all of them lead to your future. Thus, the direction of one's life is always shifting from moment to moment on account of an unending number of variables that impact the plethora of options available in any given moment."

Julitha's explanation seemed overly heavy with philosophy. I didn't find it especially helpful. But it didn't matter. What mattered was her repeated reassurances about my eventual return. I tucked the shell I'd been examining into my bag.

"For you, my dear Traveler," she continued, "what I saw—what I felt—is your most likely course toward that which you desire most, to return home. The brightest path towards this desire leads to the Traveler in West Scapah. And your guide on this long journey is Lord Loxley."

I discarded my next shell, wrinkling my nose in distaste at the thought of being in Lox's company for weeks on end. It would be worth it, though, if the end result of the journey meant I would be home and reunited with Kimberly. I forced myself to re-focus on what Julitha was telling me.

"The connection between you and the Traveler feels brightly lit; yet, at the same time, full of shadows. I am intrigued by this paradox. And I am indeed tempted to travel with you and see for myself the enigma that is the Traveler."

My tone was hopeful when I asked, "Do you mean you are re-considering? Will you come with us?"

The Diviner chuckled as if I'd said something amusing. "Only tempted. My work is here."

"Do you think this Traveler in West Scapah has Traveler's Dust?"

Julitha's brow wrinkled as she examined the pink-hued shell she held. "I do not know, but it seems unlikely. The Astromancer in the Western Duchy has never been a Keeper of the Dust. Nor do I know how it came to be that West Scapah even hosts an esteemed Traveler. But have a little faith, Meredith. All shall be revealed to you in a manner and at the time when you are ready to receive the clarity you seek. Upon arrival in West Scapah, and with the help of Lord Loxley, you can reassess and determine your best course of action. You can trust him, you know," she added when she saw me grimace. "He is a good man, despite the wrong you perceive he has done to you. His intentions are pure and his desire to protect the people of these Lands is unparalleled."

I tossed aside the shell I'd been examining. "But, Julitha, when you did my 'reading', you said *the one I despise cannot be trusted*. And Lox told me the Traveler in West Scapah was an imposter. Now you're telling me to trust Lox?"

Julitha laughed in unsuppressed delight. "My dear Traveler! Your Lord Loxley is *not* the one you despise."

"What?" I halted and stared at her.

She stopped as well. Still smiling, she tilted her head to the side as she studied me. "Although I do not know to whom I was referring when I Divined that statement, I do know two things; first, that the identity of the person to whom I was referring will become clear to you at a given time in the future; and, second, that it was not to Lord Loxley I was referring when I spoke those particular words."

"It wasn't?"

Julitha chuckled at my astonishment, then gestured for us to resume walking.

"It is evident that you currently despise Lord Loxley's decision to Call you here. But Meredith, his one action—which you have interpreted as abominable from your slanted perspective—does not represent the whole of him any more than one of your regretful decisions represents the whole of you. You have convinced yourself that he is wholly unworthy of your esteem. Furthermore, your devastation at this turn of events is heightened precisely because you held him in high regard prior to discovering the circumstance of your Calling. No one enjoys seeing their hero fall from a pedestal. But, Meredith, heroes do not belong on pedestals. No one does. Truly, your feelings of disdain, although valid, are misplaced."

Had Julitha made this observation when I'd first arrived, I would've argued with her. But now, only a handful of hours after meeting this remarkable woman, I instead found myself contemplating her astonishing assertion. Could I separate Lox's choice to bring me here with no way to send me home from the whole of the man himself? *Don't throw the baby out with the bathwater* type of approach? I didn't know if I was capable of doing that.

I stared unseeingly at the shell I held as I digested Julitha's words. In the deepest recesses of my heart, I could acknowledge that Lox was not a cruel and heartless man. But he *had* wronged me. What he'd done was unpardonable. Wasn't it? Or was the Diviner right? Perhaps it was his *decision* I despised. Regardless, I had no intention of ever forgiving him. I absently slipped the shell into my canvas sack.

Julitha interrupted my pensive reflections.

"Feelings are nothing if not complex, are they not? The incredible range of human emotion fascinates me. It is why I love what I do."

"Complex, yes. Fascinating? I'm not so sure."

"Shall I tell you what I have personally come to know about the ever so fascinating Lord Loxley?" Julitha asked.

I was afraid this arresting woman was about to divulge particulars of a past love affair with Lox, details I had no wish to know. I scrambled in my mind for a way to change the subject. When the Diviner began chuckling, at my expense it seemed, I stared at her in astonishment.

"Rest easy, my dear Traveler. I am not, nor ever have been, one of the many women captivated by Lord Loxley—although I acknowledge there is much about the man to inspire such adulation from our fair sex. It has become clear to me during our short time together that you are very drawn to him, yes?"

I stooped to retrieve a shell, deliberately refraining from meeting her gaze. Lox was a compelling, attractive, intriguing, charismatic, and incredibly sexy man. I knew I couldn't convincingly deny my attraction for him so I remained silent.

"Do not be alarmed, Meredith," she said. "Your feelings would not be obvious to any but me. A well-honed intuition is a consequence of my vocation." Julitha hesitated, as if debating whether to share her thoughts. She gave a small shrug and continued, "Although more than four years have passed since I last saw Lord Loxley, I would hazard a guess he reciprocates your deep affection."

I knew he was as attracted to me as I was to him. That had

become clear at the felter's cottage. But he cared more for his selfish pursuits than for my happiness. "His feelings don't matter one iota," I retorted, finally willing to meet her penetrating gaze. "I'll be gone at the first opportunity. And anyway, he's married."

Before I lost my nerve, I decided to ask Julitha what she knew of his marriage. "Have you met Lox's wife? What's she like?"

Julitha snorted. "That bitch?"

I stopped and stared at the Diviner, gob-smacked by her crude language. Up to this point, she'd been the epitome of refinement.

She saw the look on my face and burst into laughter. "It is not jealousy that makes me describe her so, my dear Traveler. As I said, I am not one of those women who adore Lord Loxley. But I understand why many do." She touched my arm, urging me to continue walking. "But he is no more in love with his wife than I am. She is a loathsome woman, wicked to the core, and a traitor. She should be tried for sedition and then banished back to the Garden Archipelago from whence she came."

"Wow." My eyes sightlessly scanned the beach as I tried to picture this version of Lox's wife. "Wait." I stopped again as I realized the full extent of what Julitha had just shared. "He's not in love with her?"

"No, thank the gods." She gestured toward a large, bleached driftwood log. "Come, let us sit for a time. I have a jar of sweet tea in my bag and some scones. While we rest, I shall regale you with the tale of Lord Loxley's treacherous and despicable wife. Perhaps many men have been so ill used, but none, I dare say, deserved it less than your Lord Loxley. And, if I may be so bold as to hazard yet another guess, I am certain my tale will inspire within you a great deal of compassion for this man, for he has been sorely wronged. Perhaps you'll even find it in your heart to forgive him."

"Yeah, not likely," I muttered.

While Julitha took a seat on the log, looking elegant and refined despite the rustic setting, I hunkered down on the beach and rested my back against the driftwood. I unzipped my boots and nestled the soles of my bare feet against the sun-warmed, smooth shells. Then, with a jar of warm tea in my hand and sampling more of Julitha's delicious confectionaries, I tucked my legs under my skirt and angled myself so I could regard the Diviner as she shared the tale of Lox's doomed marriage.

CHAPTER 3

*D*iviners must never interfere in personal decisions or cajole those they serve to choose one path over another. Rather, a Diviner's role is to convey only what insights are received, whether they provide clarity at the time of sharing or not. The recipients are never hindered by a Diviner's personal opinion and can thus freely choose and shape the trajectory of their own paths.

As a Diviner, Julitha served the people of her district, a three-day journey from the royal city of East Scapah. She was content in her seaside cottage serving the families who lived simple, uncomplicated lives and made their living as tradesmen and fishermen. But after three consecutive nights of the same disturbing dream that foreshadowed unspeakable tragedy descending on their Lands, she knew she must travel to East Scapah and request a personal audience with the Chancellor.

Upon arrival at Court four days later, she was informed that Lord Loxley was entertaining a delegation of diplomats at his country estate a further half-day's journey away. Finally arriving at Hawkwood Heath late that same afternoon, and because of her status as Diviner, Julitha was soon granted an audience with the high-ranking leader. Although he'd been entertaining a dozen or so guests on his large, sweeping lawn—where the ladies nibbled on dainty sandwiches and the men played a game with sticks, colored balls, and nets—Lord Loxley excused himself to meet his unexpected guest.

Julitha hid her nerves as best she could as she and the Chancellor began to stroll on the pathways that wound through his expansive gardens. Summoning the confidence that came as a result of her status as Diviner, she relayed her fear that turbulence would come to these Lands if an enigmatic foreign lord from the Lands Beyond the Veil of Mist—an obscure region shrouded in great mystery and ancient animosity—would be allowed to settle with his mysterious entourage in the royal city of East Scapah. Julitha was relieved when Lord Loxley received this information with due seriousness. He informed her that the court-appointed Diviner had also spoken of the potential for doom if the Grand Duchess trusted these foreigners who had not yet darkened their shores.

Emboldened by his acceptance of her counsel, Julitha then relayed the secondary information from her dream concerning a secretive, exotic woman who hailed from the Garden Archipelago, a grouping of islands in the northern Indigo Seas. Julitha warned the Chancellor to beware of this strikingly beautiful woman who was shamelessly selfish and artfully manipulative, and whose sole goal was to permanently attach herself to an abundant and endless flow of wealth. Julitha had not been shown anything specific, she admitted, but she felt certain this woman had the potential to bring ruin to him personally as well as disaster to the Duchy he served.

By this time in their conversation, they'd come full circle and were very near where Lord Loxley's guests continued to entertain themselves on his lawn. It wasn't until the Chancellor stopped walking and addressed her that Julitha realized he was furious, not about the content of her message but at her audacity to deliver it. It was then she realized her mistake. The dread she'd felt since first having the dream had only partially been founded on the content of the message; her trepidation had actually been due to her intuitive knowledge that her message—at least about the woman—would be delivered too late.

In a clipped tone, the Chancellor proceeded to rebuke Julitha for her unwelcome interference in his personal life, dismissing her concern and instructing her on the boundaries within which a Diviner divined. His tone and words made her feel like a child. Rather than argue or interrupt, Julitha turned her gaze toward his high-ranking guests. Her eyes were drawn to a woman dressed in an embroidered polonaise costume with a frilled skirt in a shade of crimson that complemented her platinum locks and perfect skin. The creature was incandescently beautiful, and Julitha knew she was regarding the woman about whom she'd dreamt and who would be Lord Loxley's downfall.

When she took her leave of Lord Loxley, Julitha's heart was heavy with disappointment as the Chancellor was already well caught in the conniving woman's intricately crafted web. The fact that he was already besotted had been plain for anyone to see; yet Julitha, a Diviner, had failed to grasp his state-of-mind prior to sharing her warning. She wasn't unduly troubled about having angered the Chancellor. It was unlikely she'd ever see him again. But she was uneasy on account of the vague and undefined feelings of doom that lurked like an invisible menacing shadow around the woman, whose named she later learned was Toriah.

Julitha journeyed back to East Scapah, arriving late in the evening. She planned to enjoy an extended visit with her cousin, a bachelor in his forties who lived above his apothecary shop. Although she'd been expecting the news, Julitha had been disappointed when, three days later, court-appointed bellmen went through the streets announcing that, in two weeks' time, the inhabitants of the royal city would celebrate Lord Loxley's marriage union with the Lady Toriah.

Julitha had fully intended to spend two handfuls of days at her cousin's in the bustling city that she rarely visited. But she chose to depart after only half that time on account of a disturbing misunderstanding with the apothecary's assistant, a young woman named Prin. The assistant had been trying unsuccessfully to catch the eye of a certain young man who, upon meeting the beautiful, copper-haired Diviner, had become obsessed with Julitha. Caught between the young man's unwanted advances and Prin's vicious dislike, and with her cousin incapable of doing much more than wring his hands in utter helplessness at the unexpected drama, Julitha had cut her visit short.

Julitha later learned that, within days of her departure from East Scapah and as foreseen, the Grand Duchess did indeed receive an unprecedented delegation of merchants, ambassadors, and explorers from the Lands Beyond the Veil of Mist who'd arrived in a flotilla of ships with colorful sails. In an effort to mend historic animosities and build profitable trade relations, the Grand Duchess welcomed them, hosting multiple court functions and formal celebrations, including the wedding of her cousin to the enchanting Toriah. In due course, the foreign lord and his delegation departed the royal city. Julitha had breathed a sigh of relief when she'd received news of their leave-taking, although she hadn't been able to ignore the niggling worry about this unprecedented delegation. Much later, she finally understood her underlying concern when she heard news that the foreign delegation had been welcomed by the Grand Duke in the Western Duchy. But as the distant royal city of West Scapah was located in the far northwest corner of The Lands of Vendome, Julitha allowed her concerns about these foreigners to wane.

But the true reason Lord Loxley despised Julitha, she explained, was not on account of her warning him about the woman from the Garden Archipelago; rather, it was about what occurred many months later. As he was wont to do after weeks of functions at court, the Chancellor and his new bride relocated to his country estate of Hawkwood Heath. Soon after settling in the idyllic countryside, rumors began to spread that the marriage he'd so imprudently embarked upon showed signs of strain. The frivolously passionate young woman he'd married despised the tame and quiet existence of the country and longed to return to the glitter and excitement of daily life at court.

At about that time, Julitha received a secret missive from her apothecary cousin. He was seeking his cousin's advice on a matter he felt he could entrust to no one but her. He shared that it was public knowledge the Chancellor was eagerly anticipating the arrival of children, and then divulged that he was conflicted beyond endurance on account of his most secret customer—none other than the Chancellor's young wife—to whom he'd been dispensing herbal contraceptives.

In her return letter, Julitha gave her cousin frank counsel. She advised that, just as it was her duty as a Diviner to share her knowledge without attempting to influence an outcome, so too was it his duty as an apothecary to provide remedies that gave his customers the ease they were seeking. It was not his place to interfere or judge. She stated it would be inappropriate for him to involve himself in the marriage of any of his patrons, including that of the high-ranking Chancellor and his wife. Thus, Julitha strongly counselled, the right action for the apothecary was no action at all and to do nothing to change the present state of affairs.

Unfortunately, Prin stumbled upon Julitha's letter in her master's cluttered desk. She still blamed the attractive Diviner for her own failed romance and immediately recognized how she could use the Diviner's missive to harm the reputation of the hated woman. The girl thus ensured Julitha's letter was secretly delivered into the hands of the Chancellor that very same day.

Julitha later learned from her cousin that, rather than confront his wife about her deceit—as revealed in Julitha's letter—Lord Loxley instead visited the apothecary. There, the Chancellor coerced Julitha's cousin into replacing Toriah's usual infusion with a benign herbal concoction that carried no contraceptive qualities. Predictably, Toriah became pregnant.

Following a difficult and unpleasant confinement, she gave birth to a boy who was given the name Axel. Although it was no secret that Lord Loxley was now desperately unhappy in his marriage, it was also evident to anyone who encountered him that he was overjoyed and indescribably proud to be a father.

Meanwhile, and seemingly unrelated to Lord Loxley's private issues, trouble had been brewing in the Lands of Vendome on account of the foreign delegation. Instead of returning to the Lands Beyond the Veil of Mist as they'd led their hosts to believe, they'd sailed their ships around the Jutland Peninsula, north along the western coastline, and inland up the River Atha to the royal city of West Scapah. For reasons Julitha did not know, the Grand Duchess had sent repeated ambassadors to her brother's Duchy, but every one of these men had been killed by what people were calling the thunder and lightning of the gods.

Soon after, the Grand Duchess herself traveled to West Scapah accompanied by her Council, her new husband and consort, Lord Corian, and her cousin and his young family. Within days of arriving in the distant royal city, rumors began to spread that Lord Loxley's wife and the foreign Lord Rodmyrrah had embarked upon an illicit love affair. Julitha speculated that this highly inappropriate and improper behaviour formed part of the reason why the Grand Duchess and Lord Loxley shortened their visit to the Western Duchy.

Rumors of the tragedy that occurred on the day of their departure rippled through the Twin Duchies and reverberated far beyond its borders and shores. Julitha understood that the Chancellor and his wife and toddler son had been granted a large suite of rooms in the Royal Residence. As their servants scrambled to ready themselves for their unexpected and premature departure, the embittered couple became embroiled in a heated argument when the Lady Toriah announced not only that Lord Rodmyrrah wished her to remain West Scapah, but that she was choosing to stay. The Chancellor was understandably horrified. He'd known for quite some time that the woman he'd so spontaneously married cared nothing for him, although he'd convinced himself she loved their son. But now she was willingly casting away her relationship with the child, and this decision was anathema to him.

At the height of their argument and in a fit of pique, Toriah seized some of their belongings a servant had set aside to pack and flung them over the railing of their third-floor gallery apartments. One of the items she'd inadvertently snagged was the small blanket their toddler son slept with every night.

Neither of the toddler's parents nor any of their harried servants noticed when little Axel trotted onto the balcony to retrieve this treasured object that was his comfort. The piece of cloth lay entangled in a nearby tree whose branches reached towards the balcony. The child, with no apparent fear, clambered onto the wide stone balustrade, intent upon reclaiming his precious blanket.

Passersby on the courtyard below shouted with horror when they saw the child, but their cries came too late. Axel tumbled to the paved marble courtyard below, dying on impact, and condemning the Chancellor and his wife to the ranks of the Desolate.

CHAPTER 4

I shivered when Julitha relayed what she'd heard of the days that followed; how Lox had ridden beside the carriage that bore the hastily constructed coffin, stopping only when necessary for fresh mounts and a few hours of fitful sleep, and making the journey to Hawkwood Heath in a record number of days. How those close to him had described him as a man whose soul had been cracked open with grief; and how he'd fallen to his knees and wept when he'd laid his treasured infant son to rest in his family's mausoleum.

From Julitha's account, I now understood why there was a permanent well of sadness in the depths of Lox's amber eyes. I could not imagine what he'd gone through seeing his infant son's broken body. Julitha was right. I did indeed feel a deep and great sadness for him, although it angered me more than a little that he'd been so stupidly susceptible to the charms of a beautiful woman who was, by all accounts, conniving, greedy, petulant, spoiled, and self-serving. Were all men so ridiculously predictable when faced with an attractive woman?

Realizing my perch on the beach had become uncomfortable, I rose, taking a seat beside Julitha on the sun-bleached log.

"You mentioned that Lox and Toriah have joined the ranks of the Desolate," I said, breaking the long silence that followed her heartbreaking tale. "What did you mean by that?"

"I don't know what word or phrase you use in your world, but when we describe a parent who has lost a child to death we refer to them as One of the Desolate."

A week ago, when I'd stood at my brother's graveside, the only comfort I could muster was the knowledge that my emotionally fragile mother had not lived long enough to bury her eldest son. I stared at the incoming surf as I considered Julitha's comment. Children whose parents die are orphans. Husbands and wives whose spouses die are widowers and widows. But my world did not have a word to describe parents whose child had died. "We don't have a word for it," I stated, mystified as to why not. Perhaps because it was so unthinkable.

During Julitha's telling, a picture of Toriah had begun to form in my mind. I'd never understood how a parent, including my father, could walk away from his or her children. My father hadn't been particularly kind or loving, yet I knew first-hand the kind of pain that type of abandonment caused. Clearly, Toriah and my father were cut from the same cloth as it seemed she'd been as willing as my father to abandon her parental role at the first opportunity.

"Why would Lox have married such a horribly unsuitable woman?" I asked in an accusing tone.

"I have puzzled that out myself. Aside from his short-lived fascination with Toriah, Lord Loxley has a reputation for being sensible. He is well loved for his wisdom and fairness, and highly respected for his devotion to duty. I believe I finally understand, though. You may discover this for yourself, if you see this unfaithful woman while you're in West Scapah. The truth of the matter, my dear Meredith," Julitha said, giving me an indulgent look. "Toriah resembles you."

"What? *Me?*" I stared at Julitha in dumbfounded amazement.

Julitha chuckled. "I have now concluded, correctly I believe, that you and Lord Loxley formed a very strong bond during the short time you spent together all those years ago. And I suspect that Lord Loxley was initially attracted to Toriah because, in many ways, she reminded him of you. Maybe he did not even know it at the time, but I feel this must be the case."

"But you said she was beautiful." As soon as I spoke, I clamped shut my lips. I had not meant to say something so ridiculously inane.

"Toriah is beautiful. Strikingly so," Julitha responded, taking my silly comment seriously. "But Lord Loxley is not, and never has been, despite what you may think of him at the moment, one of those men who is beguiled only by surface beauty. No. Toriah intrigued Lord Loxley because of her spirited effervescence. You have that same quality."

I barely managed not to snort in derision. Julitha's assessment might once have described the girl I had been, but it had little in common with the woman I had become. Despite her Gift, Julitha was ignorant of the fact that I hadn't lived up to the potential of that spirited child.

Julitha tilted her head in what I now knew was her habit while deep it thought. Her gaze was intent as she studied me. "That is not where the similarities end, though. There is the way you move."

I swivelled my head to gaze at her, my eyes wide with astonishment. "The way I move?"

"There is an unrestrained element in how you gesture, in the manner in which you stick out your chin, and in the way your eyes flash. From the little I saw of Toriah—and the short time I've spent with you—it is obvious you share this physical language. Based on the time you spent together in your youth, Lord Loxley has, perhaps unknowingly, compared every woman he has since met to his memory of you, and of how being with you made him feel." Julitha nodded as if she'd just solved a complex mystery. "I suspect he has been quietly and silently cherishing you all these years, whether he knew it or not."

"Julitha, you're putting way too much significance on a youthful encounter. It was a childish infatuation on both our parts. No more." I pictured the Polaroid photograph that Lox insisted on keeping despite the fatal consequence should it be discovered in his possession, and realized my words didn't ring true. When I met Julitha's gaze I read amusement in her expression. "What's so funny about that? I'm being perfectly serious."

I hadn't meant for my tone to be sharp, so I deliberately softened it as I continued. "I know you're a Diviner, and I don't mean to criticize your..." what would I call it? Her calling? Her profession? "...vocation. I know you see Lox and me sharing a 'path' to West Scapah to find this other Traveler, but that is where our paths will diverge. If you're right—and I'm choosing to believe you are—then, as soon as I get to the royal city of West Scapah, I'm going home and I'll never see him again. Oh!" I gestured impatiently at her growing amusement. "This whole conversation is absurd."

"My dear Meredith, I think you misunderstand me. My statements about Lord Loxley's feelings for you were not Divinations. They were simply my opinion as a woman who has become an expert at observing others."

I stared at her in open-mouthed dismay. "You mean they have nothing to do with your Gift?"

"Ah!" Julitha crowed triumphantly. "You have faith in my craft. That bodes exceptionally well for the Divination we have yet to perform. I am so very pleased."

Julitha jumped to her feet. "Let us put aside all dismal talk and amuse ourselves doing something that is both pleasurable and useful. We shall return home and assemble your travel wardrobe."

I pulled a face, feeling conflicted at the thought of spending weeks traveling with Lox. On the one hand, I felt pity and compassion for him on account of the tragic tale Julitha had

shared. Yet, on the other, thinking about his decision to br.
to his world with no means to return me renewed my ane
nism. Julitha's suggestion to focus on stocking my tra.
wardrobe was a welcome distraction.

I brushed bits of shells from my feet then reached for my
boots, smiling at Julitha's childlike delight as I pulled closed the
functional zippers.

As we began to pack our tea things, and although I didn't want
to dampen her spirits, I felt compelled to speak forthrightly about
my unwavering objective. "Julitha, just so we're clear, I will travel
to the royal city of West Scapah with Lox—and I'll try not to hate
him for *every* minute of that journey—but I'm only willing to go
because I need to find this other Traveler. I have no intention of
creating an image of any kind of the foreign lord. I will not
comply with Lox's plan. Your story about Lox is horribly sad, and
I do feel compassion for him. But it hasn't changed my mind. Not
about that."

Julitha's eyes met mine and she suddenly grew very still. For
the third time that day, I was held captive by the intensity of her
searing gaze. When she spoke, her words were electrifying.

"Meredith, you must understand that we desperately need you
to perform your magic and capture Rodmyrrah's likeness. The
result of your aid will change the course of our future. Like a
landslide into a river, it will dam the threat of war. I speak now
with the full art and knowledge of a Diviner who is overstepping
her bounds to influence your actions. But I also speak from my
heart as a woman who serves and loves the people of these Lands.
Think, Meredith! Imagine every young man you know in your
world. In your mind, put them on a battlefield with a weapon of
destruction in their hands. Do they want to be there?

"Imagine the women and children of your world," Julith
continued. "Would you not want to prevent them from becʳ
widows and orphans? Would you not want to preveʳ
from joining the ranks of The Desolate? What of·

nd corn and your pastures of domesticated beasts? Do you
to see those crops ruined in battle and littered with human
pses? Picture the massacre, Meredith. I implore you to see the
waste, to feel the hunger in the bellies of children when winter
comes and there is no bread to eat."

Julitha grabbed both my hands, squeezing them tightly.

"Meredith, I know you feel that what Lord Loxley and the
Grand Duchess did by Calling you here with no way to send you
back was unforgivable. And I know the countless thousands of
lives you could save are nameless and faceless to you. But I also
know that even in your world it is one thing to deliberately
choose the path of warrior and live on the frontier or go to sea in
battle against invaders, but quite another to be conscripted into a
war on the very soil you have tilled. Meredith, you must not
doubt that *you* can liberate our Lands of so much wasted death
and misery. Will you not do this one deed? Will you not put aside
your personal resentment of Lord Loxley and at least consider
how, with a few strokes of ink, you can prevent such needless
waste and devastation?"

"Julitha!" I finally found my voice. "I'm not refusing because I
resent Lox. I'm refusing because it would result in someone else's
death! I can't be an accomplice to that."

Julitha suddenly deflated and released my hands. "My dear
Traveler, please forgive my outburst," she said with earnest regret.
"You are not required to justify your decision. Not to me, and not
to Lord Loxley. My words were unjust, and I am so very sorry. I
cannot fathom how I allowed myself to overstep my bounds and
speak in such a discourteous manner. It was inappropriate, and it
is not my place to do so. Can you forgive me?"

"There's nothing to forgive," I said, feeling a little overwhelmed by her passionate self-recrimination.

Julitha draped her canvas sack over one shoulder and then re-
tucked my arm into hers, gently tugging me forward. "Do you
speak from the heart, Meredith? I do so hope your words are

sincere. I assure you, your road is your own. It is not my place or my choice to sway you." She briefly rested her other hand on my forearm. "Please know that you have my enduring friendship, Meredith. Always. It makes no difference what you decide. Please, if you believe nothing else, then believe that."

"I do, Julitha. And thank you." I also spoke with utter sincerity. Even though I'd spent so little time in her company, I dearly wanted us to remain friends for the short time our paths converged.

At my words, Julitha's light-hearted mood returned. "Enough of serious discourse then," she decreed, waving her hand gracefully as if it held a magic wand. She looked me up and down. "Traveler or no, pretty clothes are a must."

CHAPTER 5

I was deep in sleep and awoke to the feel of a hand firmly shaking my shoulder as a voice whispered my name. Opening my eyes, I saw Julitha perched on the side of my bed wearing an ivory velvet and lace dressing gown. Her flawless skin glowed in the soft light of the lamp she'd placed on my bedside table.

"What is it?" I asked in alarm, pushing up onto an elbow.

"All is well," she said as she gently pushed me back onto the pillows. "Do not fret, Meredith. Now," she instructed, enfolding my hands in hers. "Think of your niece."

I noticed then that she had Kimberly's shirt draped across her lap. "Now?" I asked stupidly, my brain foggy with sleep.

"Yes. Hold my gaze, but call to mind your favourite memories of your niece. This will open the channel of your mutual love. I will do the rest."

In my drowsy state it was easy to do as she requested. I sank into the pillows and looked into Julitha's mesmerizing eyes as I thought of Kimberly. I imagined her as the enchanting toddler who'd stolen my heart when I was little older than Kimberly was now. I pictured her on her seventh birthday, or maybe it was her eighth, singing with my brother as she proudly strummed her new guitar, its adult-size dwarfing her. I saw her again, older this time, perhaps twelve or so. I'd taken her to the waterpark at the giant mall in Edmonton. We'd laughed so much that day. Then I saw her as she looked now, at sixteen, her sandy blond hair dyed an unbecoming black. She was sitting propped up against the pillows on her bed and wearing a black tank top as she read by the light of her bedside lamp. Her hair was pulled into a messy tangle on top of her head and her face was free of cosmetics and jewelry. I noticed she was wearing what looked like my wristwatch, which struck me as odd. I found myself moving until I was hovering above her right shoulder. It *was* my wristwatch. Odd. Even more odd, the time it displayed was exactly the same as when we'd first arrived in the Lands of Vendome. I was distracted then as Kimberly turned a page in the book she was reading. I shifted my ethereal focus until I could read the loopy cursive writing scrawled across the lined pages. What I saw there so startled me I jerked forward, narrowly missing smacking my head against Julitha's chin.

The Diviner released my hands and leaned back, exhaling heavily as she regarded me. The shadows of the lamp emphasized new lines of exhaustion on her face.

"There you are, then," she said with a tired but satisfied smile. "That was less taxing than I anticipated. If I did not know better, I would say you have the blood of Vendome in you. That was your niece, yes? What made you startle so dramatically? We could have observed longer but for your reaction."

"That was *real?* It wasn't a vision of something I wanted to see?"

Julitha gave me an indulgent smile. "You know it was real, do you not? But what made you startle? It did not seem to me that what your Kimberly was doing was particularly unusual."

As I settled more comfortably against my pillows, I smiled in contentment. My worry for Kimberly's safety had entirely evaporated. I found myself answering in a tone that radiated my delight. "Two things, Julitha. She was wearing my wristwatch." I gestured at my arm as if that explained everything. "It's a time piece that straps onto your wrist. I was wearing it when we came to this world. I thought I'd lost it, but Kimberly told me she found it." I chuckled. "I can't imagine why she's wearing it. It's stopped at the exact same time we arrived here."

"I see."

Julitha clearly didn't see, but her polite response made me smile.

"What was the second thing?" she asked.

I grimaced self-consciously. "Well, when we first arrived in this world, I told Kimberly that I'd written detailed accounts of meeting Rikka, Jaybex, and Lox in my childhood diary." I shook my head. "She must have gone to my townhouse and found them. That was the book she was reading." I was a little embarrassed knowing Kimberly had full access to the details of my schoolgirl crush on Lox, but my feelings of relief that she was back in my world far outweighed any discomfort I had over the contents of my childhood diary.

"What time is it, Julitha?" I asked, looking toward the dormer window where wooden shutters blocked the glass.

"Almost dawn. It was worth it, yes? You will rest easy now?"

"Yes, Julitha. Thank you so much."

She rubbed her temples wearily, but still managed a wide smile. "I am glad your fears have been allayed, Meredith."

"Please, call me Meredee."

"How delightful. Meredee, it is."

"Julitha, why did we have to do this at dawn? What relevance is the timing?"

"None whatsoever. At least not in the way you are implying. I chose dawn because, after the oblivion of sleep and at your precise moment of waking, I knew you would be emotionally open. That openness allows me to follow those threads that have become, over the years, saturated with love for your niece. My exertion and my present exhaustion are on account of the effort of bringing you with me so that you could also see her and thus have the proof you require. That is not something I usually do, but it is what makes my Gift unique, if I choose to employ it in such a manner."

"I see." This time it was me who did not see. But my lack of understanding was irrelevant given I felt like I'd been released from a dungeon.

"If you have no more questions, then I will take my leave, Meredee." Her tone rang with pleasure as she spoke my nickname.

I smiled, then briefly rested my hand on her forearm, urging her to remain seated for a moment. I could see that our session had visibly drained her; conversely, it left me feeling strangely invigorated. "Julitha, I don't know how to thank you. I feel…"

"Relief," she finished for me. "You feel an inordinate amount of relief. Such welcome feelings will renew your spirit and prepare you for what is to come."

"Yes. I've done a complete one-eighty." At her puzzled look, I added, "I now feel the exact opposite of what I had been feeling."

Julitha nodded in satisfaction. "Then I have succeeded in what I set out to do." She stood, smiling down at me. "Meredee, I am afraid you will be on your own when you break your fast. I will likely sleep deeply for many hours. Will you be able to manage?"

"Of course. Don't worry about me, Julitha. I'll be fine."

As soon as the door closed behind her, I dragged the coverlet from my bed and crossed the room to the cushioned bench in the gabled alcove. I folded open the wooden shutters and saw the first hint of dawn with its promise of light on the eastern horizon. As I settled into the cushions and tucked the blanket around me, I thought about the contents of my diary. I stared unseeingly out the window as reel upon reel of those cherished memories flashed onto the screen of my mind like a treasured home-movie rescued from a dank and dusty attic.

PART II

RENEWAL

CHAPTER 6

$\mathcal{T}$he third and final time the children from the Lands of
Vendome visited my world was July first, twenty-two
years earlier. There are three reasons why I can remember that
date so exactly. It was a national holiday, Canada Day. A trip to
Sandpiper Lake on any day was thrilling, but on a national
holiday it was extra special. The second was because, in the late
summer of that same year, my father deserted our family. The
third reason was because on that day I met a boy unlike any I'd
ever met before. Or since.

I remember having my beach bag slung over my shoulder as I
made my way downstairs in our big, rambling house. On the
landing, I happened to glance out the window, then whooped in
delight when I saw Rikka and Jaybex emerge from the woods
followed by a boy I'd never seen before. I raced down the stairs
and through the kitchen, ignoring my mom and Marilyn who
were busy packing coolers with food, pop, and ice. I practically
flew out the kitchen door.

Moments later I was exuberantly chattering with Rikka and
Jaybex. They introduced their companion as their cousin, Loxley.
He was a full head taller than the twins and, with his sand-colored

45

hair, did not resemble his dark-haired cousins. Unlike the twins, he was enormously displeased to find himself in my world.

"You look as miserable as my cat Minx after he fell in the fish tank," I said to him, which, as intended, made Rikka and Jaybex chortle with mirth.

"Lox is a stickler for rules," Rikka explained, when he didn't join their laughter. "He is angry that we tricked him."

When I glanced at Lox, as Rikka called him, he lifted a shoulder slightly but said nothing. He could choose to be a spoil-sport, I decided, but I wasn't going to let that ruin my day. I returned my attention to Rikka and Jaybex. "It's so cool you're here today. It's Canada Day, and we're about to leave for the lake. You have to come, too."

"Will your brothers be accompanying you?" Jaybex's tone of forced casualness did nothing to hide his trepidation.

I could hardly fault the boy for his nervous concern. On that first visit, the three of us had managed only a very narrow escape from my older, bigger brothers after we'd instigated what Rikka later dubbed The Inglorious Tree House Battle. On their second visit, when we'd booby-trapped the same tree house, we'd made an equally narrow escape.

"They'll go bananas when they see you, but don't worry about them. Marilyn and my parents will be with us. Besides, all that was ages ago. It's summer holidays now!" I could see they didn't understand what I meant by summer holidays, but Marilyn was calling for me and I couldn't take the time to explain.

"Come on." I gestured for my visitors to follow me but then stopped abruptly. "Wait. You don't have swimsuits." The boys were each wearing dark knee-length shorts and white shirts and Rikka was wearing a shapeless muslin dress in an unflattering pea green that fell past her knees. All three wore ugly, clunky shoes.

"We wore the most nondescript clothes we could find so that we would not stand out."

I raised my eyebrows at Rikka's comment, but refrained from

commenting on their dreary attire. "Follow me," I said, glancing over my shoulder to ensure they trailed behind as I hurried toward the house.

I saw my dad had already reversed the station wagon out of the garage. He looked ridiculous as he stepped out of the car wearing his perfectly pressed Bermuda shorts. Summer had come late this year and his thick, powerful legs were whiter than my mom's good tablecloth. Marilyn was overseeing where my towheaded brothers were stowing the blankets and picnic items in the car. My mother was nervously checking and re-checking the contents of her purse like she always did before we went anywhere. I called out that we would be right back, and then gestured for my friends to follow me through the house. In the laundry room I grabbed two swimming trunks from the stack of clean clothes my mother had folded. I tossed the larger pair to Lox and the smaller pair to Jaybex, then retrieved an old swimsuit of mine for Rikka from the Rummage Sale box behind the laundry room door. "This one will fit you. And here's a towel each." I grabbed three of the biggest towels I could find and distributed them to my friends.

Carrying their swimming clothes and towels, they silently followed me out of the house. I could hear Jaybex's footsteps lag as we approached the car where my brothers had just climbed into the middle seat. As was usual, space had been left for me in the backwards-facing bench at the rear of the station wagon.

"There you are," my dad snapped impatiently as we approached the car.

Marilyn was already in the front seat of the station wagon. I could see her using the rear-view mirror to adjust her hairband.

"Who are your friends, Meredee?" my mother asked in her timorous voice.

She looked overwhelmed by the arrival of three additional children. I felt a twinge of conscience but was distracted when her words gained my brothers' attention. When they saw us, all three jutted their heads out the open window behind the driver's door and started hollering about how these were the kids who'd wrecked their tree fort. I responded by yelling at them that we'd dish out more as soon as we had the chance.

Our exchange was interrupted when my father roared at us to shut the hell up, which we did. None of us wanted him to lose his temper and then do something irrational like cancel the trip to the lake, a reaction that would have been entirely characteristic for the moody, unpredictable man.

"Mom, you don't remember me asking you if they could catch a ride with us?" I was admittedly ashamed at taking advantage of my mother's guileless fragility but, in this instance at least, it was necessary. "Their dad had to work and their mom is taking care of their sick Grandma. I'm positive I told you."

Predictably, my brothers started a round of fake retching, but I ignored their juvenile antics.

"Their dad drove off with their beach bags," I quickly added, thinking on my feet and prevaricating with practiced ease. "I've lent them some of our stuff."

"No way does that retard get to wear any of my clothes!" Tommy, the youngest of my three brothers, stuck his head and shoulders further out the window in wild-eyed consternation.

"Don't you call him a retard," I retorted hotly. "You're the retard. Tom Thumb retard." Tommy hated that he was shorter than most everyone his age, even the girls. As his little sister, I felt it was my duty to take every opportunity to push his very sensitive, vertically challenged button.

"Pearl, make them stop bickering," my dad warned.

Without my older sister's willingness to step in and take charge, parenting would have overwhelmed my mother. But that didn't stop my dad from making statements that made her feel inadequate.

"Children," my mother said in her timid voice. "Let's all get along now."

48

"They can stay here if they want to fight," my dad continued, ignoring my mom. "They can argue over who weeds the garden and who mows the lawns."

That shut us all up.

"Well," my Mom said. Her gaze darted about like a chick-a-dee flitting from twig to twig. "I wish you had reminded me of this before we packed the car, Meredee."

Marilyn, finally finished fussing with her hair, poked her head out the open door on the driver's side. "Meredee, you should have told *me*. Boys, get out of the car and rearrange the picnic things to make room for Meredee's friends. You can sit in the back this time. Meredee and her friends will ride in the middle."

Marilyn didn't wait to see if my brothers would do as they were told. They would. We didn't mess with Marilyn any more than we did with our dad. She turned back to the rear-view mirror and began applying yet another coat of lipstick as my mother got in beside her.

"Make it snappy," my Dad said in a huffy tone without offering to help. "If we delay any longer, there won't be any point going at all."

My brothers quickly and efficiently redistributed the picnic things to make room for themselves in the back seat. Moments later, my Vendome friends and I climbed into the middle. Rikka looked aghast when her shoes made dusty imprints on the picnic blankets that were now stacked on the floor behind the front bench-seat, but I waved away her concern. The blankets would soon enough be full of sand. I slid over to the passenger side with Rikka beside me and a picnic jug at our feet. Jaybex followed his sister willingly, but Lox had to be coaxed into the car with urgent gestures from his cousins. He narrowly avoided having his fingers pinched when my Dad slammed the door closed.

I knew my friends had never before traveled in a car. From what I'd gleaned so far about their world, they had old-fashioned things like horses and swords. I could understand Lox's hesitation given it was his first visit to my world; at the same time, I was beyond proud of Rikka. She was more adventurous and fearless than her brother and cousin combined.

My dad got behind the wheel and started the car. "Jesus Christ, Marilyn," he grumbled when he was forced to adjust the rear-view mirror. "You have a compact in your purse. Why can't you use it?"

"Because it's compact," Marilyn retorted matter-of-factly, patting her hair to make sure it hadn't fallen out of place in the last five seconds. She was the only person in our household who wasn't intimidated by our dad, probably because they were a lot alike. Except Marilyn actually did have a heart, whereas I was often convinced my father did not.

My dad put the car into gear and then accelerated along the drive that circled our house. After a few turns we were on the highway and heading toward the lake twelve miles west of Bellecourt.

Lox and Jaybex were both rigid in their seats as we gained speed. Had Rikka not been grinning with delight, I might have felt sorry for the boys since it was their first time speeding down a paved highway at sixty miles an hour. Then Jaybex let out a yelp and ducked his head into his lap. I could see his fingers groping for the spitball that was stuck to the back of his dark hair.

I flipped around in my seat and slapped my brother Frank on the back of his head. I would have slapped the other two as well, but they were out of reach. "You are cruisin' for a bruisin'! I'll sock it to you big if you don't stop." I spewed. Then I turned to the front. "Marilyn, they're shooting spit balls!" I grabbed the back of the front seat, but accidently pulled Marilyn's hair, which caused her to screech at me.

At the same time, Tommy was taunting in a sing-song voice, *"Up your nose with a rubber hose."*

"If you all don't pipe down," my dad roared, "I'm going to turn this baby around and there'll be no picnic for anyone. You hear?"

When my dad used his military-general voice—he hadn't risen high enough in the ranks to issue orders, but he had served—we listened. I once overhead my brothers saying that our father had been dishonorably discharged from the army. When I demanded to know if it was true, they'd taken my interference as insolence and used it as an excuse to drag me into the hayloft of our sagging barn and tie me to a beam. They told me they'd be back in an hour and warned me they'd sic the communists on me if I told on them. A long time passed before I dared to start yelling for help. Marilyn eventually heard me. The boys always claimed they meant to come back for me but simply forgot. Marilyn believed them, but I didn't.

As I sank back into my seat beside Rikka, I could hear my brothers whispering. I turned around and gave them a you-better-watch-out glare, then silently slapped Tommy's hand away as he reached out to pull my pigtail, at which point we embarked on an unacknowledged truce.

I leaned in front of Rikka and pulled on Jaybex's sleeve. "Never mind them," I said in a soft tone. "As soon as we're at the lake they'll hang out with their loser friends."

Lox leaned forward, glanced warily at the back of my dad's head, and then addressed me quietly. "How is it that we can travel at such a speed without horses?"

Rikka managed to take everything in stride and just have fun. Jaybex was less courageous—although always willing to follow Rikka's lead—but this boy? He was a total stick in the mud. He and Marilyn would get on like a house on fire, I thought. Not that Marilyn would ever give a boy of twelve the time of day. "It's the 20th century here, you know," I responded, as if that explained everything.

Lox gave me a quizzical look. For the first time, I noticed the unusual color of his eyes with their burnt yellow flecks. He stared at me for a long moment, then leaned back and gave his attention to the passing scenery whipping by his window.

"I did not bring my sword with me today," Jaybex confided to me in an undertone.

He balanced the spitball in his palm as if considering its potential as a return missile. I swiped it, cranked down my window a couple of inches, and threw it out before rolling my window back up. Jaybex couldn't know that one more episode really would make my dad turn this baby around.

When Lox saw me roll my window down and up again, he turned to examine the knobs on his door. With a second wary look at my father, he rolled his own window down a few inches, then up, then down all the way. Then he stuck his head out the window as if he were a dog. I reached in front of Rikka and Jaybex to punch his arm, and then hissed at him to crank his window back up and leave it closed or he'd get us in trouble. He did as I asked, but was grinning in delight, which completely altered his appearance. I found myself staring at him for a moment before my attention was diverted to Jaybex, who'd just repeated his regretful confession.

"You don't need a sword where we're going, Jaybex. But you do need to know how to swim. Can you all swim?"

All three nodded.

In no time we were pulling into the crowded parking lot at Sandpiper Lake. As we spilled out of the station wagon, my dad bawled at us to help bring the coolers, picnic jug, blankets, air mattresses, pump, lawn chairs, and towels to a spot of his choosing. As soon as that task was accomplished, my brothers took off. My dad, whose moods swung from mad to glad in the blink of an eye but who was always happy and charming around neighbors and friends, used the foot pump to fill the mattresses with air only because Mr. van den Klaver was doing the same thing right next to us.

When I insisted my exotic friends accompany me to the change rooms, Rikka had to drag Lox away.

"It is ingenious to fill a mattress with air." Lox declared as he reluctantly joined us. "But how do you prevent leakage?"

"Lox!" Rikka's tone was like Marilyn's when her patience was wearing thin. "If you intend to ask questions all day, you will spoil our fun." She turned to me. "He always wants to know how things work. And not just in your world. He does it all the time in ours, too. Do not show him Barbie and Ken or he will take them apart just so he can put them back together again."

I gave Lox a you-better-not look despite not having my Barbies with me.

After we changed into our swimsuits, we returned to our picnic spot where I snagged two of the air mattresses, handed one to Lox, and then lead them at a run toward the shoreline. From that moment on, the day was glorious.

By lunchtime, I'd entirely changed my opinion of the twins' cousin. Lox, despite his thoughtful inquisitiveness, spoke with an unaffected playfulness that frequently had me in stitches. We sat on our damp towels in our wet bathing suits as my mom handed out paper plates loaded with potato salad, soft buns, and crunchy pickles. My Vendome friends had never seen disposable plates before let alone plastic forks. Mom also distributed bottles of ice cold Pepsi. Rikka and Jaybex didn't care for the fizzy drink, but Lox loved it. He politely accepted a second when my mom offered, impressing her with his good manners.

After lunch, my mom asked Mr. van den Klaver to take a group photo of us with our Polaroid camera. Then, to my delight, she spontaneously took a snapshot of me and Lox. My visitors did not know what was happening at first, but when my mom handed me the undeveloped exposure, I held it on my palm and told my friends to watch. All morning Lox had been asking what that was and how this worked and what that was for, so I knew he would be delighted with this invention that I felt sure did not exist in their world. But, as our two images slowly spread like spilled ink across the small plastic square, I was flabbergasted by their distraught reactions. Rikka and Jaybex both let out a bloodcurdling scream that generated a dark scowl from my dad. Rikka further surprised me by refusing to look at it again. I was puzzled and for the first time disappointed by her reaction. Jaybex completely over reacted. He had tears in his eyes and said he didn't want Lox to die. That's when Rikka jumped up and grabbed Jaybex by the hand, demanding he go swimming with her. As usual, Jaybex did as his twin instructed.

The photograph clearly frightened Lox as well, but it also captivated and intrigued him. He demanded to know why our world indulged in such heresy. I didn't have a clue what he meant, but I explained that we took lots of pictures and put them in albums and frames. Despite my reassurances that what he was looking at was perfectly normal, he remained both deeply disturbed and extremely fascinated by the Polaroid.

Later that afternoon, I brought my new friends to the baseball diamond to eat popcorn and watch a ball game, giving a play-by-play of the rules to Lox the entire time. After that, Lox and I floated on an air mattress as we idly watched Rikka and Jaybex tossing colorful beach balls in the shallow waters near the shore. By this time, I'd developed a massive crush on Lox, an attraction that, in a matter of only a few hours, had formed deep roots.

While we floated on our shared mattress, Lox peppered me with questions I was all too eager to answer. But when he asked—for the umpteenth time—how the station wagon could actually propel us forward without horses, I groaned and punched his shoulder in exasperated affection.

"Enough, Lox," I laughed. "I'm not an encyclopedia you know."

"What is an en-cy-clo…what was it you said?"

I thoroughly enjoyed the awe that danced like amber dragonflies in his tawny eyes when I explained things about my world. I did not know any other boy who was so serious and smart, and yet so curious and quick to laugh. And who seemed to be as fascinated with my company as I was with his.

"An encyclopedia set is a series of important books," I explained after I taught him how to say the word. "Kind of like the dictionary I described earlier except, instead of definitions, the encyclopedia gives a summary of everything there is to know about everything and everyone important in the world, with pictures and maps included."

"Truly?" Lox said in awe. "I would like to read this en-cy-clo-pe-di-ah-set."

"You can't, Lox! It would take you months to read it. There's, like, thirty books in the whole set."

"When we get back to your estate, if my cousins and I have not yet returned, will you show me this en-cy-clo-pe-di-ah-set?"

"Sure, along with my Spirograph, my Lite Brite, our telephone, my Slinky—"

"And your picture of the man on the moon."

"That's not mine. It's in Frank's room and we would risk death if we entered."

"I have already risked death by having my photo-roid polo…"

We laughed hilariously. "Pol-ah-roid pho-to-graph," I enunciated.

And then my Dad was hollering at us that it was time to help load the station wagon. We stayed in our swimsuits when we climbed into the car, our sun-kissed skin hot to the touch and our hair still wet. I'd contrived it so that Lox and I sat side-by-side between Rikka and Jaybex. I liked it that Lox's warm bare leg and arm brushed against mine. Everything about him fascinated me. The way he gestured with his hands; the way his bony shoulder blades moved on his back; the way his eyes lightened when something delighted him; the way his head tilted back when he chuckled.

In keeping with family tradition and despite having also had ice cream at lunch—although my dad took my Dixie Cup away as punishment for yelling at my brothers—we stopped for soft-serve cones at the lake's General Store. My enjoyment of this second ice-cream treat was marred as usual by my loser brothers. My new friends had never had soft serve before. When my brothers overheard them exclaiming at its deliciousness, Tommy, predictably, had to be the jerk.

"What kind of retards are you, anyway?" he accused from behind us.

"Retard triplets," Frank chortled.

"Ignoramus retard triplets," Tommy added, which made Frank and Curtis snort with laughter as if Tommy had made the joke of the century.

Before I could blast the appropriate rebuttal, Lox looked over his shoulder at them and spoke in a calm, dignified tone. "Only a fool mistakes lack of knowledge for stupidity. To be conscious of one's ignorance leads to purer and greater wisdom."

His comment wiped the grins off my brothers' faces. They stared at him like the clueless, oxygen-deprived idiots they were.

Lox met my gaze, lifted an eyebrow slightly and winked at me. My crush on him, which had already taken root, blossomed into full-blown adoration.

Once back in town, Marilyn suggested we drop my friends off at their house, but I begged for them to be allowed to come home with us. My father conceded, mostly because he wanted to go straight home and have a nap in his easy chair. At the house, I showed my friends all the things Lox and I had talked about that day, including the encyclopedia set. The summer evenings were long in July, so we went outside where I demonstrated how to ride my bike with its sparkly banana-boat seat and colorful handle streamers. They watched with open mouths and words of praise as I peddled figure eights around them, which made me feel like an accomplished acrobat. Then they took turns attempting to ride the bike, laughing and shrieking as they lurched along the drive and careened across the lawn. When my brothers returned on their bikes, Tommy made fun of Rikka, who was wobbling precariously on my bike as I ran alongside her trying to prevent another crash.

We stopped what we were doing and hurled insults at each other, which could have escalated into Round Three of the Inglorious Tree House Battle—without the tree house—but Marilyn came outside and put a stop to our antics. She ordered my brothers inside, which thankfully relieved us of their insufferable presence, then told me it was time for my bath. She also told my friends in no uncertain terms it was time for them to leave. I'd already devised a plan in case my friends were still here at bedtime; I didn't argue as I followed Marilyn into the house. I let her think my friends were heading back to their non-existent home on the other side of the golf course. In reality, once we were inside and Marilyn was on the phone with her best friend reliving every boring minute of her day, I tiptoed to the mudroom entrance and snuck my three pals up the stairs and into my bedroom.

After hurrying through my bath, I crept into my room in my nightgown and robe, hoping that my friends had not yet been whisked back to their world. I was relieved to see them, although Rikka and Jaybex were both sound asleep on my bed surrounded by my Ken and Barbie dolls and accessories, including Cheerleader Barbie with her shaved head. Lox, awake and alert, was sitting on the floor with his back to the wall. A thrill of pleasure jolted through me when I saw him, but my smile faltered when I noticed my sketchbook open on his lap. I liked drawing portraits and had been experimenting with pastels, but the end results were amateur. It embarrassed me to see him pouring over the pages.

"Give me!" I demanded in mortification as I sank to the floor beside him. He easily evaded my attempts to confiscate the large book.

"These are...I do not know how to describe what these are. I have never before seen anything so incredible. These faces are... they are extraordinary."

At his effusive compliments, I flushed with pleasure and stopped trying to wrestle the book out of his grasp. Part of me knew the only reason he was impressed was because no one in his world drew portraits, but that didn't lessen my glow.

"You are truly allowed to do this?" His voice held awe, but also fear.

"Of course I'm allowed. How many times do I have to tell you?" I could not wrap my head around the fact that, in his world, creating a human likeness in any medium was forbidden.

Lox lifted his gaze from the pages of the book and regarded me with a serious expression I couldn't read. When he leaned slowly toward me, I think I stopped breathing. I'd never been kissed by a boy before. Ever since turning nine, I'd been wondering what it would be like. As Lox's face drew nearer to mine, I closed my eyes. A moment later, I was astonished to feel the warmth of his breath on my face.

And then, just before his lips could touch mine, I felt a kind of shimmer in the air. I opened my eyes, but he was gone. In the space of a single heartbeat he'd vanished. My pent-up breath exited my lungs in an astonished whoosh as I stared in disbelief at where he'd been.

I looked at the bed where Rikka and Jaybex had been sprawled, but they too were gone, leaving only the imprint of their bodies on the rumpled bedspread.

For years after that night, I waited in anticipation for Lox's return, convinced that, when he did show up, he would kiss me for real. I imagined that kiss—which should have been my first—countless times, but it would forever be condemned to existing only in my imagination. Eventually, I had to accept I would never see him again and that he would always and forever remain the boy who'd almost kissed me.

In large part because he never came back, I became a skilled amateur portraitist, filling sketchbook after sketchbook with images of that alluring, fascinating, unforgettable boy.

58

CHAPTER 7

"*W*as that necessary?" Lox accused Julitha after one look at me.

It was late morning on my fourth day at Julitha's cottage. The Diviner and I were standing in the exact spot where she'd greeted Fredryk and me a few short days before. For a whole host of thorny reasons, I'd been feeling apprehension about seeing Lox again. I knew Julitha was, too.

Over the last few days, I sorted shells or, when visitors came to call seeking the Diviner's guidance, took long, solitary walks on the beach. Julitha had not hidden my presence from visitors, but we had made certain I never spoke with anyone on account of my strange accent.

For four days and with no pressing tasks, I had a lot of time to think. My thoughts had bounced around in my skull like the orb in a pinball machine. I re-examined Lox's motivation to call me here from every imaginable angle. In the end, I found myself concluding—in theory at least—that the task he wanted me to perform was not as monstrous as I'd first believed. It was valid—in theory—to not only sacrifice one life for the lives of many, but also to elevate the safety of thousands of people over and above the happiness of one person. Was Hitler not a case in point? I also conceded—more reluctantly—that Lox's *decision* to Call me here without the ability to send me home, although callous and selfish, was understandable when perceived from his and Rikka's perspective. But my ability to choose was taken away from me. And that was still the singular problem from my perspective.

During my long, solitary walks on the beach searching for shells, I also tried to come up with a believable story that would, upon my reappearance in my world, explain my prolonged absence. This proved an impossible task. I eventually decided that when I did make it home—when, not if—my first order of business would be to find my niece so that I could align my story with hers.

The end result of this exhaustive introspection was that I was no longer consumed by debilitating antagonism toward Lox due, in large part, to my belief that I would soon return home. I was grateful I'd had a change of heart given Lox would be my guide on our weeks-long journey to the city of West Scapah. Nevertheless, I still believed his *decision* to call me here with no way to send me home was wrong. And I remained immovable in my refusal to depict Rodmyrrah in any way. Julitha had kept her promise to refrain from trying to sway me on this matter, although that hadn't prevented her from slipping a few lead sketching sticks and a packet of high-quality linen paper into my traveling case.

Over the last few days and with no help from me as I couldn't sew a stitch, Julitha had altered a number of clothes from her extensive wardrobe to fit me. Earlier that morning I'd donned what Julitha called a walking costume, an elegant ensemble consisting of a floor-length skirt with a matching long-sleeved, tailored blouse. This beautiful honey-toned silk crepe, cut on a bias and trimmed with cinnamon accents, flattered my coloring and my curves. At first, dressing in her clothes felt decidedly odd, but it didn't take long to become accustomed to the long skirts and the rustling silks, reminding me of an interview I'd once seen of an actress in a period film. She'd complained of the discomfort of wearing a corset but in the same breath noted that authentic dress from top to bottom added to her ability to remain in character. I now understood what she meant. After only four days wearing Julitha's beautiful but seemingly old-fashioned clothes, I was beginning to feel disconnected from the modern 20th Century world from which I hailed.

Regardless, I was more than a little self-conscious in the elegant dress, so much so that when Lox made his biting remark, I at first thought he was mocking Julitha for dressing me in her pretty clothes. Then I realized he was upset because, upon meeting my compassionate gaze, he'd correctly deduced that Julitha had shared intimate details about his private life, making me wish I'd learned the knack of adopting a poker face.

Julitha, ever the gracious hostess, responded to Lox's caustic comment in her characteristic charitable tone. "My Lord, considering her sacrifice in coming to our Lands, she is owed a full accounting."

"That may be so. But it was not *your* place to interfere." Lox didn't say the word 'again', but his hostile tone implied it.

When Julitha gave a small shrug and looked away, I could tell she felt slighted by his harsh words. I felt a wave of anger toward Lox. How dare he make this warm and wonderful woman, who'd given me refuge in my time of need, feel bad? "What does it matter?" I demanded. Neither Lox, who remained tight-lipped, nor Fredryk, who kept his gaze averted as he fiddled needlessly with the straps on his saddle, responded. "Oh, for god's sake, Lox! It's not like *your* choices have been so stellar. I don't know what gives you the right to be upset with Julitha. It's not her fault. And besides—"

I stopped talking when Lox began to smile, at my expense it seemed.

"What?" I demanded.

"Meredith," Lox said with more warmth in his tone than when

he'd addressed Julitha. His eyes lightened a little as he looked at me. "I do so admire how you stand up for the people you care about. You have always been that way, have you not?"

It annoyed me beyond measure that his soft tone could so easily unsettle a butterfly in my knotted stomach, but his response also deflated the palpable tension that had arisen.

"Will you walk with me?" he asked, his tone solemn.

Even though I knew it would've been juvenile, I was tempted to refuse just because I could. But I also knew I had to have a frank discussion with him before we began our long journey. I needed to re-emphasize that I would not draw Rodmyrrah, and that my sole motivation for traveling to West Scapah was to meet this Traveler so I could go home.

"Fredryk, would you care to join me in the garden for tea?" Julitha did not wait for Fredryk's response but turned and began strolling toward her cottage. Fredryk glanced briefly at Lox before trailing after her.

"Let's go this way," I suggested, leading Lox toward the now-familiar trail that led through the woods and down to the beach.

He seemed oblivious to the beauty of the towering trees as we entered the woods. When he spoke, it seemed to me he'd rehearsed his words.

"Meredith, I need you to know that your safety is and always will be my paramount concern. If you believe nothing else, please believe that."

"I do," I said. My answer was sincere. I knew with absolute certainty that I could implicitly trust him—and by default, Fredryk—to keep me safe.

"The second matter I must share with you," he continued before I could say anything further, "is that, as of yesterday, I have confirmation that the Earl of Avercorris is indeed actively searching for you. Thus, it is now even more imperative that Fredryk and I protect your identity and keep your whereabouts a closely guarded secret. My greatest fear is that Lord Conraz, or someone in his employ, delivers you to the mind-weaver. I could not bear it if you became like Jaybex."

I pulled a face. That chilling outcome hadn't even crossed my mind. I'd earlier shared what I knew of Jaybex's fate with Julitha. She'd been understandably horrified, yet also greatly intrigued by the power of this foreign mind-weaver. She also became sorely tempted to accompany us to West Scapah, but remained duty bound to stay and serve the people who depended on her for their well-being.

"I'm going to assume you and Fredryk have a plan to prevent *that* from happening," I stated.

"Of course. We have devised a plan to travel anonymously using false identities."

I wasn't entirely sure what that meant given this world's lack of passports, but we fell silent as the track steepened and narrowed, forcing us to walk single file. Once on the beach, we resumed walking side-by-side. The sound of our footsteps crunching on crushed shells seemed over loud in the strained silence that had fallen.

There were so many questions swirling in my head that needed to be answered. I had to make a concerted effort to keep my tone neutral when I asked, "Why did you claim the Traveler in West Scapah is an imposter?"

Lox strode beside me with his hands clasped behind his back. At my question, he frowned. "Fredryk informed me of the Diviner's immediate declaration of your imminent return to your world. I do not mean to shatter what I believe is your optimism when I say I have difficulty believing it."

"You doubt her? Even after..." I struggled to find a polite way of saying *your fiasco with Toriah*.

"No," he admitted with a heavy sigh. "I do not doubt the Diviner's Gift. She is skilled in her craft. Yet, Julitha herself would admit that she does not fully understand some of what she Sees until time chooses to reveal the wisdom that had previously remained concealed. Thus, I simply cannot fathom how it is possible the Traveler in West Scapah is authentic. What little I saw of him during that grievous visit reminded me only of a dressed-up buffoon. Remember," he added, glancing at me briefly and giving me a ghost of a smile. "I have seen your kind before."

I smiled half-heartedly in return, then he looked away and continued.

"The foreign lord periodically displays his Traveler at Jaybex's court because he ever seeks to manipulate, to his advantage, the opinion of both his obsequious nobles and the credulous populace. He uses this hireling's presence as a tool to trick people into believing that the gods favor him. Despite my continued belief that this Traveler is a hoax, I have sent word ahead to my trusted friends in West Scapah. It is coded," he added in a reassuring tone, "so as not to reveal our intentions if the missive makes its way into our adversary's hands. I have asked Alberic and Lita to arrange an encounter with this so-called Traveler so that you will have the opportunity to judge his authenticity for yourself." He shook his head as if with regret. "I know you want to believe in what Julitha has Seen. But we will not have answers until we safely, and clandestinely, reach our destination."

Lox's dismal outlook made me momentarily wonder if I was being foolish to believe in Julitha's vision. But when I called to mind the compelling image of Kimberly reading my diary, my doubts vanished. Kimberly had indeed been returned to our world. Julitha had not simply given me the gift of a vision of my niece; she'd enabled me to experience a visceral reaction that was as undeniable as it was mysterious. How Julitha had the skill and the power to perform such a feat I would never know. It was yet another mystery to add to the teetering tower of inscrutable unknowns I was encountering while on this strange and unexpected adventure. But I believed in her ability, and not just regarding Kimberly's current whereabouts, but my eventual return as well. Lox could remain doubtful if he chose. But I would not.

"Lox, if Julitha believes the Traveler in West Scapah has the means to send me home, then I believe it. I *have* to believe it." My conviction was my lifeline. Without it, there would be nothing to anchor me to sanity. I wondered then about my mother and her fragile hold on reality. Had her beliefs somehow impaired her perception of the manifest world? But now was not the time to ponder such a weighty topic. The point was, I did not need Lox to agree with me. I simply needed him to escort me to our destination.

I decided then to address the very large elephant that was lumbering beside us, which was my newly acquired knowledge of his personal affairs. "Lox, I get that maybe you don't want me to know private details about your past, and that's understandable." Although I noticed his brow furrow at my words, I did not let it deter me from continuing. "I don't want you to be mad at Julitha, though. That's not fair. She's been amazing. You must realize, the only reason I'm even able to have a rational conversation with you is thanks to her."

When he smiled faintly I wondered if his humour was in response to my defense of Julitha or the image of me scratching out his eyes.

Lox responded in a solemn tone. "Upon our return to the Diviner's cottage, I shall apologize to Julitha. And thank her for her aid and hospitality where you are concerned."

I nodded, mollified, but then had to work up the courage to mention his son. "I also really want to say how desperately sorry I am about Axel. I know you would have been an amazing father. He must've adored you." Unlike our conversation after Shulha's death, this time when I spoke of death my comments were not inane but rang with sincerity. I had no doubt Lox had been a devoted and loving father.

"I worshipped him," Lox answered quietly without looking at

me. "I wish you could have met him. He was the brightest beam of pure joy in what had become a very bleak life. I gained immense pleasure from being his father; he was more than worth the nightmare my marriage had become."

I was surprised he didn't avoid speaking on this most painful subject, but I shook my head in a show of compassion. "I'm sorry about your marriage, too. Julitha told me the whole story."

Lox's laugh was harsh and devoid of humour. "She may have told you what she knew, but she most certainly did not tell you *everything*. As who but me could truly know the bitterness that thrived in the privacy of my conjugal misery?" He sighed heavily. "Perhaps I should disclose to you *my* account of the tale."

"That's not what I meant, Lox. And anyway, there's no need for you to talk about it." I was uncomfortable at the thought of becoming his confidante. Even though I was behaving reasonably with him, I hadn't forgiven him for calling me here with no way to send me home.

"There is a need." Despite his statement, Lox took his time gathering his thoughts. "I will confess to you, with the appropriate degree of shame, that even after we entered our marriage union and I learned that my wife had little love for me—all her love was for my wealth, my status, and my access to everyone of import in these Lands—yet I still desired her. I craved starting a family. I felt certain that motherhood would change her. She was very young, you see. I was older and supposedly wiser. At the time, I had the audacity to believe that I knew what was best for her. Inconceivably arrogant on my part, I now know."

Although I glanced at his profile occasionally as we walked, Lox didn't look at me and his gaze remained either somewhere in the range of his feet or on the distant trees at the far end of the beach. I was glad I didn't have a bag with me to gather shells. Our conversation was absorbing to the point where I wouldn't have noticed a treasure chest were I to trip on it, let alone finding the perfect shell.

"Forgive me for speaking of intimate moments," he said. "But if I am to share my story with you, I must be candid and forthright; not for the purpose of generating your sympathy, but because, as Julitha stated—correctly—you are owed a full account. *From me.* Perhaps doing so will make some amends for my previous duplicity."

Lox absently scratched at the stubble that darkened his jaw, then re-clasped his hands behind his back as he continued in a resigned tone.

"I was not so blind that I could not see her selfish tendencies but, as I said, I chose to believe motherhood would transform her into a woman who placed her family higher than herself. I eagerly anticipated the arrival of children not only for the joy it would bring, but also to prove myself right. In her arms I frequently—and arrogantly it seems—assured my young wife that children would inspire a love in her unlike any other. I opened my heart to her and shared my dreams of the family for which I had always longed." His voice took on a harsh, self-condemning tone as he continued. "She would laugh in what I blindly believed was delightful anticipation. I later learned—by her own taunting admission—that it filled her with glee to beguile me. I now know that playing with my emotions served as an aphrodisiac. It gave her immense pleasure and satisfaction."

Lox shook his head in self-disgust before resuming a neutral tone. "As Julitha likely told you, all along and without my knowledge, my wife was intentionally preventing the possibility of conception while, at the same time, allowing me to believe that we were doing everything in our power to create children.

"Julitha told you of the letter that came into my hands? Yes?" Lox met my gaze, but only long enough to see me nod in affirmation. "The day I read that letter, my fascination for my heartless wife evaporated. That day, I finally understood what a ridiculous fool I had become."

It saddened me to hear the scathing self-loathing in his tone.

In the short time I'd been in these Lands, I'd seen firsthand that Lox could be arrogant, a necessary trait in a leader with his level of responsibility. Now I saw a different side of his complex character. In my heart, I knew he was a good man even if I still nursed residual resentment about his decision to call me. But I knew he did not deserve to be treated so abysmally by the woman for whom he'd so publically and foolishly fallen.

"When I read that letter," Lox continued, "I wanted to put my hands around her throat and choke the life out of her."

Lox's hands were in front of him, curled into claw-like fists as if he was mentally strangling a phantom image of his perfidious wife. He seemed to realize this and re-clasped his hands behind his back.

"I initially intended to confront her, but then had the notion to trick her as she had tricked me. I went to the apothecary and shamefully used my influence to coerce him into providing my wife with a false contraceptive. I remain conflicted about having used my wife to get what I wanted, just as she had used me to access a deep well of wealth and status. Not my proudest moment. But I still believed that a child would open her heart. Yet..."

He shook his head and cleared his throat as if girding himself for what he must divulge next. "Yet, when she learned she was with child, her first action was to visit a specialized medical practitioner to terminate the life that quickened in her womb." He frowned at his feet. "Julitha would not have told you that. Few know of it. Because I did not trust her, I had the foresight to have her followed. Thus, it was when I learned of her visit to the abortionist that I discovered I would be a father. Out of necessity and to protect the child she carried, those I employed to follow her became her guards. It was also when I stopped frequenting her bed."

As I listened to Lox, in the back of my mind I was thinking of women in my world who had what I believed was the indelible right to terminate a pregnancy. I'd never personally been in a

68

position where I had to make this difficult decision—in fact, I had not been able to conceive despite years of trying—but I felt strongly that women must be allowed to retain their right to choose. What I found impossible to understand in Lox's account was Toriah's decision to abort her fetus while married to a man who would clearly love that child.

"Despite the attention of various Diviners and medical practitioners," Lox continued. "My wife's pregnancy compromised her health. I was not entirely unsympathetic toward her suffering, but predominantly I feared for the well-being of our child. When our healthy son finally came into the world, I was overjoyed." Lox smiled absently at the distant memory. "She had little interest in him, and declined to nurse him. Yet, as I predicted, by the time he was a few months old, she did indeed begin to take an interest. He was a happy and amiable baby, and she delighted in having fine costumes made for him and showing him off. It seemed to me that becoming a mother had, in fact, softened her a little. Regardless, by that time it was far too late to salvage our marriage union. We had been living separately in the same home since the day she attempted to end her pregnancy. Then, shortly before our son reached his second Birth Day, we traveled to West Scapah. What unfolded there is public knowledge." In a voice thick with emotion, Lox added, "I am certain she misses him, but surely not as much as I. Surely not." His last words were barely above a whisper.

I wished I knew what to say to ease his pain, but there were no words, in his world or mine.

"Since then, she has remained Rodmyrrah's favored and much indulged paramour in West Scapah. It is widely assumed that her public indiscretion distresses me, but please know it does not. Life without my son is agonizing; life without my wife is a gift. I do not feel less of a man because she discarded me for the foreign lord; yet, I do feel less of a leader for ignoring Julitha's forewarning and entering a marriage union with her."

It seemed to me that a great deal of tension had lifted from Lox as a result of sharing his tale. He'd finally unclasped his hands and his arms moved at his sides in a natural rhythm.

"Only a handful of people know about my wife's deceitful use of contraceptives. Fewer know of her attempt to terminate the pregnancy. And even fewer know of my equally devious trick to father a child. The other elements of my story are, unfortunately, general currency amongst the populace. I am fully cognizant that many feel pity for me. I would change that if I could. I cannot, for it would mean divulging the more intimate details of my marriage union, which I will not do. Until recently, I never felt the need to seek permission from the Priests of the Temples of the Gods to sever our union. Neither has she, for it matters not to her whether she is Rodmyrrah's wife or his mistress. She cares only for his wealth and the attention his status lavishes upon her."

Lox focused on me then. I could see he was no longer mired in memories of his past.

"If—and believe me I understand that it remains an *if* for you, Meredith—if you chose to capture Rodmyrrah's image, then Toriah's access to the prosperity of the Western Duchy will vanish with Rodmyrrah's death. As my wife, and despite her indiscretions, I will be obligated by law to provide for her. As such, I felt I must remove any right she has to my name, my status, or my wealth. In spite of the pressing political events unfolding in our Lands, I have just come from the Isle of Mathe where the High Priest resides at Sherha's Mound. I initiated a request to have the union officially severed. I must now wait and see what comes of it."

CHAPTER 8

$\mathcal{B}$y the time Lox concluded his story, we'd reached the end of the shell-strewn beach. It seemed natural to detour to the largest of the logs and sit. As I tucked the folds of my skirt around me, I distractedly noticed how the cinnamon accents made a striking contrast against the log's bleached whiteness.

"Lox, would you have shared your story with me if Julitha had not already done so?" I asked.

Lox's gaze remained on the rolling surf as he shook his head. "I truly do not know, Meredith. I have never openly discussed the events. Not even with Fredryk or Rikka." He looked at me and spoke with intensified gravity as he regarded me. "Do not misunderstand me. Exposing the intimate details of my personal suffering is not an attempt on my part to elicit your sympathy, or to manipulate your feelings, or even to alter your less than flattering opinion of me. I believe I would have refrained from raising this topic with you in large part because I hold the recollection of my childhood adventure in your world as one of the purest memories of my life; one that I did not want tarnished."

"But why were you so angry with Julitha?"

"I was angry with the Diviner because you are the last person

71

from whom I want to solicit pity; yet, that is what I saw in your eyes when I arrived."

"But Lox, the death of your son *is* tragic. What kind of person would I be if I didn't feel pity about that, and about your marriage, which was clearly no picnic?"

Lox smiled almost reluctantly. "You have always used phrases that strike me as very odd. I remember that pick-nick is how you described our meal time at the lake. Most certainly my marriage had nothing in common with that enthralling day. Indeed, it was no pick-nick."

"Well," I countered. "Your use of the word 'odd' is a significant understatement given the improbability of my even being in this world."

At my light-hearted tone, Lox's eyes lightened. He'd been a naturally serious child at twelve and had turned into a very serious man. He should smile more. He probably had around Axel.

"Meredith, I appreciate that you see fit to converse with me without acrimony. But I would like to know, had Julitha not made her pronouncement about your return, might you still feel loathing for me?"

I hesitated, thinking how best to answer. "Do you remember my sister?" I asked. I could see that my question startled him.

"Yes, most certainly. I remember everything about that day. She behaved toward you more like a mother than a sister."

"Yes, well...that's a whole other story. Anyway, she can hold a grudge like you wouldn't believe. But I've never been good at that —even if I have a good reason. Over these last few days with Julitha, I've been doing a lot of thinking. I do have a very legiti-mate reason to be upset with you, Lox. But I've also been able to deconstruct what you did and why you did it. And the only reason I've been able to do that is because Julitha has reassured me that I'm *not* stranded here. So yes, it does make all the differ-ence. I don't loathe you. I don't suppose I ever actually did," I admitted with a reluctant smile. I held up my hand when I saw he was about to interrupt. "But that doesn't change the fact that it was wrong of you and Rikka to be so cavalier with my life. That said, I do understand what led to your decision to call me here. I haven't reconciled with it, and I don't condone it—I doubt if I ever will—but I do understand what motivated you to make that decision."

"And, in your enhanced understanding, are you willing to depict Rodmyrrah's image?"

I shook my head. "No. That's what I'm trying to tell you. Lox, I'll travel with you to West Scapah because that city is where I will find this Traveler. The way I see it, he's my ticket home. And going home is my only objective. Drawing an image of Rodmyrrah? No way." I could see he wanted to argue, but he was too polite to interrupt me. "Hypothetically, I get that the ends might justify the means. Remind me later to tell you about a freak from my world named Hitler. But we're not talking hypothetical, are we? We're talking about me being an accomplice in ending someone's life. I just can't..." I shook my head. "You wasted your Traveler's Dust on me, Lox. You 'called' the wrong person. I wish there was something I could do for you that would still benefit you and Rikka and the people of these Lands. I really do. But I want it to be something that doesn't make me feel like an executioner."

"I do not want you to feel like an executioner, Meredith. That would be barbaric," he said quietly.

As he studied me, I saw again that well of sadness that marred the amber depths of his eyes. Now I knew what had put it there.

"I must tell you, Meredith, that during these last few days I, too, have been preoccupied with much internal debate. In fact, it is an irony for me to hear you say you understand my decision, for I am now conflicted by feelings of self-doubt. Not a preoccupation with which I have much familiarity." He dropped his eyes to gaze sightlessly down at his hands. "Did Rikka and I make a grievous error in using the last of the Dust to Call you here? I do not know," he admitted as he turned his head to regard me. "Meredith, do not misunderstand me, seeing you is..."

He searched my face as if the words he wanted were engraved across my brow or along the contours of my cheekbones.

"Seeing you..." For the briefest moment, he closed his eyes. "It fills my heart with gladness, Meredith. Being in your presence is like finding an oasis in the midst of a desert. That first evening, I enjoyed reminiscing with you more than words can convey." He sighed heavily as he looked unseeingly at the endless expanse of water. "But we could not have shared those idyllic moments if you had known, at the outset, the circumstances of your Calling. I deliberately chose to postpone divulging the truth to you so I could selfishly prolong the enjoyment your company brought. Later that evening, on Fredryk's justifiable urging, I resigned myself to telling you the next morning. But then Shulha..." He swallowed and dropped his gaze to his hands.

I had not forgotten Shulha's death, but I think I had forgotten that Shulha was to him like Curtis had been to me; a dearly loved member of the family.

"Then Shulha died," he added dully. "Perhaps you are right. Perhaps it was arrogant and self-serving on my part to Call you. It certainly was cowardly of me to postpone telling you the truth. And it was weak. But mostly it was self-indulgent." He met my gaze. "For my cavalier arrogance, I sincerely apologize."

Lox shifted on the log then so he faced me. "Allow me to make a pledge to you, Meredith. I do not want you to ever feel coerced by me or anyone else in these Lands. Thus, if you find that you still cannot capture Rodmyrrah's image by the time we arrive in West Scapah, I promise I will not try and convince you to act in contradiction to your conscience. I will do nothing to take away your power to choose. Not ever again."

I was moved by his spontaneous, heartfelt promise. "Thank you," I said with a relieved smile. "I'll hold you to that, you know."

Lox smiled briefly in return, then lifted a hand to tuck a stray hair behind my ear. His tender touch tingled warmly against my cheek.

"And, since I am apologizing for my actions," he continued quietly, holding my gaze. "Please know that I am grievously sorry about pulling Kimberly here with you. It is obvious how greatly you cherish her." He tilted his head as he studied me. "It would never occur to *you* to be careless with the ones you love, would it?"

His innuendo made it clear that he blamed himself for the irrevocable consequence of leaving his son unattended on that tragic day, just like Kimberly blamed herself for her father's death. I couldn't help but wonder how much wasted energy we invested in guilt and self-blame during the course of one lifetime.

Lox gave me a sudden smile that completely altered his somber countenance. "Do you recall how fiercely protective you were that day at the lake championing us when your brothers persisted in their ridicule?" Lox lifted his hand again and gently rested his palm against my cheek.

His thumb caressing my skin and the desire glowing in his magnetic eyes held me captive. "Lox," I pleaded in a soft voice. I couldn't summon the words to break the spell his touch seemed to have cast.

He leaned toward me then just as he had that day twenty-two years before. I knew he was going to kiss me and I knew that I shouldn't let it happen. For a fleeting moment, I wished to be whisked home even knowing that, if my wish were instantly granted, then the ghosts of two unconsummated kisses would doubly haunt me.

My wish wasn't granted. Instead, the touch of his lips sent a shiver through my body like champagne on the underside of my skin. In my mind, I heard the seductive voice of Etta James singing the lyrics of *At Last*. Overcome with desire, I deepened the kiss, reveling in his immediate response. My arms lifted of their own accord to wind possessively around his neck. In that moment, even if the last shuttle to Earth had been on that beach and in the last thirty seconds of its final boarding, I'm not sure I would've had the willpower to tear myself out of his embrace.

The kiss ended, slowly and languorously. I rested my cheek against his jawline, noting the abrasiveness of his bristle and relishing it simply because it belonged to Lox. I closed my eyes and filled my nostrils with his scent, reveling in the feel of his hands against my back and in my hair. When he adjusted his hold so that he could lift my chin, I met his gaze. Passion glittered in his golden eyes as I knew it did in mine. When he opened his mouth to speak, I spontaneously silenced him with another kiss. I did not want words to ruin this moment.

This time when our lips touched, I felt like a detonating cord had been lit at the core of my being. Every vein and nerve-ending in my body sizzled.

I can't say where our passion would have led had not the jukebox in my mind screeched unpleasantly as if a needle were being dragged across a vinyl record. Unlike the words of the song, Lox was *not* mine. He never would be. He belonged in his world. And I belonged in mine.

I tore my lips from his. "Stop!" I insisted as I disentangled myself from his embrace. I shifted down the log an arm's length away. It would be so easy—and gloriously satisfying—to become Lox's lover for the duration of my stay in his world. But my heart was far too fragile to survive a temporary liaison with this man. Anyone else perhaps, but not Lox. I made myself sit on my hands so that I could not give in to the temptation of reaching for him.

"I can't do this, Lox."

"Why can you not?" he demanded hoarsely.

I was thankful he at least refrained from reaching for me. I wasn't sure I had the strength to resist him a second time.

"Why can you not, Meredee?" He repeated, staring at me in bewilderment when I didn't immediately answer.

It was not lost on me that he used my nickname, the name I'd forbidden him to speak. But that was no longer an issue for me. "Because...it's...I...there's a whole host of reasons why not!"

"Name one."

"Well...for one, you're married, remember?" *That's lame,* I thought to myself as soon as I said it.

"My marriage union has no relevance," he countered, an impatient edge to his tone.

I knew I owed him an honest response, at the very least for the sake of our childhood friendship, but also because he'd been heartbreakingly honest with me. "Fine then. I don't want a short-term romance, Lox. Not with you." Looking out at the ocean, I sighed heavily as I searched for words. "The truth is, my feelings for you are not casual. They're deep and real and complex. This..." I released one hand and waved it between us before jamming it back under my leg. "Whatever this is, it has nowhere to go. Over the years, my self-esteem has taken a beating. So has yours, by the sounds of it." I met his gaze. "I've only recently figured this out, Lox, but...my life?" I shook my head. "I've just been existing. Coasting. It's taken being in the absurdness of your reality to make me realize what I want, what critical decisions I have to make. And what I know for sure now that I didn't know when me and Kimberly first landed on that beach is that I deserve to carve out some long-term happiness for myself. A holiday fling with you? Tempting, yes, but it wouldn't enhance my happiness, it would detract from it. So, let's do ourselves a favor and acknowledge that this...attraction between us is a dead-end."

I turned to look at him, but rolled my eyes in response to his look. A redneck in Bloomingdales couldn't have looked more baffled. When I next spoke, I softened my tone. "It's simple, really. I'm not able to become *your* lover without giving you my heart, Lox. I wouldn't know how to take it back when it's time for me to leave." I shrugged with finality and then lied through my teeth, forcing myself to hold his gaze. "The truth of the matter is I have no intention of falling for you. It's as simple as that." Lox couldn't know I was already well beyond the half-way point of falling for him.

Instead of looking displeased—the response I'd been expecting —Lox smiled at me. The wonder in his eyes evaporated the weariness and strain that had marred his handsome face. "Is that how you say it in your world, Meredee? You would 'fall for me'? I would catch you. And I hope you would do the same for me. For you must know, I have already 'fallen' for you."

As he spoke he reached for me, but I leaned away. "Lox!" I insisted, holding up my arm like a patrol sign. "Don't make this harder for me than it has to be, okay?" I dropped my hand into my lap. "It's not that simple, and you know it. I *am* leaving. The fact that you don't believe me is, frankly—and sorry for sounding harsh—but it's your problem." At his baffled look I rolled my eyes again. "Come on, Lox. Work with me on this, okay? I don't want to fight with you, and I don't want to shut you out. It's too exhausting. But the simple fact is, our friendship? It has to be platonic. None of this...well, it's not real. At least not for me." That was another bold-faced lie. I might not be able to convince anyone of the reality of this place, but in the short time I'd been here, my complex and complicated feelings for Lox had already worn a deep grove into my heart that was as undeniable as the Grand Canyon. But even standing on the edge of the Grand Canyon, all one had to do was face away and it would be gone.

Lox sighed heavily before giving me a resigned smile. "Meredee, I have no wish to fight with you either. I never again want to give you reason to fling words of abhorrence at me. Even so, that does not change anything about how much I love and desire you. And I hope you know that I am not being arrogant when I say I know you feel the same for me."

I looked toward the sea. The portion of my heart that belonged to the girl I'd once been was doing somersaults of delight at his deliberate use of the word 'love'. But the rational woman I'd become wished he hadn't complicated this already complicated conversation with evocative declarations. I met his gaze. "For goodness sakes, Lox, one of us has to be rational."

"What if Julitha is wrong, Meredee? What if the Traveler is a hoax, as I believe? What if you cannot, in fact, return to your world? What then?"

When he shrugged in a hopeful kind of gesture, I realized something I should have seen from the beginning. All along, Lox had been harbouring a foolish fantasy that we could carve out a future together. Underlying his justification for his world needing my so-called unique skill was a misplaced hope that he and I would somehow end up together. He'd been devastated by his wife's insincerity and his son's death, and he was lonely. And now he was attempting to bring to maturity something that had started years ago. He seemed unable to recognize there wasn't enough fertile ground in all these Lands to cultivate his illogical illusion. For me, this startling revelation illuminated much about his intentions. And it was flattering. And ludicrous. And ever so sweet. Yet it changed nothing. He was being completely unrealistic. He was making the same silly mistake of placing me on the same ridiculous pedestal I'd placed him.

"Lox," I said shaking my head and loosely clasping both hands in my lap. The moment of passion had passed and I knew I would now behave sensibly. "There is no 'what-then'. This..." I searched for a word. "This attraction between us has to fizzle out. It has nowhere to go. The only place I'm going is home. We can either be platonic friends until that happens, or...well, there is no 'or'. I'm totally serious, Lox."

He stared at me for a moment before heaving a resigned sigh. "Very well, Meredee. I will take your friendship, and gladly. I will value and cherish it, for always."

We smiled a little forlornly at each other.

"Okay, then," I said.

"Oh-kay," he echoed.

My sudden burst of laughter startled a nearby flock of sea

birds that had gathered along the shoreline. They squawked loudly in protest as they flew away.

Lox was also startled. "I did not use your word in the correct context?"

"You did, Lox. Only, it sounds hilarious when you say it. Slang doesn't roll naturally off your tongue."

"Oh-kay, oh-kay, oh-kay," he practiced playfully.

We shared an amused grin.

"Meredee, I have not felt this..." He paused then as if searching for words. "This *unburdened* in a very long while. Thank you."

"I'm glad to hear it Lox, but it has nothing to do with me. Nothing's really changed, has it? I won't create an image of Rodmyrrah. And I *am* going home."

"But everything, for me, has changed," he said with a thoughtful frown. "And it has everything to do with your presence here in my world." He shifted closer to me, but this time without the intention of reigniting our passion. "Allow me to make a second pledge to you," he declared, resuming his characteristic earnestness.

I could see him struggling not to take my hand in his.

"For the time it takes us to travel to West Scapah," he continued, "I shall put away my fears about the future. I shall only revel in the pleasure of being with you, in our platonic friendship," he added with a teasing smile. "For whatever time remains. This I shall do, and with the utmost pleasure."

I wanted to hug him then, but I squinted at him in mock ferocity instead. "If you're trying to butter me up just to get me to draw nasty old Rodmyrrah, think again."

"Butter you up?"

The suggestive look Lox gave me was heart-stoppingly sexy. I had to fight against letting the flames that flared in his amber eyes melt my resolve. It occurred to me then that I would have to be utterly committed and resolute while we traveled together over the next few weeks if I was going to be successful at keeping this captivating man at an arms-length distance.

I adopted an instructive tone to hide my internal battle. "It's a phrase from my world. You use it when you're trying to flatter someone in order to compel them to do something you want. Usually, against their better judgment."

Lox was immediately contrite. "I did know that, Meredee. I did not intend for my words to make you guarded again."

"I'm not. It's just…Let's not complicate things with flirtatious banter. Let's simply be friends."

The smile he gave me contained the full wattage of his devastating magnetism. "Friends we shall always be, on that you have my word. Meredee, you cannot fathom how vastly relieved I am to no longer be tangled up in your anger and resentment. I have had enough of such unpleasant emotions to last me a lifetime. Truly, I am simply content in this moment to be here with you, in friendship."

"Well…okay then," I said in genuine relief.

"I could not have expressed it better myself."

We both chuckled at his deliberate avoidance of slang, and then again when we simultaneously stood.

As we strolled back the way we'd come, we chatted companionably. We talked about Brebin and how difficult it was for Lox not to be with his valued friend at such a tragic time. I told him about Curtis, and then shared how I believed that Kimberly's time in the Lands of Vendome had done much to heal her.

As we walked, I deliberately kept my arms crossed so that I would not give in to the temptation of tucking my arm in his. For the weeks of our shared journey, I would have to subvert all thoughts about how irresistibly sexy, attractive, amazing, and absolutely, utterly fascinating this man was. But I promised myself that, when I got home I would buy an entire art store's stock of sketchbooks. And I would fill every page with his arresting face.

CHAPTER 9

*A*fter Lox and I returned from the beach, I changed into my riding clothes—a camel-coloured blouse in a plain-woven linen and a voluminous pair of midnight green trousers made from a durable but high-quality cotton twill. A handful of days ago I could not have imagined being in a calm state of mind while readying myself for a journey with Lox. A *double*-handful of days ago, I thought to myself, I could not have imagined the mind-blowing reality of reuniting with my childhood friend in a world that was not my own.

I went to retrieve my saddle bags where I'd left them on the window seat, but paused as I looked out into the inviting yard where I'd first sat and had tea with the warm and welcoming Diviner. I did not have a view of the sea from here, but with the window open I could smell the invigorating and singular scent of salt and seaweed. Julitha must have sent word to her groom on a nearby farm to request delivery of my saddled horse, for it was in the shady lane standing next to Lox and Fredryk's mounts. Despite Lox's directive to leave immediately, there was no sign of my travel companions or Julitha.

Earlier, Julitha had helped me pack my borrowed clothes and toiletries in a finely handcrafted pair of worn leather saddlebags. I'd promised her, upon reaching my destination and before leaving for my world, I would arrange to have everything returned. But she'd only smiled and assured me that it was no hardship for her to replace these items. I'd just added the walking costume to the bags, which were now stuffed full; a grey dress made of silk charmeuse; a second pair of riding trousers; two blouses; a beige tightly-knit, poncho-like wool sweater; and two nightdresses, one in lightweight cotton and the other a heavier cotton-linen blend. Julitha had also given me a supply of soft cambric linen underclothes and a navy hooded cloak that she said was woven with wax-covered threads to give it waterproof properties. The only items I'd arrived with—Kimberly's shirt and the warm and serviceable wool shawl Fredryk had purchased for me —were also packed, and I was wearing my supportive, under-wired bra as I felt strangely vulnerable without it.

I'd forgotten to ask Lox about my 'Bellecourt clothes', but I assumed he still had them. I wouldn't need them until reaching my destination, but I would certainly change into them before being sent back. I would have trouble enough explaining my absence let alone if I showed up wearing Julitha's clothes.

I reached into the left saddlebag and retrieved a small oxblood velvet pouch, letting the contents fall into my palm. It was a neck-lace Julitha had made and infused with safe-travel blessings. She'd shaped the edges of a coin-sized shell pendant into a smooth, perfect circle, and painted a miniature replica of the beach below her cottage in its concave indent. The pendant dangled from a perfectly matched string of tiny pink-hued shells. Scared of losing it, I'd decided I wouldn't wear it until I went home. I knew I'd treasure it always.

So much had changed for me in the days since my arrival at Julitha's cottage. I'd initially dismissed her claim that the wind chimes at her door were infused with healing powers, but I believed it now. For all intents and purposes, my life had been over the day Lox had confessed he'd stranded me in his world. But after spending time with Julitha in the safe and soothing sanctuary that was Spring Willow Cottage, I'd gained clarity about the reasons Lox had called me here; about Kimberly's well-being; and about what I truly wanted—to go home and embark on a new, more fulfilling life of my own choosing.

When I saw two strange men striding out of the cottage and across the yard toward the horses with Julitha trailing behind, I did a double take. I barely recognized Lox. He was wearing a misshapen hat and loose clothes suitable for a labourer. Fredryk had shaped his heavy stubble into a salt-and-pepper goatee and appeared handsome and prosperous in his expensive-looking clothes. Lox had told me we'd be traveling with false identities, but I hadn't realized he and Fredryk would reverse roles. It was a brilliant idea. The seemingly minor changes didn't at first explain why each man looked so different, but then I realized Lox had altered his posture, drooping his shoulders and scuffling his feet, and Fredryk held himself like a man of importance. The ease with which the appeared to adopt these modified personas made me suspect they'd done something like this before. Perhaps many times before.

I put the necklace back into the velvet pouch and stuffed it deep into the saddlebag, then buckled the clasps. With a bag in each hand, a wide-brimmed hat on my head, and the woolen cloak over my arm, I took one last look at the cozy dormer room and left.

Once my bags had been secured behind my saddle, I turned to hug Julitha, thanking her profusely for all she'd done. Our farewell was particularly poignant for me because, although she would be able to "see" me if she chose, I knew I would never see her or hear anything about her ever again.

As my traveling companions and I left the Diviner's cottage on horseback, I turned in my saddle to wave at Julitha where she stood at her gate waving to me in return. I kept her in sight until we went around a bend and she and her cottage were lost from view. I was eager to embark on this journey that would ultimately allow me to return home, but I was also sad knowing I'd never again see the lovely woman with whom I'd forged a deep and abiding friendship. Wishing for a distraction, I asked Lox to tell me about the disguises they'd adopted for our journey. I learned that they'd indeed adopted these identities on multiple occasions in their covert attempts to gather information about the mood of the people who inhabited these Lands. For the duration of our journey, Fredryk was a prosperous silver mine owner who, if anyone asked, was intent on sourcing a new supply of the specialized shallow copper vessels that were required to smelt his silver. I was his mute sister accompanying him for the simple pleasure of the autumn journey, and Lox was our servant. On those occasions when our small party would encounter travelers, I was to refrain from speaking so as not to evoke any curiosity about my strange accent. If my silence was questioned, Fredryk would explain that I'd been born mute and, although I could hear, I'd never learned to speak.

As we traveled north, the breathtaking vistas of the spectacular, coastal scenery distracted me from my melancholy at leaving Julitha. I had to commit these images to memory as, not for the first time, I had to stop myself from reaching for a camera. It seemed somehow amiss not to have the capacity to take photographs. Something else struck me as odd, but it took me a while to figure out that it was the absence of modern sounds of machinery; a plane overhead, a chugging truck or motorcycle on a distant road; a generator near a homestead; or even a tractor in a field. This lack of machine-induced sounds was decidedly odd.

Shortly before dusk on that first day, we turned inland toward the foothills. We'd mostly seen pastures and fields of crops in various states of harvest, but these soon changed to gently sloping hills covered in vineyards. Although I was sad to leave the ocean behind, the beauty of the rolling hillsides beneath the setting sun kept me just as spellbound. Not long after as we crested a high hill, I caught my first glimpse of the distant mountain range that marked the border between the two Duchies. Over the next two days as we continued to travel toward the mountains, I began to understand why this spectacular range had been named the 'Folded' Mountains. In the right light, the tree-covered hills and valleys truly did resemble folds of rich velvet in variegated shades of green that were now dotted with the splendour of burgeoning autumn hues.

The settlements and townships through which we passed as we journeyed north and west, some quite large and others barely more than a cluster of buildings, consisted mostly of dwellings constructed of local ivory-hued stone. Hostels and inns were plentiful along the winding, cobbled streets in the numerous towns and villages. The splendour of the countryside and the picturesque townships were further enhanced by mild weather, although Lox assured me I would need all my layers once we reached the mountains.

Lox also informed me about the milestones on our long journey. We would reach the border city of Ballindale on our fourth day of travel. It would then take about nine or ten days to traverse the Folded Mountains on a well-traveled trade route, and a further six or seven days to cross the rugged terrain of the downward sloping western plateau before we would descend through a sequence of valleys to reach our final destination of the royal city of West Scapah on the River Atha.

This plan took me by surprise, as I'd assumed we would be visiting Rikka before making our way west. Illogically, I was conflicted about reuniting with the woman who'd so arrogantly approved of snatching me from my world to serve her needs in this one. I still could not imagine a circumstance where I would justify doing the same to her, or anyone else for that matter. Regardless, a part of me was disappointed I would not have the chance to see Rikka. Perhaps I would write a letter to her before I left, telling her how angry I'd been about her decision but also explaining why I would not draw Rodmyrrah. And wishing her well, of course.

Despite the fact that my traveling companions knew I had no intention of drawing the foreign lord, they were still determined to arrive in the city of West Scapah in time for the annual Coronation festivities. These public events, which spanned two days, would provide spectators, including me, with multiple opportunities to observe Rodmyrrah. It was for this reason that our days began at first light and did not end until dusk.

When we'd first begun traveling and despite my double-take when I glimpsed Lox in Julitha's yard, I didn't believe that his disguise would truly fool anyone. But his astonishing ability to modify his posture and speech took me by surprise. By the time we'd passed through the first town, I concluded that his tentative gait, submissive mannerisms, and rough speech were no less than Oscar worthy. Fredryk, too, acted the part of master exceptionally well. On those occasions when people tried to engage me in conversation, they readily accepted Fredryk's explanation of my inability to speak.

At one point in our travels, Lox pointed to the road that led, with half-a-day's journey on horseback, to the Astromancer's estate where he'd expected me to arrive. I wondered then if I would ever know why Kimberly and I had landed on that lakeside beach near Conraz's hunting lodge.

All in all, I felt like I'd embarked on a backcountry adventure holiday in some remote country in my world that had not yet embraced Twentieth Century practices. My only real problem in those early days of travel was trying to accustom my backside to sitting in a saddle. As often as was feasible, I dismounted and walked to avoid the discomfort of that unforgiving perch.

As I often couldn't speak while strangers were in earshot, I had a great deal of time to reflect. Some unfamiliar feeling kept tugging at the peripheral edge of my thoughts. It took me some hours to tease it closer, but I finally realized that, for the first time in years, I was happy.

CHAPTER 10

*A*t the end of each long day of travel, Lox would book Fredryk and I separate bedchambers at an inn, deliberately chosing accommodation that neither man had previously frequented. Lox was usually assigned a pallet on the floor in the servants' quarters. If there were none available, he would be relegated to the hayloft above the inns' stables, a circumstance that did not seem to trouble him in the least. I couldn't help but respect the fact that he willingly humbled himself to play the part of servant to his own servant in order to do what he could to quash the threat of war. I also found myself reluctantly intrigued and entertained by his exceptional acting ability.

Despite the fact that they took extra precautions with their disguises while we traveled in the region near Lox's massive family estate—bypassing it would have added days to our journey—Fredryk was recognized on two occasions. Thankfully, neither instance had any adverse effect, except to increase my fascination with the man my childhood friend had become.

One day, after lunching on delicious meat pies in a small village, Lox left us briefly to make a few purchases. I was standing beside my horse when an older man on crutches recognized

Fredryk. The fact that Fredryk was not in the company of the Chancellor was clearly a disappointment to the man; nevertheless, he implored Fredryk to give Lord Loxley a message of deep gratitude for providing a home for him and his family. Later I learned that the man had lost a leg in a tragic accident. No longer able to pay rent on the cottage he shared with his widowed daughter and her young children, the landowner had evicted the family from their home. When Lox learned of this injustice, he'd provided them with a cottage on his own estate until the man could once again earn an income, which he was now doing as an apprentice cobbler.

Fredryk was recognized a second time the next day in circumstances much the same, except this time by a woman who appeared to be in her mid-thirties. She also asked Fredryk to deliver a message of thanks to the benevolent Chancellor. Apparently, she and her husband, with the help of their seven children, farmed a small landholding where they raised pigs and sold them at market. Unbeknownst to them, their fence had broken and six of their prized sows had wandered into a marsh where they'd suffocated in a pool of quicksand. The farmer and his wife had not been able to save the sows and their livelihood was almost completely wiped out. When Lox learned of their predicament, he replaced all six sows with the agreement that the farmer and his wife would deliver to Hawkwood Heath half a dozen piglets every year for six years. The woman had been effusive with Fredryk in her thanks as, without the sows, they would not have had sufficient means to provide for their large family.

In both cases Lox had not been in earshot when these people encountered Fredryk. I later overheard Fredryk and Lox discussing these episodes, and saw Lox's genuine pleasure at the continued well-being of these two families.

Another surprise while traveling incognito with my two companions was discovering that Fredryk was, in fact, not the one-dimensional, taciturn, and unpleasant man I'd pegged him to be. Playing the master, Fredryk interacted with the strangers we met in a confidant, authoritative manner, engaging them in expansive and boisterous conversations on a wide variety of topics. In return, he gained a comprehensive knowledge of the mood and gossip of the people, including information that the Earl of Avercorris was indeed offering a monetary reward for information leading to the whereabouts of a foreign, fair-haired woman.

When we were able to discuss this news freely in the privacy of my bedchamber, both Lox and Fredryk exhibited grave concern. They made me renew my promise to remain mute and do nothing that would draw attention to me. Considering the vagueness of the Earl's description, I didn't take it seriously, but I did upbraid Fredryk for failing to discover the value of the reward.

Lox and Fredryk decided it would be prudent for me to take my evening meal in the privacy of my rented room rather than in the taproom where most of the other guests dined. That way I would not inspire curiosity from either locals or fellow travelers. As a result, Fredryk would pay extra coin so that the innkeeper would provide our 'servant' with a tray of food each evening for Fredryk's 'sister' who was feeling indisposed from a long day of traveling. I ate in the privacy of my bedchamber with Lox for company while Fredryk dined alone in the public taproom. This routine gave Lox and I the opportunity to talk freely and Fredryk the chance to glean information from locals and other wayfarers.

After his shared meal with our fellow travelers, Fredryk would join us in my room where he would give Lox a full account of all he'd discovered. From these reports I learned that, as Chancellor to the Grand Duchess, Lox was responsible not only for building relationships with foreign ambassadors to foster and stimulate trade relations, he also advised Rikka and her judicial leaders on what actions would be fair and equitable, and he worked closely with the military leaders to secure the Duchy on its borders and coastlines.

Rumors had already been rife throughout the Duchy that a secret alliance of nobles, who'd transferred their allegiance from the Grand Duchess to her brother the Grand Duke, were planning a coup in East Scapah. If these rumors were true—which Fredryk was trying to discover—it made it difficult for Lox or Rikka to know who they could trust. Despite this uncertainty, it was common knowledge among the populace that the Earl of Aver-corris had openly and arrogantly transferred his loyalty to the Grand Duke. It was also suspected—but not yet proven—that the Earl was the leader of this alleged and treacherous alliance, and that he had been agitating to merge the Twin Duchies into one country presided over by the Grand Duke. Those who were loyal to Rikka—a growing minority, they feared—were adamantly opposed to their Grand Duchess being ousted from her rightful throne. Both camps were becoming increasingly vocal about who was suspected of being a traitor. The end result was that hostilities were escalating within and between the previously harmonious regions.

Because of rising tensions, Rikka had been forced to dilute the strength of her patrols on her Duchy's northern boundaries where deserts separated the Twin Duchies from the marauding tribes inhabiting the Lands of Char. Beyond those Lands, Lox told me, was the Northern Realm, which consisted of fourteen tribes ruled by a King. Many other lands, including the Garden Archipelago, stretched beyond these, their closest neighbors. Rikka was, albeit surreptitiously, also increasing the number of warriors in her standing army. Her fleet of ships, which regularly patrolled the eastern and southern coastlines, were similarly on high alert.

Fredryk was clearly discomfited when he was forced to deliver news of the increasing frequency of open criticism directed at the Grand Duchess. These slurs were often made by influential merchants who complained that her soured relationship with her brother adversely affected their ability to conduct profitable trade. As I listened to Fredryk's account each evening, it became evident that this growing condemnation for Rikka aggrieved Lox deeply, especially given the fact that few people knew Jaybex was the victim and not the perpetrator of this upheaval.

Rikka had not lost hope when it came to her brother. Apparently, she'd consulted medical practitioners and Diviners to discover whether Jaybex would be permanently damaged when —*if*—he was ever released from the mind-weaver's hold. No one knew the answer, but they all agreed Jaybex's mysterious and debilitating state-of-mind had to be kept a secret from the general public for as long as possible in order not to incite panic or deflate hope for a peaceable solution. Unfortunately, until Rodmyrrah was successfully dealt with, no one could say with certainty that Jaybex would ever recover.

Lox informed me that, seven years before upon the coronation of the twin rulers, few members of the populace would've taken more than five minutes to comment on the political decisions and activities of the Grand Duke and the Grand Duchess. Where formerly there had been contented complacency and trust in their rulers, people now spent a great deal of time expressing their discontent. The tensions were at their highest in the border towns where family units were being torn apart by conflicting loyalties that created enemies amongst relatives, and pitted brother against brother and father against son.

When I asked Lox how the Priests of the Temple of the Gods factored into this political crisis, he explained they had no civil authority. They were an order of men who were tasked with interpreting and enforcing the Six Precepts that had been established upon the founding of the Lands of Vendome in ancient times when Venlandian Kings still ruled. As servants dedicated to the immortals, the Priests did not involve themselves in political upheavals within the Twin Duchies; rather, they only intervened and imposed the will of the gods—through force if necessary— when one of the Six Precepts was broken. The highest of these Six Precepts—that gods and winged beasts could be rendered as images while humankind and four-legged animals could not—was the very reason I'd been Called here. I already knew from Lox's earlier explanation that these Priests had the power to publicly condemn, and execute, any subject who dared defy this Precept.

As a result of gleaning this broader and more comprehensive understanding of the political situation in the Lands of Vendome, I reached the reluctant conclusion that the key to quelling any hint of war and reinstating peace in the regions did indeed rest in the removal of Rodmyrrah in a manner that could not be challenged by the influential traitors who'd aligned with him. Despite this conclusion, I still had no intention of drawing the man. Regardless, as I rode with my companions through the towns and villages and along the thoroughfares that wound through the countryside, I often found myself doing exactly as Julitha had implored, visualizing the people of these Lands being subjected to the ravages of war, leaving them injured, widowed, orphaned, or dead.

During the long hours of travel, especially in congested areas where I could not speak for fear of being overheard, I had lots of time to reflect on what I would have done had I been in Lox and Rikka's shoes. As leaders, they were responsible for the well-being of hundreds of thousands of people. Thinking about it logically and from the standpoint of preventing war, it seemed I really could find no fault with their plan. Their history of relying on Travelers of Old in times of great need made enlisting my aid a logical solution. Because of my sketchbook, Lox knew I had the ability to capture a person's true likeness. If they successfully utilized my skill as an image-maker, they could covertly and publicly provide 'proof' of Rodmyrrah's transgression against the Highest Precept of the Gods. A transgression of this magnitude would, in turn, provoke the Priests to call forth the deadly

Warriors who served them, and the heretics—both Rodmyrrah and the artist who'd had the audacity to capture his image—would be subsequently executed. This public denunciation, I now reluctantly believed, was the only way to neutralize the threat of war.

Lox's talk of heretics and executions seemed unreal, as if it belonged in a history book under a chapter heading, The Spanish Inquisition. But it was real to Lox and his first priority remained protecting my identity. Lox and Fredryk's conversations planted a knot of anxiety in the pit of my stomach, but not for my own safety. As I had no intention of creating a likeness of Rodmyrrah and therefore was not concerned about becoming the target of the deadly Warriors, it seemed our first priority should instead be protecting Lox's identity. He was the one with a price on his head if he entered the Western Duchy. I did not for one moment believe a god hurled a bolt of lightning from the sky, but something had killed Rikka's ambassadors. On top of that, if Rodmyrrah and his treacherous cronies weren't stopped, war would ensue. I was haunted by the opposing mental images of holding a guillotine-like pen in one hand if I drew Rodmyrrah, while wielding a giant-sized version of the grim reaper's scythe in the other if I did not. Visions of other deaths also troubled me; innocent people dying in towns ravaged by war or, worse, Lox being killed on a field of battle. Yet I insisted—to myself, since we never openly discussed it—that I would not draw Lox's enemy.

On a lighter note, the highlight each day was when Lox and I shared our evening meal in my rented room. We'd adopted an unspoken agreement to steer clear of subjects that would mar our growing camaraderie. We didn't discuss the task he and Rikka had devised for me, and we also avoided discussing my departure. Instead, we talked only of things that brought us pleasure. The outcome of one such conversation challenged my perception of Fredryk, and gave me greater insight into Lox's most dedicated friend and servant.

It was the end of our third day of travel and, as per our established routine, Fredryk spent his evening meal conversing with guests in the common room while Lox and I dined in my bedchamber. I'd earlier changed out of my travel clothes, sponged them and myself clean, and changed into my grey silk charmeuse dress. That night, when Fredryk rejoined us, he found Lox and I laughing so hard that tears shone on both our cheeks. I'd been regaling Lox with my version of the day Rikka, Jaybex, and I had rashly instigated The Inglorious Tree House Battle with our only weapon a boy with a wooden sword. My brothers and their friends, who were older and bigger, outnumbered us. Rikka, Jaybex, and I had no choice but to flee across the sacrosanct fairways of the golf course that bordered my childhood home. As we fled, we had to dodge clusters of irate golfers who brandished their clubs in frustration, and evade other golfers who chased us in their electric carts. Lox and I were in stitches when I described how my brothers and their friends—who'd followed us across the forbidden fairways—had been caught. They'd been subjected to severe consequences imposed by the small town's police chief. Rikka, Jaybex, and I had escaped unscathed and unpunished, an outcome my brothers considered a travesty of justice.

As I recounted the tale, it hadn't taken long for our contagious mirth to deteriorate into uncontrollable fits of side-splitting laughter. It was at this point Fredryk knocked on my door and entered. Upon seeing our mirth, he immediately frowned in what I interpreted as his usual censorious disapproval of me. Lox, who seemed unaware of Fredryk's displeasure, gleefully suggested he send himself down to the innkeeper to purchase a bottle of evening spirits so that his 'master and mistress' could imbibe in a nightcap. Because we were both still consumed by intermittent and semi-hysterical splutters, he had to make several concerted efforts to compose himself before he could finally depart the room in convincing subservience.

At Lox's departure and in the face of Fredryk's scowl, my humor evaporated.

"What, you're going to bawl me out now for making your master laugh?" I accused. "That's pushing your disapproval of me too far, Fredryk."

Fredryk and I hadn't warmed to each other in the days since leaving Julitha's cottage. I assumed he regarded the friendship blossoming between his master and me with disapproval in large part because I refused to perform the task for which I'd been Called. It often seemed to me that Fredryk could barely tolerate my presence.

I expected a caustic remark in response to my sarcasm, but his next words surprised me.

"It's been years since I have seen my lord laugh like that," he said in a tone that held an equal mix of awe and gravity.

I realized then that the reason for Fredryk's furrowed brow had not been disapproval but astonishment.

"It was a joy and a pleasure to behold," he added in a sincere tone. "Thank you."

Fredryk had never before given me any kind of praise, had never once thanked me for anything, and had never acknowledged the wrong that had been done to me. The gratitude and sincerity he now directed toward me on behalf of his master was so unexpected it left me speechless and flustered.

For a short time following that conversation—a very short time—Fredryk and I established an unspoken truce where we both made a conscious effort to be friendlier with one another. Unfortunately, while Lox and Fredryk continued to play their reverse roles to perfection, I failed miserably at the one request made of me—to keep my mouth shut and call no attention to myself. My actions in Ballindale the next evening made Fredryk so incensed that we quickly found ourselves back in the familiarity of our frosty and firmly entrenched friction.

CHAPTER 11

*L*ate the next afternoon, Ballindale came into view. I was riding beside Fredryk with Lox trailing behind us. Upon cresting the last rise and seeing the panoramic view of the expansive, bowl-shaped valley, I drew my horse to the side of the road. I had no camera and wanted to stop and absorb the beauty of this unexpected vista.

The city was nestled in the foothills of the Western Duchy, a region Rikka's ambassadors—including Lox—had been forbidden to enter on pain of death. I worried that it was too risky for him to enter the Western Duchy and continue on to the royal city of West Scapah, but Lox assured me that, as long as he and Fredryk maintained their disguises, we would all be safe.

Flags in every color imaginable flew from rooftops and spires, giving the city a lively, festive atmosphere. Lox had previously informed me that the town's name originated from the muddy winding River Ballin—an old Venlandian word for brown—that snaked its way through the valley. Most of the town lay on its western bank, with the eastern bank hugging the rocky bluff upon which we stood.

Fredryk drew his horse to a halt beside me and 'our servant' stopped slightly behind us. I smiled over my shoulder at Lox to indicate my delight with the view, but was surprised to see him exchanging a look of concern with Fredryk.

"What is it?" I said, checking first to make sure no nearby traveler would hear or see me speak.

Lox pointed with his chin. "The flags. It appears we have reached Ballindale on the night of the Cast Away Festival."

A large group of wayfarers were passing by, preventing me from asking what the castaways were.

"The resulting crowds will either be to our advantage and make us anonymous," Fredryk observed. "Or be to our disadvantage. Dare we assume no one in this crowed of revelers will recognize us?"

I wanted to argue that that there was no way Lox, in his present disguise, would be recognized. He was too good an actor. But again, the presence of strangers forced me to remain mute.

Lox addressed Fredryk in his servant-speak. "How far b'yond Ballindale be the next inn?"

"We would be traveling well into the night before we reached it." Fredryk gestured towards a road to the south of the city. "We could, however, bypass the city and make camp in the woods on the opposite shore."

My face fell at Fredryk's suggestion. Although I hadn't complained about my sore, aching thighs and buttocks, I'd privately asked Lox for a remedy. That morning, he'd promised to take time in Ballindale to shop for sheep's wool to pad my saddle and salve to soothe my chafed skin. Part of the reason the thriving city looked so inviting to me was because I knew Lox would be making these purchases.

He correctly interpreted my look of dismay and nodded at Fredryk. "To Ballindale, then."

"Our venture may come to naught," Fredryk bleakly observed as we nudged our mounts back onto the road. "With these crowds, we may not find an inn with vacant rooms."

We navigated down a curving wide thoroughfare paved in intermittent rows of bricks that, I assumed, gave a kind of grip for those traveling up the hill with loaded wagons. Like us, most of the travelers with whom we shared the road were heading into the city rather than away from it. Once on the valley bottom, we bottle-necked onto a wide, sturdy-looking bridge. The sound of the horses, cattle, and carts traversing across the wooden slats, mingled with the calls and shouts of townspeople, merchants, soldiers, and travelers, reverberated riotously, and the racket only served to heighten the festival atmosphere of the bustling town.

We made our way along crowded lanes lined with colorful awnings above market stalls displaying a wide assortment of food and goods, including a row of stalls with tubs of fragrant spices in rich, vibrant colors that had me longing once again for my camera. I took in the enthralling sights and sounds as my docile mount, who needed little direction, obediently followed Fredryk's slow procession through the crowded, cobbled streets.

When my eyes fell on a wig seller's stall, I jolted up in my saddle as an idea came to me. I almost called out for Fredryk to stop, but remembered just in time I was meant to be mute. I turned to look over my shoulder and caught Lox's attention, then gestured enthusiastically at the booth. Lox immediately deduced what I was after and smiled before he called out to his 'master'. In the next moment, Lox was off his horse and approaching the merchant. I would rather have picked out a wig myself, but I also knew that doing so might have made me memorable to the wig seller. Lox and Fredryk were nothing if not painstakingly cautious.

While Fredryk and I waited for Lox, I took in the activity in the expansive square. Stilt walkers dressed in colorful jackets and flowing red pantaloons wove through the crowds. Jugglers threw colorful hoops and balls while a family of acrobats performed stunts balanced on a thick rope strung between two buildings. As I watched, two acrobat children who couldn't have been more than six or seven years old did one last balancing stunt before dismounting. While the adults continued to perform more difficult manoeuvres, the children retrieved colorful cloth bags and what looked like maracas, shaking these at members of the audience until they laughingly, or begrudgingly, dropped coins into the bags. My eyes moved to the center of the square where a group of people stood with their backs to me near a tall fountain. I couldn't see what held their attention but the sound of their unified laughter briefly filled the air. My gaze was caught then by a strangely empty corner of the square where a lone woman sat on a small platform decorated with colorful flags and flowers. No one seemed to be giving her any attention, and nothing enlightened me as to her purpose for being there.

Lox returned with a paper-wrapped package. As he tucked it carefully into his saddlebag, he gave me a secretive and enigmatic smile under the brim of his hat.

Before remounting, Lox gestured at a street urchin lounging nearby and asked if he was interested in earning some coin. The boy nodded eagerly, listened intently to Lox's instructions, then ran ahead of us as we resumed our trek through the crowded city, going into every inn we passed to ask about vacancies. I was beginning to worry that Fredryk had been right and we wouldn't find lodgings when the boy came out of a tall, narrow inn with a faded sign above the lintel that read 'Rooster's Comb'. He went straight to Lox and I was relieved to hear him deliver the news that there was one room to be let. Lox handed over some coins and the boy looked up at Lox with unsuppressed delight. Clearly, Lox had given him more than the child expected.

I dismounted stiffly and gave my reins to a young stable lad before following Fredryk into the noisy common room. Lox trailed after us with our saddlebags.

Every table in the large room was filled. Numerous servers, who expertly balanced massive trays filled with jugs of ale, wines, and plates of steaming food, hustled through the throngs. No one spared us a second glance.

Fredryk led us through the crowds to a long counter where he quickly caught the innkeeper's attention and requested the room that was available to let. The innkeeper did not pause in his activity of filling pitchers with ale but immediately frowned and shook his head.

"I told the boy my only vacancy is a small attic room with a single cot." The innkeeper had to practically shout to be heard above the din of conversation. He glanced at me briefly before he turned his attention back to Fredryk. "Your lady can sleep there, although the quarters won't be to her standards. You and your servant can find a bed of hay in the stables if you're willing. I'm afraid that's all I can offer." The innkeeper raised his voice to drown out Fredryk's dismayed response. "You'll find no rooms in Ballindale this night no matter what inn you make your inquiry. Not on Cast Away night. The attic room is available only because my wife was saving it for her nephew. We just got word not ten heartbeats before you arrived that he's laid up and won't be coming. Take it, else you'll lose it to the next wayfarer who darkens my door."

"Very well," Fredryk responded in a resigned tone. "We shall take it."

They haggled briefly over the price, and Fredryk begrudgingly placed a generous number of coins on the counter. The innkeeper expertly scooped them up with one hand while using the other to keep the tap flowing, shouting as he did so for someone named Brita. Moments later, we were following a young serving girl of about fifteen through the crowd. She stopped momentarily to instruct a boy to prepare and deliver an urn of hot water.

We trailed after her up flights of stairs that got steeper and narrower with each level. After five flights, we finally arrived on a tiny landing that boasted one small, dirty window. Although it let in a dusty patch of sunlight, it looked like it had been shut for at least a century. Since there was only sufficient room for the girl and me on the landing, Lox and Fredryk waited on the top few steps of the stairwell. The girl opened the door with a large key she'd withdrawn from her pocket, handed it to me with a small curtsy, and then silently squeezed past Fredryk and Lox to resume her tasks in the crowded taproom below.

I stepped into the room, which was barely bigger than my walk-in closet at home. It boasted a cot on one side and a narrow, unstable looking sideboard on the other above which hung a cracked mirror. A rickety screen on my left shielded, I assumed, a chamber pot. The room was stuffy and I immediately went to the small window in the gable, relieved to find that I could push it open. I took a moment to admire the amazing view then turned and pounced on the package Lox had just laid on the bed beside my saddlebags.

I tore it open, revealing a short, black bob with a blunt fringe. "It's perfect," I breathed in delight.

"I deliberately chose something very different from your natural look. It might be to our advantage as we continue our journey."

I absently removed the wide-brimmed hat I'd been wearing and tossed it onto the bed as I turned to face the mirror. I tugged on the wig, tucked in the few stray hairs that escaped my braid, and then stared mutely at the dramatically altered image reflecting back at me. I shook my head experimentally. The bobbed hair bounced unfamiliarly against my neck and chin. I grinned at my reflection.

"So? What do you think?" I turned to the men and struck an exaggerated pose. "Do I look like the exotic fair-haired foreigner the Earl of Avercorris is trying to find?"

Fredryk and Lox were hovering at the doorway of the small room. It seemed my new look had struck both men dumb.

I sucked in a breath as a delightful thought came to me. "Lox, will you take me to the Festival? With this wig and your disguise no one could possibly suspect who we really are. And Julitha packed cosmetics for me. I didn't think I'd need them, but I can use them to alter my appearance even more."

Both men looked troubled at my request, but I babbled on excitedly.

"I can't possibly remain in *this* stuffy room all evening. And my joints will seize up if I don't go for a walk soon. And I'm sure I've got a thousand saddle sores. There's no way I could sit for another moment on anything, horse, chair, or bed. Please let's go to the Festival."

"It's too dangerous," Fredryk stated.

I ignored Fredryk, keeping my gaze on Lox, who seemed as intrigued as me with the idea of taking in the Festival.

"Lox, it would only be dangerous if I opened my mouth, right? Which I won't do. I promise. It will remain tightly zipped." I gestured as if zippering my lips closed. I could tell from Lox's expression that my use of the colloquialism amused him, especially given his fascination with the simple invention that closed and opened my tall boots.

"Oh-kay, oh-kay, oh-kay," he finally said.

I chuckled at his playful rejoinder. He'd been using the word 'okay' at every opportunity. It injected humor into whatever we were discussing at the time, although the joke was always lost on Fredryk.

Above the hum of distant conversation, we heard a set of footsteps ascending the stairs.

"That will be the boy with hot water," Fredryk warned.

"Come downstairs after you have bathed." Lox said, giving me a lopsided smile and a playful bow, before switching to his servant-speak. "It shall be my honor to accompany you t'the celebrations, m'lady."

CHAPTER 12

A little later, after a surprisingly refreshing sponge bath in the airless room, I studied my reflection in the cracked mirror. I'd dressed in the honey-toned silk walking costume and donned the wig. The black-haired woman with the kohl-rimmed eyes and the rouged lips and cheeks looked nothing like the Meredith Whitby who'd met Conrad Avercorris two weeks before. It dawned on me then why Kimberly had dyed her hair and worn all that heavy make-up and gruesome jewelry. If you stopped looking like yourself, you could more easily stop behaving like yourself. With her disguise in place, Kimberly had successfully transitioned into the persona of rude, belligerent teen.

As best I could, I smoothed out the wrinkles in my dress, then left my room to navigate the steep stairs. With each step, the noise volume increased. When I came to the top of the final staircase, I saw Lox standing below waiting for me, his hair still wet from his own wash. As expected, his stance perfectly personified the bored, yet attentive servant who'd been forced to wait upon his demanding mistress.

When he casually glanced up and saw me, his magnetic eyes blazed with a surge of heat that stopped my descent and took my breath away. The din in the room faded into the background. Over the last few days, Lox and I had made a concerted effort to nurture a platonic friendship. Now, I belatedly realized that our blossoming friendship had, in fact, caused our mutual attraction to increase rather than diminish.

Lox finally dropped his gaze and the spell broke. I breathed again and the clamor of the crowd resumed. I inhaled deeply, cursing my weak-kneed attraction for this man. My involuntary response renewed my belief that our relationship had to remain platonic. With my conviction restored, I moved to join him at the foot of the stairs. When our eyes met, his gaze held only guarded interest. "The master sent me t'accompany you t'make your purchases, m'lady."

I nodded, then followed Lox out of the noisy room. It was not yet evening, but with Ballindale tucked at the foot of a looming mountain, the sun had already disappeared. This lack of direct sunlight was welcome, as the day had been warm. Lox, ever the professional, trailed me by half a stride, pointing out interesting landmarks in his servant-speak and sharing anecdotes about the town's history. At an apothecary's shop, I waited outside while he purchased some ointment for my chafed skin. When we eventually arrived at the congested square, he bought each of us a fragrant bun that was stuffed with the perfect blend of spices, vegetables, and goat meat. He also ordered ale for himself and a tumbler of delicious chilled, white wine for me, which he explained was from grapes that grew in the region near where Julitha lived. The benches and tables in front of the baker's stall were filled to capacity and we were forced to remain standing while we ate. This was fine with me not only because of my tender bottom, but also because it gave me an opportunity to people watch. It dawned on me then that I'd forgotten to ask Lox who the castaways were and why there was a festival for them, but my lack of knowledge did not hamper my enjoyment of our outing.

Lox and I ambled along the merchant stalls. The wide assortment of goods was a feast for the eyes, showcasing items from functional pottery and fine clothes, to intricate jewelry and well-crafted weapons. When I paused to admire some beautiful wool shawls as soft and luxurious as cashmere, Lox informed me that 'the master' had provided him with sufficient coin to make my purchase. I knew this was his way of saying he wanted to buy one for me. Enchanted, I spent considerable time choosing, and finally settled on a light-weight, oyster-colored shawl embellished with a vibrant border of peacock feathers. It was too warm to wear it so the merchant neatly rolled it and tied it with a string, handing it to my 'servant' to carry.

By dusk, our meanderings had taken us to the lone woman I'd spotted earlier. I now saw she was perched on one of two low stools on the flatbed of a wagon whose sides had been let down. Flowers, wreaths, and ribbons decorated the otherwise plain, wooden platform.

Lox touched my elbow and gestured toward a row of stalls that displayed an assortment of sheepskins. I nodded my head vigorously—I would welcome the extra padding on my saddle— and then pointed to my feet to indicate I wished to remain where I was.

"Please may you wait here, m'lady, until I return," he said in a tone of attentive subservience.

I watched Lox engage one of the wool merchants in conversation, impressed yet again at how he could so convincingly shake off his natural authoritative persona and embrace the role of servant. As he began to haggle, I turned and strolled a few steps closer to the wagon, curious about why the woman sat alone. She looked to be about fifty years old with rich brown hair twisted into a loose chignon. She was wearing a seal brown dress patterned with marigold flecks and made from what looked like cotton broadcloth. Her hands rested calmly in her lap but her roving gaze was passing searchingly over the faces in the crowds with an air of peaceful expectancy. When her eyes fell on me, her clear-eyed gaze so reminded me of Julitha that I couldn't help but incline my head and smile. I was about to turn away and head toward Lox when I realized she seemed to have interpreted my casual nod as an invitation of sorts. I eyed her with apprehension as she rose, descended the roughly built wooden steps, and approached me.

When she stopped in front of me, I saw compassion in the milk-chocolate depths of her eyes.

She held her hands out expectantly. "Greetings. I am Marintha."

Her voice had a warm husky tone that made me think of fine cognac. Her name also cleared up the mystery of why she reminded me of Julitha. She was a Diviner. I was still a little taken aback that my friendly smile had caused her to approach me, but I hesitated only briefly before placing my hands trustingly in hers. Perhaps with our hands clasped I would be able to see Kimberly again. If so, and unlike what I'd done with Julitha, I would refrain from jolting myself out of that insightful vantage point.

The instant our hands touched, I realized I'd been foolishly naïve in assuming that clasping hands with Marintha would be similar to the experience of touching Julitha. I'd forgotten that each Diviner had their own very unique skill. Marintha's ability was nothing like Julitha's. In less than a heartbeat, I went from feeling carefree to being slammed by a colossal wave of sadness as if a lifetime of hurts had been concentrated into that one potent moment. A current seemed to pass through me, like an electric surge, opening a valve into a reservoir of painful memories I'd mistakenly assumed were long buried.

Astonishment widened Marintha's eyes. "You are not from these Lands! You are a—"

I frantically shook my head. In that moment, it was the constriction in my throat that caused my muteness, not a deliberate attempt on my part to maintain the role Lox had devised for me.

Instead of finishing what she'd been about to say, the Diviner smiled and shrugged. "It matters not," she said. Then she turned and, still clasping one of my hands, led me back the way she'd come.

Before I knew it, I'd mounted the steps beside Marintha and allowed her to gently push me onto the second stool. I barely noticed this, for I was focusing all my energy on suppressing the emotional tsunami that seemed to be pushing me on a cresting wave toward a precipice of heartache. Confused by the surging emotions that were bubbling just beneath my surface, I was incapable of processing what was happening with any degree of understanding.

I almost jumped out of my skin when Marintha, who stood beside me with one hand lightly resting on my shoulder, tilted her head back and uttered what I can only describe as a ululation. Her unusual cry caught the attention of a number of people passing by the platform. I badly wanted to flee, yet I was as rooted to that spot as an ancient tree. Then Marintha ceased her ululations, pulled up the other stool, and sat facing me. When she gripped my hands in hers and I met her gaze, our surroundings faded into the background. As I'd experienced with Julitha, I was powerless in that moment to tear my eyes away.

She spoke in a calm, kind tone, saying, "As long as you see yourself as the wounded child of a father unable to show love, you will never access all of who you are."

I stared at her in dumbfounded amazement. Based on the compassion in her eyes, I'd been expecting her to say something about Curtis's recent death—although I couldn't have explained how she would've known—but I certainly hadn't expected her to mention my estranged father. He hadn't been in my life for twenty-two years. But, as she continued, I finally understood who the castaways were.

"Your father may have cast you and the rest of your family away," she continued, "but you need not suffer from this injustice any longer. Child, I implore you, allow the frozen pockets of pain that line the walls of your heart to thaw. Doing so will change nothing of what your father did or did not do, but it will change everything of what resides within you."

At her words, I had the sensation of being in a dream despite my wakeful state. I seemed to be standing on a sandy beach. Somehow I knew to look down and saw a wooden chest upon which was inscribed my name. As I stooped and lifted the lid to reveal the contents of the chest, I somehow knew that, metaphorically, I was looking into my own heart. Inside were all the hurts of my past; my father's abandonment that caused my mother's permanent break with reality, Jillian's teenage betrayal, Sheldon's selfish rejection. I also saw something else, something that surprised me. There was an abundance of love, far more than could be contained in such a limited space, yet it was endless. I had a moment of intense clarity then; that endless stream of love resided within me. It had the power to neutralize all my past hurts. Within my very own heart, I had all the love and support I would ever need to shape myself into the person I wanted to become.

These revelations felt as tangible as running my fingers through a chest full of priceless jewels.

The dream-scene evaporated when the Diviner released my hands and stood. She kept one hand on my shoulder, signalling me to remain seated. But, had I tried to stand in that moment, I would've fallen.

I turned to look at what had caught the Diviner's attention, startled to see that a small group of people were now gathered expectantly in front of the wagon. It seemed the Diviner's ululation had summoned them, although many others in the square barely gave us a passing glance.

"One has come who has been Cast Away!" Marintha announced to this rapt audience.

Her unassuming statement finally loosened the constriction that had been blocking my throat. I dropped my face into my hands and wept. As a result of my past hurts, the shining 'me' at the core of my being had retreated to a private refuge in the furthest corner of my heart where I'd soothed the pain of my perceived unworthiness in sheltered isolation. I could not fathom how Marintha had known how much those past rejections had diminished me.

While I wept, Marintha continued to address the small gathering. "Will you agree to offer your healing to this woman so that she can shed the oppressive cloak of the Cast Away?"

I felt the Diviner resume her seat on the other stool. She gently lifted my hands away from my face and handed me a handkerchief. My spasm of weeping ended as quickly as it had begun. I suddenly felt light enough to float. I could not fathom how any of this was happening, but I had sense enough to simply allow this cathartic process to run its course. I smiled tremulously through my tears as I wiped my face with the handkerchief, then exclaimed in dismay when the black kohl and red rouge soiled the fine linen. This time when I met her gaze I saw the light of laughter in her eyes.

With a raise of an eyebrow, Marintha directed my gaze to the press of people who stood expectantly waiting. When I turned to look at them, I immediately spotted Lox. My heart jolted. I'd forgotten all about him. I had, in fact, forgotten all about Ballindale and my black wig and the impossible circumstances that had brought me to these Lands. As I met his gaze, I noticed his handsome features were marred by shock and concern. He seemed about to shed his servant persona and looked poised to act. What action, I couldn't say. It wasn't as if I needed rescuing. I was in no danger. I gave a slight shake to my head, hoping he grasped that I did not want him to draw any attention to himself. He seemed to understand and I saw with relief that he would remain where he was.

The Diviner's next words reclaimed my attention.

"By presenting gifts to you, these people show that you are worthy of love. Their tokens are meant to erase the pain from those who have been Cast Away."

I distractedly wiped away the last of my tears as I tried to absorb what she was telling me. "Gifts?" I asked stupidly. As if that was what I cared about! What I really wanted to ask was how, in such a short time, she'd freed me from an emotional burden I hadn't even known I'd been carrying.

The Diviner nodded. "Gifts! From the people, to symbolize healing; gifts, to validate the Cast Away's worthiness; gifts that will dispel the resentment you harbor in your heart and thus make space for love; gifts that, in the giving of them, will set you free."

I felt a tug on my skirt, and turned to see a girl of about four years of age in the arms of a man I assumed was her father. Both of them were smiling shyly at me. The child was holding out a miniature rag doll the size of my hand. Her smiling face was like a beam of sunshine breaking through the clouds after a violent storm. Seeing no other alternative, I tentatively reached out and accepted the doll.

"Bless you, miss," she said in a sweet voice.

I took a deep shuddering breath. "Thank you," I mouthed in a quiet, trembling undertone. The father nodded deferentially to me and then moved aside.

A grandmotherly woman stepped into their place. She grinned

at me unselfconsciously despite the gap where her front teeth should have been. She held out a pair of lace gloves. When I took them from her she reacted as the girl had, saying, *bless you, miss,* before also stepping aside.

And so it went on until there were dozens of small gifts at my feet. The people who'd already presented their tokens stood to the side. I was nervous about why they remained, but I could not ask Marintha as I was too preoccupied accepting the offerings and hearing the *bless-you-miss* over and over again like I was some kind of celebrity or saint or super hero.

By the time the three dozen or so people had finished presenting me with gifts, it had grown fully dark. Lamps had been lit in the square and on the buildings and street corners. Overhead, the sky had filled with stars.

The last person to present me with a gift was a crooked old man who handed me a delicately painted object about the size of a button. I whispered my thanks, but instead of giving me his blessing and turning away, he instructed me to tuck his gift into my chemise to keep the heart of the man who loves me close. I nodded again and quietly repeated my thanks, but he looked at me and gestured expectantly at my chest with a gnarled hand. After a startled exclamation—much to the amusement of the onlookers—I carried out his instructions and tucked the button into the lace edging of my bra. He did not need to know that it wasn't a 'chemise'.

Then the Diviner stood and, smiling down at me, pulled me up to stand beside her. I'd been so focused on what was going on around me that I'd temporarily forgotten the soreness of my thighs and backside. As I rose, I had to make a concerted effort to stop myself from massaging my aching bottom. I was still confused as to why this surge of generosity had made me the surprised and undeserving recipient of both a cathartic emotional healing as well as a large quantity of delightful gifts, but what was clear was that these proceedings were drawing to a close.

"Now it is your turn to give a gift," the Diviner instructed. "Upon this final exchange you will be free of the bondage of the one who cast you away."

"I didn't bring...I don't have..." I stammered under my breath.

"You can throw coppers or, if you have none, chant a rhyme or tell a joke. Entertainment pleases them the most."

I gaped in consternation at the group of gift-givers who looked back at me in expectant anticipation. My eyes fell on Lox who was fumbling with the moneybag at his belt as he moved toward me. I could give these people his coin, yes. But, after their indescribable generosity, it would feel wrong if my token of appreciation came from something that did not belong to me.

Without thinking, I turned to the Diviner and blurted, "I will sing."

Behind her shoulders, I could see the multitude of unfamiliar stars in the night sky. Immediately, my thoughts went to Kimberly. I closed my eyes and pictured her singing *Starry, Starry Night* as Jazper steadily rowed her across that terrifying lake. Their lives had been spared because of that song. I breathed deep and then I, too, began to sing. As the haunting melody rolled off my tongue, I knew my voice, while not equal to Kimberly's, had never before sounded so pure and my tone and timing had never before been so perfect. I opened my eyes and looked up at the star-filled sky and sang as if Kimberly and Curtis were somewhere in those endless depths gazing upon me.

On the last note, I dropped my gaze from the beauty of the starry night and took in the sea of faces. The crowd had grown significantly and people were staring at me in mesmerized silence as if I'd put a spell on them. In the flickering lamplight, I saw that some cheeks even shone with tears. The silence in the square reminded me of the response Kimberly and I had received in the felter's cottage after we'd sung. There, too, we'd been greeted by stunned silence. I pictured Shulha, her hands on her pregnant belly and her face beaming as she announced she would name her child Singer.

And then, as if I'd been hit by a lightning bolt, I realized what I'd done. No one in these Lands sang. No one even knew what singing was.

What better way to advertise who I was, where I was, and with whom I was traveling than to display my otherworldly talent in front of a captive audience? In my mind's eye, I saw the bright lights of a flashing marquee and knew that the Lox's enemies would see it too: *Lord Loxley and the Traveler, in Ballindale!* Lox had been forbidden to enter the Western Duchy on pain of death. If he was discovered here and subsequently targeted by the so-called thunder and lightning of the gods—which I'd dismissed as nonsense—then his assassination would be entirely my fault. All this time, I'd been adamant I could not be responsible for the death of the faceless stranger I was summoned here to draw; now, inadvertently, I would be responsible for the death of a man I had grown to profoundly admire and love.

Panic overwhelmed me. When I called Lox's name, my voice rang out like the single peal of a bell. It broke the strange spell of silence my performance had cast. When I could no longer find him in the teeming sea of faces, terror almost overwhelmed me. Had he already been identified and killed? But then the wagon tilted. In the next moment, I felt his strong arms wrap protectively around me.

"Someone will collect the gifts later," I heard him say to the Diviner in an authoritative, clipped tone that was at odds with his servant attire. Then he hustled me off the platform in a very un-servant-like manner.

His rage was palpable. And irreproachable. He had every right to be furious with me. My spontaneous, reckless singing had, in one fell swoop, annihilated our goal of anonymity.

With a grip that kept me pinned securely to his side, he thrust his way through a crowd that had morphed from rapt awe into a noisy, unruly mob. As the crowd pressed in on us, Lox had to forcefully shove back against the crush. Even so, copious tentacle-like hands reached for me as if I were Jesus or Mother Theresa or Madonna. I sagged against Lox, but he yanked me roughly upwards.

"You cannot collapse!"

Lox's sharp, impatient tone felt like a needle being driven into my heart.

"You must walk, and fast, for I cannot carry you through these throngs," he commanded.

And then I heard someone say, *"By the gods, that's Lord Loxley!"*

A ripple seemed to pass through the crowd.

I stumbled, sobbing in despair as the full realization of what a senseless fool I had been hit me.

* * *

LOX KEPT an iron grip on me as he slashed his way through the horde of people. After numerous failed attempts to outmaneuver our eager pursuers, we finally made our escape down a shadowy alley, our success attributable almost solely to the fact that we were sober and many of those who pursued us were not. Once safely away, Lox stopped. He roughly jerked the black wig from my head, stuffing it into his pocket. He put down his parcels as he shrugged out of his shapeless coat and then wrapped it around me to conceal my conspicuous dress.

His rough treatment and angry scowl made me feel like an errant three-year old, but all I could muster in response was a pathetic whimper. On an emotional level, I'd been wholly and completely drained. By the time Lox and I finally made it back to the Rooster's Comb, I was stumbling like a drunkard.

Fredryk was on a bench in front of the inn sitting in a casual pose as if entertained by the inebriated stranglers staggering along the relative quiet of the dimly lit street. Even in my exhausted state and despite his calm veneer, I could sense the tension that wound inside him like a coiled spring. When he saw us, he casually sauntered over. When he spoke, his harsh undertone belied his relaxed stance.

"What's she done?" he demanded.

Even if I could have summoned the energy to object to Fredryk's acerbic accusation, I knew I had no innocence to claim. I was guilty as charged. I deserved Fredryk's uncensored wrath.

Lox ignored his question. "Lead us by way of the back entrance."

We followed Fredryk through a rear door and then made our way stealthily up to the attic. After we'd safely crowded into my room—my closet—with the door closed, Lox turned and confronted me.

"You badger me about not being honest with you? Yet you fail to tell me that you are one of the Cast Away? When did this happen?"

I'd been assuming he would castigate me at the earliest opportunity for opening my mouth after all the care he and Fredryk had taken to maintain a low profile. Instead, he was demanding details of an event that had taken place in what seemed to me another lifetime. My brain couldn't process this unexpected turn.

"What difference does it make?" I pleaded, weakly shrugging out of Lox's coat and collapsing onto the bed.

I could not remember a time when I'd been so utterly depleted of emotional and physical resources. I closed my eyes, glad that, for the time being, I could set aside my concern for Lox's safety. As long as Fredryk was nearby, Lox would not be harmed.

"People were calling for the Cast Away. And for you, my lord," I heard Fredryk say. "I could not comprehend why. But I did learn that it's been years since the Diviner has identified a Cast Away. I did not comprehend that *she* was the one hailed as such."

"I as well. But Fredryk, her gift to them was to sing."

I had my eyes closed and so could not see the expression on

Fredryk's face, but I could imagine it well enough based on the silence that greeted Lox's remark.

"I'm sorry," I mumbled.

I felt Lox remove my boots and lay a blanket over my still form. Then my surroundings faded as I drifted off into the blessed oblivion of sleep.

CHAPTER 13

Sometime later I awoke from a strange and disturbing dream. In it, my father and I had been in the north pasture of the acreage where I'd grown up and where my sister Marilyn now lived with her husband Jim and their four sons. It was daytime, but we were enveloped in an uncharacteristically thick fog. My father was wearing his military fatigues and carried a rifle over his shoulder, something I'd only ever seen in pictures as he'd retired from the military long before I was born. Although he was the age he'd been on the day he'd vanished twenty-two years before, I was my present age. In the dream, I kept calling out to him. I knew he heard me because he would pause and look over his shoulder, but then he would resume running up the sparsely wooded hill. No matter how many times I called for him or how hard I ran, he remained elusive. And neither of us ever crested that hill.

As I lay on my cot somewhere between wakefulness and dreaming, I heard the sound of breathing and knew that Lox was in the room with me. I reached out a hand into the darkness and found him lying on the floor next to me. As soon as I touched him, he woke.

"Hold me?" I whispered simply.

He immediately rose and joined me under the blanket. As soon as his arm slipped around me and pulled me close, I fell back asleep.

When I woke the next time, I saw by the light from the small window that it was barely dawn. I lay with my back spooned against Lox's chest.

I moved my head slightly so that I could see his face. His golden-brown eyelashes curved in a crescent under his closed eyes. A faint smattering of freckles dusted his tanned cheeks. In slumber, the lines of anxiety that often marred his brow were absent. He looked unusually peaceful. For the first time, I noticed hints of grey in his stubble. I dropped my gaze to linger on the shape of his full lips and thought about those kisses we'd shared on the beach behind Julitha's cottage; potent kisses that had inspired my resolve to keep our relationship platonic. Everything I'd said then was still true. If we became lovers, then it was highly possible—probable—I would go home with a very wide crack in my heart.

But the Cast Away ceremony had changed something deep within me, as if the stores of love and worthiness housed in that imaginary treasure chest actually had filled my heart to the point of overflowing. Now that I'd had the benefit of sleep, I was feeling a kind of euphoria. The doors that had once trapped my hurts deep inside had been sprung open and the pain released. I felt eager and free, almost drunk with potential. I now knew that, even if my heart were to crack, it would not destroy me. I could and would mend.

When Lox's lips moved into a smile, I raised my startled gaze to meet his beautiful eyes. I was instantly mesmerized by the mixture of concern and adoration reflected in their depths. When I saw he was about to speak, I shifted and placed two fingers on his lips, then rolled all the way over so that I faced him. After a long moment in which we seemed to share all kinds of conversations in our silent gaze, I gently replaced my fingers with my lips.

We would become lovers now, and I wanted no words to spoil these first magical moments. On a practical level, I knew I was taking a risk with more than just my heart. We had no condoms. But given the three years I'd tried unsuccessfully to get pregnant while married to Sheldon, I found myself dismissing my small spark of concern.

Lox's response was tentative at first, but my eager lips and demanding hands quickly ignited his passion. When I paused to help him unfasten the small, cloth-covered buttons of my dress, I saw his hands trembling. Regardless, we managed to strip me of the cumbersome dress in less time than it takes to say my full name—Meredith Elizabeth Helen Whitby—until all I still wore was my 20th century bra.

When Lox looked down at me and frowned, I experienced a moment of trepidation. Now that I was practically naked, did he no longer desire me? Was I too plain? Too chubby? Were my generous curves unappealing?

Then I realized Lox was looking at the impression beneath the lace of my bra that made it look like I had a third nipple on the underside of my left breast. I giggled in relief as an image of the gnarled, old man filled my mind. Lox's face also cleared. He brushed a teasing finger around the outline of the button. His feather-light touch made me shiver with delicious anticipation. When he edged his fingertip under the lace of my bra, I gasped with pleasure. He nudged out the painted object and held it up for a brief moment between his thumb and forefinger before carefully tucking it under my pillow. Then thoughts of anything other than Lox's touch evaporated as I removed my bra and reveled in the feel of his fingers, hands and lips leaving trails of fire on my skin.

For the first time in my romantic life, I was unselfconscious about my naked body, about my so-called physical flaws, about what I might look like to the man who was making love to me. Instead, my hands were eager and confidant as I reached for the fastenings of his clothes. His exploration of my body hampered my efforts to get him undressed until finally—blessedly—he tore off his own clothes. The bliss of our bodies lying skin-to-skin was indescribable.

Our lovemaking was explosive and over far too quickly. We lay panting on the narrow bed, our skin slick and shiny with perspiration. It seemed we were each reluctant to break the spell our lovemaking had cast. But Lox finally spoke. His words nearly broke my heart. It was all too evident that he, too, had been shaped by the betrayals of the people to whom he'd given his love and trust.

"Please, Meredee, I beg of you," he said as he stroked my cheek with a fingertip and gazed into my eyes. "Do not regret this. I could not bear it."

It cost nothing for me to fulfill his heartfelt plea. I shifted so that my chin rested on his chest and my naked body draped along the long length of his. The cot was narrow, but if we'd been in a king-sized bed in a five-star hotel, I would still have lain in just this manner. I wanted every naked inch of me touching every naked inch of him. I raised my eyebrows suggestively. "I was thinking more along the lines of *repeat* rather than *regret*." I was happy to see I'd made him smile.

"Kiss me again, Lox," I begged as I slid up his body and pressed my lips to his.

As we made love, more slowly this time, Lox's exploration of my body seemed to stop time as if there was only us in all the world. He interspersed his caresses with tender words of adoration that melted my heart.

The morning sun was streaming through the small window by the time Lox reluctantly rose from my bed. He looked a different man, young and carefree.

I didn't want him to leave, so I posed in my best imitation of seductress.

As he shrugged into his clothes, he shook his head at me and said with a smile, "Fredryk will be wondering where his servant is. I am long overdue."

I pulled a face. "No," I argued. "Fredryk will be wondering why you would leave a naked, willing woman alone in her bed." I made a grab for him, but he laughingly evaded me despite the tiny room.

I rolled onto my belly, watching him. Dressed, he came to the bed, perching on the edge beside me. I shivered as he ran a finger lightly down my buttocks, stopping at my thighs where my skin had chafed from the incessant hours in the saddle. Our wild lovemaking and his bristly stubble had reddened my fair skin even more, although in the throes of passion I hadn't given my physical aches a second thought.

"Did I hurt you, my sparrow?"

"What? Of course not."

"This looks sore."

"It is sore." I propped myself up on my elbows and looked over my shoulder, trying to see the backs of my thighs. "I know how to make me forget just how sore?" I curled my fingers into his hair and brought his head down so I could kiss him, but Lox reluctantly pulled away when I tried to deepen the kiss.

"You are a distraction, Meredee; of that you can be certain. But we cannot delay resuming our journey." He gave me an indulgent smile as he cupped my cheek with his palm.

I wanted nothing than to stay here with him all day, naked and hot and sweating on this thin, lumpy mattress in this stuffy, perfect little room. This attic was our piece of paradise. I did not want to end the spell that had been cast. I did not want to rejoin the land of the living where I had to worry about Lox's safety, and where I had to sit on a saddle—sheepskin padding be damned.

Lox rose and went to where he'd left his purchases. "Put your worries aside, darling Meredee," he said, rooting through the items. "Sufficient remedies have been acquired."

"Can't we stay here, even just for one day?" As he approached me with the jar of salve, I rolled to my side and ran the fingers of one hand lightly along my naked breasts and down my abdomen in open invitation for him to renew our lovemaking. "You won't regret it," I promised. I'd never been bold in this way with any previous lover, but it felt natural and easy with Lox.

He caught his breath and laughed quietly as he knelt beside me, setting the jar on the bed. "By the gods, Meredee. How am I to function if you continue to behave in such a manner?"

I trailed a fingertip along his thigh until my hand rested in his lap. His very obvious response to my touch made me laugh softly. "Seems to me you can function just fine," I teased, moving my hand to stroke him.

He sucked in a breath and pushed my hand away. "I was not referring to that and well you know it," he said in a voice husky with desire. "I highly doubt I would ever have trouble functioning in this manner with you. Here," he added, holding out the jar of ointment. "Once in the morning and once in the evening. Apply it liberally."

When I sighed in exasperation and took the jar from him, he looked pleased. "I could happily be naked with you all day, my sparrow, but we simply must not delay our journey any longer. I am truly sorry. You cannot possibly know how sorry." He leaned in to plant a quick, affectionate kiss on my lips, briefly pinning my roving hand in his. He stood then and moved to the door where he paused to regard me. "I do adore you, my darling Meredee," he said in a soft, husky tone. "Did I remember to share that fact with you?"

He had. Too many times to count.

And then he was gone, and I was left lying on the bed, my face in my pillow, butterflies in my stomach, and a silly grin plastered on my face.

CHAPTER 14

*D*espite the danger we were in and the added
precautions we were forced to take, the journey from
Ballindale to West Scapah felt euphoric. Lox and I drifted through
each day as if we lived in an insulated bubble filled with delight
and discovery.

Only two things gave me cause for concern during that
portion of our journey. The first was the ache in my heart when-
ever I considered our inevitable parting. I was under no illusions
that the Lands of Vendome offered any kind of permanency for
me, but at the same time, the thought of never seeing Lox again
made me inconsolably sad. My second cause for concern was, of
course, Lox's safety.

Our fellow travelers were abuzz with gossip that Lord Loxley
had been seen in Ballindale with a black-haired woman who not
only was a Cast Away—already a rare occurrence in these Lands
—but who also had a vocal gift unlike any other. A rumor began
to spread that the Chancellor of the Eastern Duchy was secretly
making his way to the royal city of West Scapah so that he could
present the Grand Duke with a priceless gift of a foreign lady who
used her voice to enchant her audience. Wayfarers were now

looking at every black-haired woman in hopes of spotting the peculiarly gifted companion of the Chancellor.

If only I had accepted his bag of coin, I berated myself. If only I had not sung, I would not have generated any interest from the crowd beyond the gift exchange. Recognition of my well-known companion would never have occurred. But because of my foolish decision in Ballindale, those who served Rodmyrrah's interests would be on the alert for Lox's arrival in West Scapah. I still did not believe that some god might hurl a bolt of lightning from the sky to kill Lox, but clearly, someone or something had killed those other ambassadors. What heaped ashes on my burden of guilt was that Lox had not once reprimanded me for the foolhardy choice I'd made that night, although Fredryk's scowls and dark looks certainly made up for it.

Because of the news that was now racing ahead of us to West Scapah, we were forced to take added precautions to conceal our identities. I could not look like the blond Traveler that Conraz would recognize, nor could I look like the black-haired, kohl-eyed woman who'd sung in Ballindale.

Before departing Ballindale, the three of us met in my small room where Fredryk wordlessly handed me a rounded sack that I, at first, thought was a rather well-stuffed pillow. I found his actions puzzling since Fredryk had never been remotely attentive to my comfort. Lox laughed at my baffled expression before congratulating me. When that remark still didn't clear up my confusion, he informed me that I was now 'with Fredryk's child' and then chuckled at my look of horror at finding myself promoted from Fredryk's sister to his wife. Nevertheless, with my baby-on-the-way disguise and with my blond braid tucked under my hat, I resembled neither my true self nor the black-haired Cast Away woman every profiteer on the road hoped to spot.

When I rested my hands on my rounded belly for the first time, my blouse no longer tucked into my trousers, I couldn't help but picture Shulha. In my mind, I could see her announcing with certainty and pride that she would name her baby Singer. I shared a glance with Lox. I could see from his forlorn expression that he was remembering the exact same moment.

In addition to providing me with a baby bump, Fredryk also acquired a handful of grey horsetails. He'd stitched short lengths of these to the inside of Lox's hat. From a distance, our 'servant' would be mistaken for an older and overly scruffy retainer—as long as he kept his hat on. Within a couple of days, Fredryk had a full beard peppered with grey. He also regularly combed ash into his otherwise dark hair. With these additional measures at disguising our identities, Lox and Fredryk felt certain none of us would be recognized.

But my traveling companions were nothing if not cautious, insisting we bypass towns and avoid public inns. Fredryk periodically left us as we rode along the well-traveled route to purchase food and supplies in the market towns. But each evening Fredryk led us off the main thoroughfare well away from any settlement to make camp in the woods. Lox and I would build a little lover's nest of springy boughs and mounds of moss in sheltered alcoves well away from where Fredryk would sleep, giving us the privacy we craved. As soon as we lay down together, we made love, often laughing and giggling in our mutual delight and haste.

Each day before we rode, I lined my saddle with sheepskin padding, which made a significant difference to the comfort of my ride. I also regularly massaged the ointment Lox had purchased onto my tender skin. As a result, by the time we left the Folded Mountains behind, my chafed skin had almost fully healed.

Strapped behind my saddle was a small chest filled with the gifts given to me at the Cast Away ceremony. Fredryk had retrieved these from Marintha that night after I'd fallen asleep. I was not at all tempted to open the little box, concerned its contents would overwhelm me again with the same strong emotions I'd experienced on Cast Away night. At some point before my return I intended to re-examine all the treasures it held. The only item from that night that was not in the trunk was the button, which I kept tucked into my bra.

In the light of day, I discovered it was both painted and carved with a minutely detailed image of a sparrow, a bird I'd always admired for its impressive ability to survive the harsh Alberta winters. Lox told me that, in the Lands of Vendome, the sparrow was sacred to the goddess of love, which explained why he'd begun calling me 'my sparrow' in private. Just as the old man instructed, I kept that button nestled near my heart. Both Lox and I were careful each night to ensure it was tucked safely away before we made love. Each morning Lox would check to make sure I'd replaced the button, although I teased him that he was just using that as an excuse to look down my shirt. I'd also taken to wearing Julitha's necklace tucked under my blouse, superstitiously believing that her 'safe travel' charm would help keep Lox safe.

At every opportunity when it was safe to do so, Lox and I talked. One of the first things he told me was that when he'd listened to me sing that night in Ballindale, he'd been as spellbound as the rest of the crowd. Thereafter, at every opportunity when it was safe to do so, I sang for him. His favorite soon became *Top of the World*, a Carpenters song, the lyrics of which seemed especially appropriate given the emotional highs we were sharing. But when I tried to coach him to sing it with me, I was forced to conclude that he was excruciatingly tone deaf.

What troubled Lox the most about the night I sang was the shock of discovering I was a Cast Away. I explained to him that, several weeks after he and his cousins visited my world, my cantankerous father suddenly disappeared only to resurface two months later and announce that he was leaving for good. Thanks to what he called a lucky strike in the stock market—I seemed to recall he'd called it his golden goose—he at least provided financially for us kids. Accounting this to Lox then forced me to launch into a lengthy explanation of fairy tales and 20th century economics.

In turn, Lox informed me that it was a rare event for a Diviner to identify one who'd been Cast Away because desertions by parents rarely occurred. Family units were treasured and protected in the Lands of Vendome. The Cast Away Festival was thus an opportunity to celebrate and give thanks for the bonds of family by exchanging gifts, a ritual that didn't sound much different than my world's traditions around Christmas and Thanksgiving.

As we traversed the Folded Mountains, Lox and I did not mention the foreign lord, or what to expect when I met the mysterious Traveler, although Lox did speak eloquently, proudly, and frequently of his little son. I got the sense he hadn't spoken of him to anyone since the boy's death, and I was pleased he could so freely speak of him with me.

One afternoon, while we were traversing a quiet stretch of road with Fredryk far in the distance scouting out a convenient location to rest, I learned how Lox first met the man who would become his most devoted friend and servant. Fredryk had apparently been hired to provide warrior training to the young lord shortly after Lox had been orphaned as a young lad of thirteen. Lox described this young Fredryk, fourteen years his senior, as a skilled and experienced fighter, a modest, generous-hearted young man who was not only wise but also quick to laugh. Although Lox did not divulge intimate details of Fredryk's personal story, he did tell me that Fredryk had been deeply in love with a young woman named Cathandra. A few days before their scheduled nuptials, it was believed she'd taken a shortcut along the cliffs above the sea near her village, only she never returned. It was assumed she'd slipped and fallen to her death on the rocks below. Despite the months Fredryk spent scouring the coastline, her body was never recovered from the pounding sea. Fredryk had been twenty-eight years old and Lox fourteen, but Lox remembered how much Fredryk had cherished his fiancé and how Cathandra had adored Fredryk. Since her disappearance, Fredryk had not made any effort to enter a marriage union, although many women over the years had tried to entice him. Instead, he'd devoted his life to serving the young lord who eventually became the Chancellor of the Eastern Duchy.

As I could not imagine Fredryk either in love or carefree, I found myself covertly studying him with renewed curiosity when he rejoined us.

In this manner, talking as often as it was safe to do so and sharing our blankets at the first opportunity after striking camp, we made our way toward West Scapah. On the day I got my first glimpse of the western royal city, I felt an almost overpowering sense of depression. My time with Lox had shrunk from weeks to mere days, possibly only hours. I desperately wanted to meet this Traveler and be assured of a route home; yet at the same time, I was dreading saying goodbye to Lox. I wasn't ready to shatter the snow-globe perfection of our mountainous journey. I hadn't told Lox, but I was regularly fantasizing about how this Traveler would help me put a whole new spin on a long-distance relationship. If this man knew how to travel between worlds, why couldn't I do the same, and regularly?

Perhaps, if I had not been so preoccupied, I would have had a premonition of the twin horrors that would be revealed upon reaching the royal city. Instead, I continued to ride toward West Scapah with the belief that my biggest problem was how I would mend the cracks that would soon appear in a heart that no longer belonged solely to me.

PART III

REVELATION

CHAPTER 15

little more than four weeks after arriving in the Lands of Vendome and one day behind schedule according to Fredryk, we approached West Scapah much like we had Ballindale, from a bluff high above the city.

As we crested this final rise, we nudged our horses to the side of the road so I could have a clear view of the sprawling city that blanketed both sides of the sparkling River Atha. Multiple bridges of varying designs and widths arched handsomely over the glittering waterway that wound lazily through the town and that seemed, even to me, overly congested with barges and boats. The oldest area of the city was located on a rise of land above the west bank. Inside the high, fortress-worthy stone wall was the sprawling Royal Residence that covered acres of land. A less formidable wall encircled most of the sprawling outer city. From the number of buildings tucked against its outer flanks, it was clear the metropolis had spilled over its edges decades ago. Tall buildings and spires shot up above the homes and shops, and domes of copper and gold gleamed in the sun. In celebration of the coronation anniversary, orange pennants—the colors of the

Grand Duke and Grand Duchess's family—decorated many of the spires, bridges, and gateways.

A steady stream of visitors, merchants, and artisans flooded into the city to take in the festivities, including the final event— the Coronation Parade—that was scheduled for the following afternoon. Horses and carriages, wagons and ponies, men pushing carts and adolescents pushing wheelbarrows heaped with goods to sell, all made their way along the teeming thoroughfare. In the distance, I saw sentries patrolling on foot and on horseback. Their polished armor, including their orange-plumed helmets, shone in the sun.

Reaching our final destination of West Scapah meant I would not only have to say goodbye to Lox, I would have to disappoint him by refusing to create an image of Rodmyrrah. I'd become deeply conflicted about this, wrestling with the knowledge that my refusal made civil war in these Lands pretty much inevitable. Not only would thousands of people be killed in the ensuing battles, one of those battles could very well claim Lox's life. Even if I never saw him again, I desperately wanted him to live a long and happy life. The image of Lox being killed on a battlefield within weeks of my departure haunted me.

As I stared down at the city I was both eager and dreading to enter, my thoughts drifted to Kimberly and the reunion that now loomed on the edge of my horizon. I wondered how she and the rest of my family were dealing with my extended and unexplained absence. My remaining two brothers, who lived with their families 3000 kilometres away in Ontario, would likely not be overly concerned. We hadn't ever been close. But Val and Marilyn—and Jim and my four rambunctious nephews—would find my absence both puzzling and worrying.

Fredryk nudged his mount forward and the three of us silently rejoined the flow of travelers moving down the gentle slope towards the city.

When we were about five hundred meters from the city's edge,

Lox brought his horse abreast of mine to inform me—in his practiced, deferential tone—that my shawl had slipped from one shoulder and had snagged on my stirrup. Although his words were appropriately servant-like, his eyes under the floppy brim of his ugly hat held the promise of what would occur between us when we gained privacy later that evening—privacy he'd earlier promised would include a luxurious bath and a soft bed. The look in his heated glance knocked me breathless and caused a blush to stain my cheeks, which in turn made him grin in triumphant delight.

In the split second after Lox reached down to untangle the shawl from my stirrup, I heard a sound I would never have expected to hear had I remained a hundred years in the Lands of Vendome. It was the unmistakable thundering clap of a single bullet being fired from a high-powered rifle.

CHAPTER 16

I had firsthand experience of the sound a rifle makes when it's fired. After my father deserted us and my mother was hospitalized, Curtis—the kindest of my three brothers—made a special effort to include me in some of his activities. He once let me tag along when he and my other brothers went to the local rifle range for target practice, although Frank and Tommy only tolerated my presence because I helped line up rows of empty tin cans. Curtis had let me fire his rifle, but after it kicked painfully into my shoulder, I lost interest.

The single crack of the rifle being fired and the reverberating echo sounded as if the sky above the wide, bowl-shaped valley had been ripped apart by two giant fists. Pandemonium erupted on the busy thoroughfare. Animals—horses, dogs, cows, sheep, and goats—scattered in all directions. Their brays and barks of fear combined with the screams of my fellow travelers created a discordant racket. In the midst of this bedlam, my terrified horse reared, almost unseating me.

As I sawed on the reins in a desperate attempt to remain in my saddle, I shrieked at Lox to take cover. Even in the chaos, I knew the bullet, which had thankfully missed, had been meant for him.

Despite all we had done to disguise ourselves, he'd been recognized.

Lox ignored my screams, or perhaps he didn't hear them as he fought to control his own panicked mount. In horror, I saw him make a grab for my horse's bridle, and I screamed again for him to take cover.

Less than a handful of seconds after the first bullet had been fired and as I clung to the neck of my rearing horse, my screams were abruptly silenced when warm blood sprayed my face. A second, piercing thunderclap sliced the air. My horse buckled and fell, taking me with it. Then I was on the ground, partially pinned under its dead weight and looking in horror at my mount's shattered skull. I felt no pain in that moment, only the terror of knowing a third bullet could whiz by at any moment and find its true target.

I watched in horror as Lox, completely exposed, vaulted off his horse and ran to my side.

"Get down, Lox! Christ Almighty, get down!" I grabbed him by the shoulder and jerked with all the force I could muster.

In that moment, while I feverishly wrestled to keep Lox's head down, I saw a man dressed in dark clothing jogging up the far hillside carrying the weapon I realized had just been fired. At the treeline, he paused and glanced over his shoulder. Although he was too far away for me to make out any details, I could see he was clean-shaven and seemed tall, with a solid, athletic build. Then he was gone, taking the threat against Lox with him.

Excruciating pain suddenly erupted in my lower leg, and I cried out in agony. Fredryk suddenly appeared at Lox's side. Together, they heaved the dead animal up. I crab-scrambled out quickly from beneath the horse's crushing weight.

When Lox squashed me against his chest, I practically sobbed with relief. I clutched at him, feverishly examining the spot where I'd seen the assassin. It seemed he'd taken his shots from behind one of the giant boulders that dotted the cleared hillside but had then fled into the more distant tree line.

Lox was cradling me in his arms demanding to know if the blood on my face and clothes were mine. I was alternating between reassuring him that I was fine to thanking every god out there that he wasn't dead. Fredryk—ever the professional—was the only one of us who had, amidst the chaos, successfully maintained his false identity. In a severe tone, he demanded Lox behave like the servant he was and allow his master to see to the injuries of his pregnant wife. Fredryk's harsh reprimand brought us both to our senses.

Lox glanced over at the wayfarers who'd gathered to gawk at us, then quickly dropped his chin so that his face was hidden under the brim of his hat. His eyes met mine. I'd never seen him work so hard to adopt his servant persona, but he released me and moved aside, allowing Fredryk to take his place.

"Lambert," Fredryk said loudly, for the benefit of the gawkers. "It looks like the danger has passed. Remove my lady's belongings from her mount. Then find a carter who would be willing to haul it away."

Lox and I shared a last, intense look before he left to do as his 'master' bid. Fredryk was holding me much like Lox had, and I desperately wanted to shove him away and go after Lox, but I knew I couldn't. For the moment, especially with the attention we were getting, we had to convincingly play our parts. I knew Fredryk's acting barely belied the fury and fear that was seething just below the surface of his own tightly controlled emotions. I felt a spark of compassion for Lox's devoted servant.

A woman hurried toward us announcing she was a medical practitioner, but Fredryk tersely declined her offer of help, pulling the hem of my wide trousers down so they covered the distinctive zippers of my boots. The woman backed away with an offended frown, but then was called over to help a young boy who'd sustained a head injury.

"No talking," Fredryk needlessly ordered under his breath.

His blameful tone made me want to snap at him, yet I also saw his fear as he looked in Lox's direction where Lox was talking to a group of men who seemed to have a number of carts and wagons in their train. Fredryk would've drawn the same conclusion as me. Lox had been recognized. It was only a remarkable stroke of luck that Lox hadn't been killed in the same manner as Rikka's other ambassadors.

Regardless, since I'd repeatedly shouted at Lox to take cover and repeatedly reassured him I was unhurt, all within earshot of the very people who were milling around us like rubberneckers at the scene of an accident, it was absurd for me to now pretend I was mute. I could only hope that, in the pandemonium, no one had taken note of my strange accent.

Fredryk shifted so that he could assess how badly I might have injured my leg.

"Help me up," I demanded instead, keeping my tone low so no one overheard.

"Remain still," he muttered.

My newfound compassion for Fredryk evaporated. "For Christ's sake, Fredryk!" I hissed in an undertone. "Stop with the mollycoddling. The sooner I stand on my own two feet, the sooner they'll all stop gawking."

With a glance toward our fascinated audience, Fredryk reluctantly helped me stand. Once on my feet, I tentatively tested the extent of my injury. My ankle was painful, but it was no more than a mild sprain. A lucky happenstance given I'd just survived being flattened by a dead horse.

Another onlooker, concerned by the advanced state of my pregnancy, approached to offer her assistance. Once again Fredryk firmly refused assistance, but more politely this time. I did my best to give the woman and the other spectators a reassuring look, but I knew I was nowhere near as good an actor as my travel companions.

I tugged on Fredryk's coat sleeve, pulling him out of earshot. I had to lean on him as we stepped away, but I limped only a little. "There's a man with a weapon up there." I whispered, furtively pointing at the tree-lined bluff. "That's what killed my horse."

A vague part of my brain was computing that the assassin—who must've encountered Lox at some point in the past and had known the truth behind the rumor of Lox's imminent arrival—had likely been examining every wayfarer who approached from the east through the magnifying scope of his very effective killing machine. This weapon could only have come from one place: My own world. I could only conclude that the thunder and lightning of the gods these people feared was, in fact, a trained sniper with a weapon unlike any this world had ever known.

It occurred to me then that Lox had been recognized because, in the second before that first shot had been fired, he'd discarded his guise of servant to openly and outrageously flirt with me. That momentary lapse—intended for my eyes only—had been seen by the assassin. The shooter had known, despite Lox's disguise of grey hair and scruffy beard, that the Chancellor of the Eastern Duchy had finally arrived, as rumored, in West Scapah. The fact that neither of the two bullets had found their intended target could only be attributed to a string of bizarre flukes. If Lox had not spontaneously moved to release my snagged shawl in that precise moment when the first bullet was fired, and if my horse had not reared and taken the second bullet, Lox would now be dead.

No one from these Lands would conclude that the man on the faraway hillside had caused the death of my horse. In their minds, the invisible hands of their gods had engineered the bedlam. Even now, the stunned onlookers were marveling amongst themselves about how the gods had seen fit to cast their wrath upon a mere horse, and one being ridden by a pregnant woman, no less. I didn't know where the first bullet had landed, but it didn't appear to have claimed a victim, animal or human. I wanted to scream at the gawkers that this had not been the work of a god. This was a man from my world with a rifle. A mercenary who'd been hired to kill Rodmyrrah's enemies.

Fredryk barely glanced at the distant tree line. Instead, and for the benefit of the gawkers, he said, "Calm yourself, dear," then feigned concern for his pregnant wife by condescendingly patting my forearm, which infuriated me.

I grabbed his hand and squeezed his fingers as hard as I could. "Don't bloody dear me!" I snapped under my breath. I jerked him further away from the spellbound onlookers. They would either interpret my actions as that of a shrewish wife or fitting behavior for someone in a 'delicate condition' whose horse had just been killed by a capricious god.

"That was no thunder and lightning of a god-damned god," I sputtered. "I'm telling you, a bullet, fired from an instrument of death from my world and meant for Lox, killed my horse."

Fredryk pulled his hand free of my grasp, giving me a look that clearly indicated his disbelief.

I continued in an undertone. "Lox is still in danger from an assassin who is hidden in those trees. That's where I saw him." With a small gesture, I indicated the tree line. "He's got a weapon from my world that can shoot a projectile from a great distance. He was behind one of those boulders, there, when he took his shots."

Fredryk studied me with an assessing look for a moment then turned and led me—limping—to where our remaining two horses were being held by a boy of about eight who was all agog. The mounts were skittish, but otherwise unharmed. Lox was busy redistributing my belongings, and he gave me a concerned look as we approached. Fredryk handed the boy a coin and dismissed him. As soon as the boy was gone, I quietly shared my theory with Lox. Unlike Fredryk, Lox did not need convincing.

"This man could be readying himself for another attempt to harm me?"

I had to dial down my panic so that I could assess the situation with logic, which took a herculean effort on my part. "I think the immediate danger has passed," I finally said. "If he could've taken his shot from the tree line, he wouldn't have been down by the boulders, right? No, he's gone. For now, at least," I added.

Fredryk was looking up at the hillside and shaking his head in disbelief. "Even from the cover of the boulder, the distance is too great. It's not possible."

I must've looked ready to erupt, for Lox touched my forearm briefly before he spoke in a reassuring tone. "Do not fret, Meredee. As you said, the immediate danger has passed. But tell me, do you believe we will be safe from this man you call a sniper once we reach Alberic's home?"

"Not *we*, Lox. You! Will *you* be safe?"

"Meredee, you must resist focusing on thoughts that cause panic. Simply tell us what action is best, now, given your understanding of what you saw."

I took a deep yoga breath, then another, distracted suddenly by the confusion around us. Herders were still working with their dogs to gather and sort their livestock, and carters were reloading their spilled goods, some of which were now ruined.

A terrifying thought occurred to me. "He could be in the crowd right now. He could kill you with a knife instead of a bullet."

"If this assassin does exist, he will do no such thing."

Fredryk's dismissive tone grated on my frayed nerves, but Lox spoke in a calm voice before I could voice a heated retort.

"Think logically, Meredee. Killing me with a blade would not be effective. The populace must witness the thunder and lightning of the gods. Only then will they know the gods caused my death. No, if I am to be targeted, it will be by this weapon you describe, and only that. My death in such a manner would reinforce the belief that Lord Rodmyrrah has the power to direct the gods."

"Right. You're right." Lox's logic made sense and his tone

calmed me, allowing me to think rationally. "Okay, his first attempt to kill you failed. So he'll be looking for another opportunity, right? The most important thing then is to make sure he doesn't know where you are. Oh my god," I exclaimed as another terrifying thought occurred to me. I could see in Lox's gaze how much it was costing him not to take me into his arms as panic made my voice rise. "He might already be ahead of us and setting himself up on some rooftop in the city. We should leave right now! We've already wasted too much time."

"Keep your voice down," Fredryk reprimanded, then added, "That would only make sense if he knew our route, which he does not."

"Fredryk is right, Meredee. Do not give in to your fear. We shall see our way through this. I promise you."

I realized then that Fredryk was livid with me. This attempt on Lox's life was entirely my fault. I dropped my face into my hands briefly before lifting my eyes to meet Lox's troubled gaze. "This is all my fault," I said in a low tone. "It's because I sang in Ballindale that you were recognized. Your enemies suspected you would come here. They knew exactly where to wait for you. And they came this close to killing you," I added, holding my index finger a millimetre above my thumb.

Lox also lowered his tone and spoke with his characteristic authority. "But they did not succeed, Meredee. Look at me. I am unharmed. And will remain so, with your help. As this is a weapon of your world, we shall rely on you to guide our decisions now. For that, you must keep a clear mind. Rest assured, we shall take the precautions you subscribe to keep us all safe. For now, you must remain focused on our next course of action. It is no secret that the cloth merchant and my father were great friends, so perhaps this man will guess that Alberic's home is our destination. We shall await darkness then, before approaching his home, and then only gain access through the servant's entrance.

Meredee," he added, seeing my uncertainty. "Alberic's compound is walled and guarded. We *will* be safe there."

"We should go into the city openly and take a room at an inn," Fredryk stated. "That will fool a watcher, if there is one."

Our conversation was abruptly cut off by the arrival of a group of mounted guards who came galloping up the hill. They were demanding an account of the situation, and onlookers were pointing at us.

"Keep your voice down," Fredryk warned, giving me a reproachful look before jogging over to greet the guards with the appropriate level of deference.

I heard him explaining that his pregnant wife had been traumatized by the death of her horse in such an unexpected manner. It wasn't hard for me to look convincingly shell-shocked.

It appeared that Fredryk was answering the guardsmen's questions to their satisfaction, so Lox moved to finish strapping my belongings onto the two remaining mounts, including balancing my horse's tack on top of Fredryk's saddle. I tucked my beautiful shawl—now bloodstained—into a saddlebag and then rolled up the sleeves of my blood-spattered blouse. Lox joined me, pouring water from his canteen so that I could wash my face and hands. Then the guardsmen ordered Lox to assist half a dozen other men in hefting the corpse of my poor mare into a cart. I felt sickened by the sight of the dead animal and the dark circle of blood that now soaked the road. It so easily could've been Lox's corpse being deposited into that cart and his blood seeping into the hard-packed dirt.

As I looked away, my eyes fell on Fredryk's bulging saddlebags. Shuffling over to his horse, I began unapologetically rooting through his things until I found his flask of evening spirits. I took a generous gulp of the fiery liquid, then another, but the foul drink did nothing to diminish the tentacles of fear that had sunk their claws into my belly.

CHAPTER 17

I ignored the throb in my ankle as I rode into the city on Lox's horse. Just like Ballindale, the town was packed with revelers, but this time I derived no pleasure from their high energy. Lox walked between the two horses, with Fredryk on the other side. Although the animals shielded most of Lox's body, he was a tall man. Seeing his head so vulnerably exposed caused a churning knot of fear to anchor itself in the pit of my stomach. I scrutinized every rooftop and every window of every building fully expecting to see the shadowy figure of a would-be assassin.

Each time we stopped at an inn along our route, we were turned away. The Coronation Festival had drawn crowds, filling every available room. Finally, Fredryk found one vacant room at a dilapidated inn for which he paid an exorbitant sum. The room was small and filthy, but I didn't care. I was weak with relief that Lox was finally indoors. We would remain there until darkness fell.

After I changed out of my bloodstained blouse and removed the pillow from under my clothes, Lox wrapped my swollen ankle with strips of cloth torn from one of his shirts. Then he and I sat in rickety chairs with my foot elevated in his lap while Fredryk stood at the wall by the window staring out at the crowded street. Once in a while Lox and I would murmur quietly together, but for the most part we all remained in contemplative silence.

As we waited, I tried to sort out how it was possible that someone from my world had been hired as an assassin in this world. More than two years ago, Lox had seen the alleged Traveler, albeit from a distance. He'd dismissed the man as a hoax because, in Lox's words, he was a buffoon dressed in exotic, colorful robes and turbans. Was it possible this buffoon and the man in the dark clothes were one and the same? Or, was there more than one Traveler in West Scapah? And, if the Traveler I sought was this assassin, then my mission to return home would be that much more complicated. I would be dependent on a hardened criminal, one who was tasked with killing my friend and lover.

When darkness finally fell, we gathered only our most essential belongings. Lox refused to let me carry the saddlebag that held the items I didn't want to part with—Kimberly's shirt, my Bellecourt clothes, and my toiletries. One of Alberic's servants would be sent to retrieve our remaining items and the two horses. One-by-one, we crept stealthily out the back of the dilapidated, noisy inn. My ankle throbbed in my boot despite the tight wrapping, but I kept up without complaint as Fredryk led us through the poorly lit side-streets and alleyways. I was so focused on moving with stealth I almost jumped out of my skin when an unexpected boom assaulted my senses. My immediate thought was that a rifle had been fired again, even though I recognized that this sound bore no resemblance to a gunshot. I whirled around and then slumped in relief when I saw Lox behind me, unhurt.

He was gazing intently over his shoulder in the direction of the noise, which I belatedly identified as the synchronized beating of a handful of drums. Lox gestured for Fredryk and me to turn and follow him out of the alley, murmuring to me that the 'noise-makers' heralded the coming of a royal cortege.

A few moments later, we stood behind a row of spectators who'd gathered on the edge of the wide thoroughfare. As the cortege approached, a couple of onlookers shouted in derision, which instigated a short-lived brawl. The remainder of the bystanders were cheering and seemed eager and excited at this unexpected diversion.

From my vantage point standing slightly in front of Lox, I watched as six elaborately uniformed men marched down the middle of the street toward us, effectively scattering wayfarers off the road. For about ten or fifteen paces, they beat a thundering, unified rhythm on large base drums looped over their shoulders. Then they marched in silent unison for the equivalent number of paces before once more resuming their rhythmic pounding. If I had not been so worried for Lox's safety, I would've been captivated. This spectacle was the closest thing to music I'd witnessed since arriving in these Lands.

On the heels of the drummers were a number of mounted guards brandishing blazing torches. They and their mounts were bedecked in ornate orange and silver regalia. Their polished armor shone like moonlight on water. Additional guards on foot in matching livery and also holding torches flanked a group of mounted dignitaries. This inner group of richly dressed men and women laughed and talked amongst themselves oblivious to the bystanders.

Lox gestured toward a bareheaded man dressed in a colorfully embroidered tunic who was mounted on a magnificent, high-stepping grey horse, identifying him as Lord Rodmyrrah.

I was finally looking at the foreign lord whose likeness Lox had brought me here to capture. As he rode toward me, I took in every detail of his handsome face. Then, without taking my eyes from him, I quietly asked Lox if the group included Jaybex or the one known as the Traveler, but Lox said neither man formed part of the foreign lord's procession.

As they drew closer, my eyes were drawn to a woman in silver and white who rode beside Rodmyrrah. Lox must have sensed my unspoken question as in the next moment he confirmed—in a flat, casual tone—that this was Toriah. Diamonds sparkled in her fair hair, on her gloved wrists, and above her impressive décolletage. Her platinum locks were swept up in an elaborate hairstyle, and her peaches-and-cream complexion looked flawless in the torch-light. As she passed, I was reminded of a young 1950's Hollywood starlet. I remembered Julitha's comment that Toriah and I bore a resemblance, but I saw nothing in this woman's beauty that remotely resembled me.

In the next moment I was shrinking against Lox, forcing myself not to raise my arm and point at the mounted man passing in front of us. "Conraz is here," I said in an urgent whisper over my shoulder.

Lox spoke into my ear. "Yes. And the man beside him is his father, the Earl."

Although the riders spared not a glance at the excited specta-tors, I was thankful we stood beyond the range of torchlight. Conraz and his father thus remained oblivious to the fact that the hunted Traveler and the banished Chancellor were within a few arms lengths of where they rode.

As soon as they passed, the three of us melted back into the shadowy alleys. Soon after, we arrived at the sprawling residence of Alberic and his wife Lita. I could see little of their impressive home in the darkness, but I was relieved that it was situated exactly as Lox had described. We entered through a small door on one side of the high wall. The privacy of the grounds with their paved courtyards, lantern-lit fountains, and lighted pathways through manicured gardens was blessedly reassuring. In the unex-pected sanctuary of the cloth merchant's palatial, inner-city estate, my stomach finally ceased churning.

My initial introduction to our hosts was thankfully brief. Lita wisely insisted the three of us be given time to freshen up before joining them for a late evening meal.

The first thing I did when left alone in the elegant bedchamber was to search the gracefully carved bureau for paper and drawing sticks, as I'd left Julitha's items at the inn. I was in luck and found what I needed. I sat on the bed—as soft as Lox had promised—and quickly stroked the bold outline of Rodmyrrah's face. I shaded the areas around his deep-set eyes, gave his dark eyebrows their haughty arch, accentuated the curve of his full lips, and set his chin in what I knew was a characteristic stance of haughty superiority.

For weeks now, I'd believed I could not possibly do the task Lox had asked of me. But that was before I'd personally jeopardized Lox's life; before an assassin had shot at him solely on account of my reckless foolishness; and before I'd acknowledged that I cared for him more than I ever thought possible. Lox's death would not rest on my shoulders. Not if I could help it. Right or wrong, I would no longer refuse to conduct the task for which I'd been Called. I could live with the guilt of helping end Rodmyrrah's life, but I could not live with the horror of knowing I'd done nothing to protect Lox from the mercenary assassin who could be neutralized by Rodmyrrah's execution.

I examined my preliminary sketch, pleased I'd captured a good likeness of the foreign lord. According to my companions, I would have ample opportunity to study him further the next afternoon during the royal pageant, which included the Coronation Parade. After that, I could add more detail to this sketch, and then create as many additional images as were needed to achieve the desired outcome.

I hid the drawing so housemaids would not inadvertently stumble upon it. Then I hurried through my bath, eager to rejoin Lox and tell him of my sudden change of heart.

CHAPTER 18

*J*n the privacy of a small but elegantly appointed room where Lox, Fredryk, and I sat at a round table and ate a simple but delicious meal of mushroom soup, fish, and vegetables, I announced to our hosts and my traveling companions that I'd committed an image of Rodmyrrah to paper and would willingly create more. Fredryk was relieved, but Lox expressed concern. To Fredryk's chagrin, Lox made me promise that I would take some time to rethink my decision. Despite my protests that I could live with the outcome of my actions, Lox remained unconvinced.

My traveling companions had already brought Alberic and Lita up-to-speed with what had occurred in Ballindale. Lox had earlier explained to me that when the medical practitioners had been preparing the first murdered ambassador for burial, they'd found a melted bolt of lightning embedded in his brain. This conclusion seemed logical to them given the sound of thunder that had been reported to accompany the instantaneous death. It hadn't dawned on me that the 'melted bolt of lightning' was a bullet and the thunder and lightning of the gods was simply a common thug with a skill and a weapon unknown in this world.

I asked Alberic for a sheet of paper and a pencil, then shifted in my seat so they could see me drawing the basic mechanics of a rifle. While I drew, I explained how the weapon worked. The 'thunder' was clearly the crack of sound the rifle made when the trigger was pulled. In the wide valley where my horse had been shot, the cliffs and trees had magnified the sound. The 'melted bolt of lightning' in the skull was simply the spent bullet.

I could not account for how such a man from my world came to be hired to work as an assassin in this one. In actual fact, it did not matter. What mattered was that my hosts, as well as Fredryk and Lox, understand that if the shooter could see Lox—even from hundreds of meters away—then he could kill Lox. I was relieved when we all agreed that Lox should not venture outside this house, not even into the expansive grounds. Lox was not particularly happy about this decision, but since he'd been the one to insist I guide our actions on this matter, he could hardly dismiss my subsequent recommendation for his safety.

Our conversation shifted then to the possible identity of this assassin. Were he and the Traveler—on whom I pinned my hopes of returning to my world—one and the same man? Alberic shared Lox's belief that the buffoon at court was in no way capable of wielding any kind of sophisticated weapon. Lita expanded, stating that many obsequious residents of West Scapah called upon the Traveler who, when 'in residence', lived in a home that flanked the Inner City walls. These toadying flatterers presented him with luxurious gifts in hopes that, by ingratiating themselves with him, they would gain access, through him, to the Royal Court. That the Traveler accepted these gifts with no apparent scruples was another reason Lox remained convinced he was an imposter. The man simply did not behave like Travelers of Old.

I pointed out the obvious flaw in Lox's reasoning, stating that neither Kimberly nor I behaved like Travelers of Old. Lox merely shrugged off my comment.

Alberic and Lita had devised a plan that would allow me to meet the Traveler. They would join the ranks of the sycophants and visit the Traveler's home the next morning bearing a gift of their finest silks that I, disguised as their servant, would carry. I could then observe and assess for myself who and what he was and, more importantly, whether I felt I could trust him to help me return home.

While the four of them debated the particulars of what would make an appropriate gift, niggles of worry frayed on my nerves. If —after observing the only Traveler, alleged or otherwise, spoken of in West Scapah—I believed he really was an imposter, then I would be no closer to finding a way home than I'd been a month ago upon first arriving in this world. I would then have to somehow track down this assassin. I recalled Julitha describing the Traveler as being emotionally inaccessible. Perhaps this was because he was a mercenary and Julitha's special sight could not penetrate his hardened heart. Even if we successfully located him, how could I enlist his help without jeopardizing Lox? If I identified myself as a fellow Traveler, the assassin would immediately know I was the Cast Away woman who'd sung. He would conclude it was my horse he'd inadvertently killed, and he would know my traveling companion was Lox. Would his price for my ticket home be divulging Lox's whereabouts? And that left me in a quandary. If I couldn't reveal who I was without jeopardizing Lox, then I would be stranded here. That outcome was intolerable. As much as I now cared for Lox, I belonged in my own world. I wanted to go home.

Lita took note of my distraction and suggested I retire with a pot of medicinal tea, to which I responded with a resounding yes. Not long after, I said a much more ardent yes when Lox slipped naked and warm and oh-so-desirable into my very large, very comfortable, and ever so enticing bed.

* * *

AFTER MAKING LOVE, I lay in the dark curled in Lox's arms with my back against his chest. When he spoke, I could feel the rumbling vibration of his voice against my skin.

"Meredee?"

"Mmhmm?"

"You know I want you to stay?"

My eyes popped open. I was already motionless, but at his words I felt my lungs freeze. I forced myself to exhale slowly and quietly. This was the conversation we'd both been avoiding.

I did not know what words would make Lox understand that, regardless of the deep and abiding connection we'd made over the last few weeks, I belonged in my modern world. My beloved brother Curtis would not be there and his absence would be dreadful, but Marilyn and Val were there, as was Kimberly. While my weeks with Lox had been amazing, our relationship had no permanency. I would go home and, once there, I would launch my new life thanks to the invaluable clarity I'd gained during my unexpected adventure in his world. I didn't confess to him that I was hoping—as long as the Traveler wasn't the assassin—that since the Traveler seemed to have the means to go back and forth, perhaps I could as well. God knows I wanted to see Lox again. And again and again. But it was all contingent on the Traveler.

I waited in silence longing for Lox to abandon this distressing subject, but he didn't.

"You know I love you," he added softly.

In response, I squeezed my eyes tightly shut. Lox had frequently declared his adoration for me, but this word was new.

"There is only you, Meredee," Lox added when I still didn't respond. "Only you, my sparrow, always and forever—"

"Stop," I interrupted. Even though neither of us had moved a muscle, I could sense him waiting expectantly. What did he want me to say? What could I say? How could I express to him that I'd never been happier than during these past few weeks? What words could I employ to reconcile my complicated feelings for him with my choice to return to my home? Even had I been able to find a way to articulate appropriate words in this painfully poignant moment, it would have been impossible for me to form them around the skyscraper constriction in my throat.

"Meredee—"

"Stop! I can't...I don't..."

I began to weep. He tried to soothe me with whispered declarations of love, but his words pierced my heart.

I turned and buried my face in his chest. When my tears were finally spent, we made love again. All the things I did not know how to say in words I infused into my caresses. I didn't want to admit to myself that perhaps I did love this amazing man. All I knew for sure was that I did not belong in his world.

Had I known that my departure would happen much sooner and more abruptly than either of us had anticipated, I would've found a way that night to choke out the three words that could've given ease to Lox's beautiful, generous heart.

CHAPTER 19

The next morning Alberic, Lita, and I departed in an open carriage driven by one of their groomsmen. I sat on a narrow perch behind my hosts, facing backwards, reminded of the station wagon of my youth.

Knowing that the Traveler was impressed with appearances, Alberic and Lita were dressed in their finest. I, on the other hand, wore a plain, taupe blouse made of twilled cotton, a floor-length, lavender skirt made from heavy broadcloth, and a snug striped vest with a peplum waist that laced across my front. My hair was held back with a scarf that matched the vest. This attire, according to Lita, identified me as a household servant. To ward off the morning chill, I also wore the nondescript wool shawl that Fredryk had purchased. My ankle was tightly wrapped inside my boot and pained me only a little thanks to Lita's poultice and willow bark tea. Beside me was a large, covered basket that held two ten-meter swaths of luxurious silk, one a bold crimson, the other a deep violet; a dozen iridescent feathers in a velvet-lined case; and three unbelievably soft pelts of stoat, which Lita told me was a white-furred weasel.

I had been fractious at breakfast. Two emotions jostled for space in my heart. One created a warm glow that flared at the center of my being every time I thought of Lox's bold declaration of love; the other was a sharp dart of pure panic. As much as I cared for Lox, I did not want to remain in his world, and certainly didn't want to be stranded here. I did not want my choice—to go or to stay—to be taken away again. Nervous about what I would encounter at the Traveler's home, the panic nearly extinguished the glow.

As the carriage jostled down the cobblestoned streets, I distracted myself by admiring the elegantly appointed homes in the grand neighborhood through which we passed. Although the dwellings were not as large as Alberic's mansion, many boasted walled compounds. Orange ribbons and wreaths to celebrate the coronation festivities decorated a number of the homes.

After a journey of what seemed to be less than thirty minutes, we halted in front of a two-storied, handsome stone residence tucked against the outer edge of the inner city wall. An ornate gate was set within a tall, wrought-iron fence surrounding a flag-stone courtyard. The centerpiece of the enclosure boasted a bubbling fountain decorated with dancing figurines of what I assumed were winged gods. I jumped off the back of the carriage and then stood to the side holding the basket while the groomsman rang what looked like a ship's bell set to the side of the elaborate gate.

A well-dressed man emerged from the front door and approached us, his posture rigid and his steps unhurried. He had an arrogant air about him that made me think of a self-important maître-d' in a posh restaurant. I assumed he was the equivalent of a butler. When the groomsman announced that Alberic—who was one of the richest merchants in the city—was calling on the Trav-eler, the manservant morphed into fawning subservience and quickly opened the gate. He made to take the basket from me, but

Alberic informed him that the precious contents would remain in my care until the gift could be presented to the Traveler.

The groomsman remained with the carriage, but I followed a few steps behind Alberic and Lita as they accompanied the servant past the fountain and into the house. The marble floor of the foyer, which was filled with light from windows in a cupola above, was paved in tawny hues of golden amber that immediately reminded me of Lox's eyes. I didn't want to think of Lox. Instead, I forced myself to focus on the servant's stiff back as he ushered Alberic and Lita into a small but richly furnished parlor. Seeing me hovering, he gestured impatiently for me to remain in the foyer. I stood near the room's open doorway as he informed the unexpected guests that he would notify the Traveler of their arrival and return with refreshments.

He didn't spare me a second glance as he strode past me and disappeared through a door at the back of the foyer. As I focused on trying to look appropriately servant-like, a random thought occurred to me that filled me with dismay and made it very difficult to stay rooted to the spot where the servant had ordered me to stand. *What if the Traveler actually* was *a Traveler, but one that hailed from a world other than my own?* This otherworldly travel was obviously possible—I was here, wasn't I? Was a third alternate universe possible? That could explain why Lox didn't think the Traveler in West Scapah was from my world. It would also mean I was hopelessly stranded.

My chilling musings were thankfully interrupted by the vigorous arrival of the master of the house. He swept past me in a blur of tangerine. I was about to surreptitiously peak around the doorframe but froze when I heard the man boisterously welcome the cloth merchant and his wife. Chills ran down my spine. The hairs on the back of my neck and on my forearms lifted. Although I could not see him, I recognized that penetrating baritone voice. My fears about a third alternate universe were unfounded. This man was indeed a Traveler who hailed from my world. His voice was one I knew well. In fact, there'd been a time in my life when I'd heard it every day. The shock of hearing it in this house in a world in which I didn't belong was mind-blowingly intense.

CHAPTER 20

I craned my head to peer into the room at the gregarious man dressed in the outlandish apparel who was welcoming Alberic and Lita as if they were visiting royalty. The light streaming in from the large windows made it difficult to see him, but it didn't matter. I knew to whom that voice belonged. The Traveler was none other than my estranged father.

Never in a million years had I considered that the Traveler in West Scapah was my father. Never! I wanted to call out to him, but I seemed to have lost my ability to engage my vocal chords. On top of that, the movements and sounds made by the three people in the room seemed warped as if they'd stepped into a slow-motion movie. Alberic gestured, but his hands were lethargic. Lita chuckled, but the sound of her laughter stuttered as if in a slow staccato of shattering glass. The sound of the Traveler's voice had become equally discordant as if being played on a corrupt audio file. I saw Alberic had lifted a hand and was beckoning me to approach, but I couldn't move. I was rooted to the spot. Then the three of them began making their way toward me, slowly, sluggishly, as if they were slogging through tepid molasses.

With the light from the windows streaming behind them and blurring my vision, I grasped at a brief flare of hope that when this man's face finally came into focus, I would not recognize him. Then he was in front of me, his large frame blocking the light. My heart sank. I was indeed beholding the familiar—older, but still familiar—face of my father. His ultra-smooth smile and perfect white teeth, evocative of a crafty television evangelist, had not changed with the passing years. A part of me wanted to collapse into a fit of hysterical giggles as I took in his attire. His robe, cinched with an elaborately embroidered sash, and his bejeweled turban might have convinced the people of West Scapah, but to me he looked ridiculous. He barely glanced at me though, his avaricious gaze drawn to the basket I held.

A hundred questions tumbled around in my head. I wanted to open the door of my skull and pluck one out, but I could not find a latch. I remained silent, handicapped by my treacherous, churning emotions.

When he lifted his gaze to meet mine, I saw puzzlement in his pale blue eyes. It was obvious he was trying to place me, and that made me unaccountably angry. A man should recognize his own daughter, should he not? *Should he not?* I felt lava leak from my eyes as my father stared at me without recognition. How dare he look at me and not know me!

As I held his gaze, it was as if I could see the cogs and wheels spinning in his impressively agile brain. Puzzlement quickly changed to recognition and then, alarmingly, to dismay and, disappointingly, to guarded calculation. I was also sickeningly aware of how quickly he recovered from the shock of recognizing me. It inspired both envy and disgust that he could regain his equilibrium so effortlessly.

My astonishment increased further when I grasped that he was searching for a way to avoid admitting he knew me. Despite how traumatizing it was to unexpectedly come face-to-face with the stranger who was my father, it was nothing like the sting of calculated rejection, although I can't say why I cared. Nevertheless, a hot needle of pain pierced my heart. It was as if the catharsis of the Cast Away ceremony was negated. Had Marintha witnessed my present turmoil, she would've been so disappointed.

Then Alberic was speaking and sound resumed with a whoosh.

"Do you know one another?" Alberic asked as he eyed first me and then my father.

"Indeed, we do," my father responded in a neutral tone.

I had been wrong. He would indeed acknowledge me. I could not have articulated why this was suddenly so important to me. Perhaps every abandoned child would feel the same, regardless of whether the parent in question was deserving of such loyalty and devotion.

My father gazed at me, absently stroking the creases on each side of his mouth with his thumb and index finger. I'd forgotten how he always did this when he grew thoughtful.

He turned his head slightly toward Alberic, but he kept his gaze on me. "I have indeed crossed paths with this young lady before," he stated, dropping his hands and clasping them casually on the knot of his elaborate belt. "At a reception, I believe?"

I felt like hot lava really was bubbling at the core of my being. How could he not acknowledge his own daughter? What had I done to deserve such ill treatment? I finally, thankfully, found my voice. "They know I'm a Traveler, Da—"

"Excuse us a moment, please." My father grasped my arm and unceremoniously steered me out of earshot.

I looked over my shoulder and registered the surprise and concern on the faces of my new friends before jerking out of his painful grip. "Don't touch me!" My harsh tone halted my father in his tracks. He did not attempt to grab me again.

Over my father's shoulder I saw Alberic and Lita approach. I turned to them. "This man is—"

"Meredee!"

My father's voice held a steely note of warning. It was the same voice that got our attention when we were kids and one that often preceded a fit of rage. A part of me hoped my present behavior would goad him into losing his temper, but he successfully hid his frustration as he turned to face his guests, who were regarding me with grave concern.

"Meredith and I know each other." He commented in an amiable tone. "Quite the coincidence, do you not agree?"

I turned to look at my father and saw his eyes held a warning, one that would have quelled me as a child. But I was an adult now. He had no authority over me.

And then it dawned on me, and my wrath sank into the pit of my stomach like a shipwreck settling on the ocean floor. He held all the cards. I had to go along with this painful charade, at least for the time being, because I could not afford to alienate him. Doing so could cost me my ticket home. For whatever reason, he did not want it known that I was his daughter. And I had no choice but to take my cues from him.

I schooled my expression as I turned to face my new friends. "Alberic, Lita, he's right." The fact that I'd just been blindsided had not, it seemed, altered my voice in any way. Shockingly, I sounded perfectly normal. "It seems a strange coincidence, I know," I said in what I hoped was a reassuring tone. "I have known..." I glanced at the man known as the Traveler. It was clear he did not want me to identify him as my father, but what was I supposed to call him? Hank? The name seemed utterly unsuitable for a man wearing a tangerine robe and a bejeweled turban. "I have known this man all my life," I amended.

My father's voice was laced with feigned pleasure as he said, "It is an absolute delight to bump into Meredee so unexpectedly."

I fought the urge to make fake retching sounds like my brothers and I had done as kids.

"I do thank you for coming," he continued, addressing Alberic and Lita. "And I propose that I not take up any more of your precious time. But, please, allow Meredith to remain. We have much news of home to catch up on...in private," he added, making it clear he wanted his guests to leave.

My father gave me a piercing look as he made his comment. I knew it was not news from home that interested him, but news explaining what the hell I was doing here.

But Alberic was not willing to be so easily evicted from the Traveler's home. "At the risk of sounding ungrateful, kind sir, Meredith should return with us." He spoke in a polite but authoritative tone. "Perhaps you would consider joining us at our home this evening? I have some fine wines I am sure would please your superior palate. You and Meredith can engage in your *private* conversation in the comfort of our expansive home and gardens."

"Alberic, Lita," I intervened. "It's fine, truly. I'll be safe here with the Traveler." Spending time with this man would more than likely test my patience, but I knew I had nothing to fear from him in terms of my safety. After all, he was my dad. "I'll walk them to the gate." I said, directing this last comment to my father.

As I made to move past him, my father shifted his body to block me so that Alberic and Lita could not see our faces. "Don't treat me like a child," I said in a furious undertone. "I won't tell them how I know you, okay?"

Without waiting for my father's permission, I stepped around him and turned to Alberic and Lita with what I hoped was a reassuring smile. "I'll walk you to the gate," I repeated as I moved toward the exit. I darted a look at my father as if daring him to stop me.

Alberic reluctantly took the basket from my hands—I'd entirely forgotten I was still holding it—and placed it on a settee near the door. As we moved across the marbled foyer, my father followed, but when we stepped outside and began crossing the courtyard, he waited in the doorway.

"Meredith, I do not think this is wise," Alberic whispered in an insistent tone as we made our way past the bubbling fountain. "Lord…" Alberic glanced over his shoulder and dropped his voice. "I cannot think what *he* will do when we return without you."

Alberic couldn't have looked more pained if he were passing a gallstone. I could almost hear him groaning at the thought of facing Lox.

"Yes, my dear, think again," Lita implored.

In an effort to be reassuring, I briefly rested my hand on her arm. "Trust me. I know this man and I have nothing to fear from him." I briefly glanced over my shoulder. My father's disingenuous smile almost made me retch for real. I lowered my voice. "I will give a full account when I'm back at your house in a few hours. I promise. There's nothing to worry about. Tell *him* to trust me on this, okay?"

It dawned on me then that if Lox were to find out how the Traveler and I were related, he might be motivated to introduce my father to the sharp end of his sword. Lox abhorred that I'd been identified as one of the Cast Away.

It finally occurred to me then why my father had not wanted to acknowledge me as his daughter. His status and reputation as a Traveler could not withstand the outcry that would be sure to follow if it became public that his daughter had been identified as a Cast Away. Regardless, all I wanted from him was the means to return home, clearly something he had. What did it matter that he couldn't, or wouldn't, acknowledge me as his child?

I saw that my father had lost what little patience he had and was approaching. I knew that his demeanor, with his hands behind his back and a benign smile on his face, masked his underlying irritation.

"Go," I said to Alberic and Lita. "I'll be fine."

"Very well, but we'll send the carriage back for you," Alberic insisted.

"Thank you, Alberic," I said, then turned and strode back the way I'd come.

I had no premonition as I entered that house for a second time that the very ground beneath my feet was about to shift again as though a bored, mischievous god took delight in pulling the rug out from beneath my feet for the fun of watching me fall.

CHAPTER 21

$\mathcal{O}$nce inside, my father barked at his startled manservant to bring the trolley of refreshments to his library.

I followed him into a dimly lit, high-ceiled room at the back of the house. Behind us, the servant wheeled the teacart, positioning it beside a large, round table flanked by six upholstered arm chairs. He then exited without a word and closed the door behind him.

I eyed my father as he removed his jeweled turban and placed it on a side table near the door. Without his headdress, I saw his hair had turned white since I'd last seen him, but he sported the same short military cut he'd always favored. He moved to the teacart, then looked at me expectantly.

"Tea?" he asked, as if it were a typical occurrence for us to encounter one another in a world far from our own and in circumstances that were utterly preposterous.

I stared at him, stunned speechless for a brief moment. "Are you kidding me?" I finally squeaked. "That's what you have to say to me? Tea?"

I clasped my hands behind my back to hide the fact that they'd begun to shake. The truth was, if I'd unexpectedly chanced upon my father in my own world, I would've been hard pressed to remain unmoved. The fact that this surprise encounter occurred in the Lands of Vendome only increased the intensity of my distress.

"Why not tea?" he countered.

He was acting as if we were two grannies embarking on our weekly gossip session.

"It seems we have a great deal to catch up on," he continued. "You're quite the last person I expected to see here. Did you find the family journals then? No," he added, holding up a hand. "Don't tell me just yet. I want to hear it from the beginning."

I had no idea what he meant by family journals, but he made it seem as if I was about to divulge light-hearted details of the latest neighborhood scandal. Questions were once again tumbling about inside my mind, but they were like dried leaves in a windstorm. Grasping hold of even one was impossible.

"Wait until we're seated and comfortable; then we can savor the telling while we swap tales."

Savor the telling? Swap tales? Was he insane?

While he spoke, he poured tea into two china cups and saucers. "Sugar?" he asked.

It struck me then as I watched him fiddle with the refreshment tray that he was far more unsettled by my presence than he let on. Perhaps the attention he was lavishing on the tea was his way of covering up that he was as shaken as I.

The realization that I was not the only one who was freaked out by this unexpected reunion calmed me a little and allowed me to begin the process of thinking rationally about this unforeseen turn of events. Most importantly, because I was entirely dependent on my father's good will to solve my current dilemma, I had to keep my negative emotions in check. He must be allowed to set the tone of our encounter. Venting my built-up resentment, which had compounded over the years, would no doubt be satisfying, but it would not serve my inherent goal of gaining the means of returning home.

As it would be in my best interest to feign detachment, I shifted my gaze to survey the room. At first glance, it seemed a multi-purpose space that combined a library, private dining room, and miniature museum. Wall sconces and lamps were lit but, overall, the room was dim and it was impossible to distinguish the patterns of the plush, dark rugs that covered most of the marbled floor. Three tall, narrow windows were set against what I believed was the east wall, but their heavy silk drapes in a rich mustard trimmed in dark navy remained closed despite the fact that the morning was already half gone. The wall opposite the windows was devoted to a display of medieval-looking weaponry, while the wall that flanked the entrance to the room was lined with shelves stacked willy-nilly with scrolls and books. A number of museum-quality, glass-topped display cabinets were interspersed throughout the central area of the large room. Two oversized wing chairs and a small pedestal table were angled invitingly in front of a fire that burned in a smoke-blackened fireplace. Dark wainscoting panels jutted out from the wall of pale stone on either side of the hearth. The paneling boasted a broad shelf at shoulder height lined with a variety of knickknacks and winged statuettes. I fleetingly wondered if the stone behind the wainscoting was part of the wall encircling the Royal Residences.

My gaze returned full circle and fell on the large bronze carving that had been given pride of place in the center of the large round table. The bronze depicted a temple-like building with miniature columns and terraced courtyards. It looked like a Greek acropolis.

"Amazing, isn't it?" My father asked. He stood beside the table holding his cup and saucer as if we were at a cocktail reception. "How are our worlds connected, precisely?" he queried amiably. "Is this a world within a world? A parallel universe of some kind? I have yet to find a satisfactory answer, although I've been mulling it over for more than twenty years. Makes me wish I had a better grasp of quantum physics." He nodded at the sculpture. "That's a replica of the Temple of the High Priest at Sherha's Mound," he added. "Have you heard of it?"

I nodded, thinking fleetingly of what Lox had told me about applying to have his marriage annulled.

"When I left the military, I was convinced that marrying your mother would give me the sense of belonging that had always eluded me."

My father's change of topic didn't entirely surprise me. It seemed he still enjoyed disconcerting people.

"But after years of mutual unhappiness it seemed futile to keep hammering a square peg into a round hole. I tried, but I just wasn't suited to being a devoted husband."

I turned away from him as I fought the impulse to lash out and list—with all the fingers of both my hands—the despicable characteristics that also made him ill-suited to being a father. Instead, I moved toward a shelf of leather bound books. I scanned the titles: *Pantheon of Gods and the Sanctity of Marriage*, and *Hierarchy of Gods; Methodology and Models*. In other circumstances, this room and its unusual contents might have greatly intrigued me, but all my senses were directed toward the man behind me who stood placidly sipping his tea.

"Why don't you stop your prowling and sit down?" my father suggested as he moved around the large table and sat in one of the wing chairs.

It took all my effort to cleave to a pretense of nonchalance as I joined him, sinking into the matching maroon chair next to his. I was not convinced my acting fooled him, but it was important to me that I at least try to maintain a calm and collected façade.

I could feel the heat from the wood-burning fire in the hearth and removed my shawl, draping it across the arm of my chair.

We sat for a moment in silence as we eyed each other. I knew my gaze reflected guarded suspicion. His eyes revealed undisguised curiosity and, strangely, pleasure. I looked away.

"You did not tell your merchant friends of our relationship?"

I shook my head.

"Good. My status in these Lands is quite elevated. I want to keep it that way. It would not serve me to have it compromised over something that took place years ago in another world, literally and figuratively. Well then, I owe it to you to share my tale first, don't you agree?"

How magnanimous, I wanted to scoff, but I bit my tongue. What galled me most in that moment was that he'd not yet mentioned my dead brother.

"What about Curtis, Dad? Didn't you get our messages?" I accused. I had to choke back tears as a surge of grief sought to overwhelm me. It was still so very hard to accept that Curtis was dead.

"What messages?" he said as he set down his empty cup and saucer on the pedestal table. "Did your brother finally dump that frumpy wife he was saddled with and make it big as a musician?"

My father was himself a talented saxophonist. Curtis and I— and Kimberly—had inherited our musical ability from him. When Curtis's musical aspirations had been hijacked by an unplanned pregnancy in high school, he and Val had given their best efforts toward raising their daughter and making their marriage work. The fact that they'd finally called it quits a few weeks before Curtis died was no fault of theirs.

"You don't know?"

"Know what?"

I saw a hint of the impatient, easily annoyed father I remembered. Any effort I might have made to couch my unwelcome news in soft words would be wasted on this cold-hearted man. "He was hit by a drunk driver on the twenty-sixth of September. We left messages on your answering machine. You still live in

Vancouver, don't you? At least, when you're not here? He's dead, Dad."

A look of horror came into his pale eyes. "No!"

When he turned to stare into the fire, I noticed his fingertips digging into the coarse weave of the chair's dark upholstery. I was unprepared for the wave of pity that washed through me. My father's reaction made it clear that, despite his decision to walk away from his family all those years ago, and despite being distant and emotionally unavailable since then, he truly did feel something for his children. His reaction to my unwelcome news about Curtis proved that he had, at least at one time, loved his eldest son. I tried to reconcile this awareness with the fact that he'd deliberately chosen a life that didn't include any of us, one in which his seven grandchildren were complete strangers to him. Regardless, at the very least, he should have been at his son's funeral.

"Don't you want to know what happened?" I finally demanded.

He started as if he'd forgotten my presence.

"What would that change?" he uttered harshly without looking at me.

"Change?" I frowned. "Nothing, but—"

"Then tell me nothing more!" he snapped in a clipped tone.

He rose and added a couple of logs to the fire. Then he retrieved his cup and saucer and moved to the table. As he poured himself more tea, he spoke in a mild tone.

"The tea is good, the best that can be had in these Lands. Maybe not as good as Ceylon tea, and a far cry from coffee. But still, a decent refreshment all-round. Are you sure you don't want any?"

It astounded me that he had more to say about the flavor of tea than he had about the death of his own son. Even now, after receiving this devastating news, his cup did not rattle in its saucer and his hands remained steady. Whatever pity I'd momentarily felt for him vanished in that instant. That he could so effortlessly recover from the shock of such paralyzing news seemed a crime. He truly was a heartless man. I shook my head in disgust as he wordlessly resumed his seat.

Then, without any prompting, my self-aggrandizing father recounted the story of how he'd become the Traveler at the Court of the Grand Duke in the Western Duchy of the Lands of Vendome. As I listened, and in spite of my aversion for this man, I grudgingly became enthralled by his fascinating tale.

CHAPTER 22

*I*n the spring of 1974, when my father was repairing the roof of our stately old farmhouse, he found a small metal lockbox tucked into an overhang in the attic. Inside were two objects: a stiff, aged leather wallet holding an undated letter, fragile at the folds and clearly very old; and a heavy, icicle-shaped stone with veins that sparkled even in dim light. The letter was addressed to 'My Son' and signed with the initials J.W. It referenced a meteorite Stone from an 'alternate' galaxy that could be used to 'travel to the Lands of Vendome'. The letter cautioned that the Stone could be fatal if over-used, and also stated that each ancestor who'd traveled using the Stone had made an account of their adventures in 'the enclosed family journals'. However, no journals were in the box.

It was at this point in my father's tale I realized he was under the false impression that I'd found these journals and had somehow used them to get here. I also remembered Julitha saying something about how the visioning process to see Kimberly had been easier than she'd expected. She'd questioned if we had Vendome blood in our veins. Perhaps the writer of the letter was an ancestor on my father's side. Hadn't Lox told me that the first

Traveler from my world had taken a Vendome bride? Was this first Traveler my ancestor? If so, how far back? Hiltha had also mentioned something about how my path was linked by the Dust of those who came before. I made a mental note to ask Lox later to tell me more about the Travelers of Old.

My father had—characteristically, I thought—dismissed the letter as nonsense and the Stone as worthless, relegating the box to a shelf in his workshop. Later that year when he was absently searching for something, his eyes happened to fall on it. Remembering the odd-looking Stone inside the box, he decided to try and identify the type of ore that glittered in its veins. After careful examination he remained mystified. On impulse, he decided to use his portable torch on the glittering veins to see how they responded to intense heat.

Holding the thick end of the pointed Stone in one hand, he passed the hot flame against the long, narrow tip. In that instant and without any warning whatsoever, he suddenly found himself standing under a large fir tree at the bottom of a hill looking up at a sprawling mansion. This 'transportation' had no ill effect on him aside from the shock of suddenly discovering he was not in the place he had just been and the warm, lush place he now stood was wholly and completely unfamiliar. And impossible, of course. Desperate to end this rather terrifying hallucination, he relit the micro-torch with hands, he admitted, that trembled. When he redirected the flame against the surface of the Stone he found himself, again in a split-second, back inside his familiar shop. Despite his intense relief, his reckless curiosity spurred his desire to investigate further. Although he initially had to work up the courage to do so, he tried this technique again, and then again, and each was as successful as the last. He timed himself each time, concluding that the same time passed in both locations, although he couldn't prove this exactly as any timepiece he took with him to the unknown place stopped working as soon as he arrived. He retrieved the letter and reread it, but the lack of detail frustrated him. He would have to find the journals. That very afternoon he conducted a thorough search of our big, rambling farmhouse, but his extensive exploration failed to turn up the missing chronicles.

I distinctly recalled that autumn day when my father had torn our house apart. His erratic, feverish behavior had severely agitated my mother. It was soon after this 'cleaning spree' he'd disappeared for good.

Believing that this ability to travel to an alternate world was the equivalent of his ship finally coming in, my father then planned, initiated, and executed a number of reconnaissance missions to determine how best to leverage this newfound knowledge and ability to his advantage.

At this point in the tale my father rose and moved to the wainscoting shelf to the left of the fireplace. One of the items on the cluttered ledge was a rectangular copper box with a domed lid. Without interrupting his tale, he opened the box and removed an object I'd never before seen but one I immediately recognized. It was the icicle-shaped meteorite.

Goosebumps rose all over my body as my father nonchalantly handed the priceless object to me. It took significant effort on my part to school my features. He could not know that I did not have in my possession something of equivalent power, or how badly I wanted to steal this Stone and run to Lox and shout *Eureka!* at the top of my lungs. This item was both the means for me to return to my world and the means of keeping Lox in my life. My heart thumped in my chest as if it had tripled in size. I'd never coveted any object as much as I coveted that Stone.

It was far heavier than I would have imagined for its size. As I handled it, a dusting of gleaming flecks stuck to my palms. I guessed this was the origin of the Travelers Dust that had been gifted to the Astromancer in the Eastern Duchy. I refocused— with difficulty—as my father continued his tale.

When he finally got his bearings, my father learned that he always 'landed' on the property of the Astromancer who served the Grand Duchess, a woman he'd never actually encountered and who he deliberately avoided for reasons he promised to explain later. In the years that followed, he taught himself how to manipulate his landing location simply by using his thoughts, which allowed him to 'land' anywhere, as long as it was a place he'd previously visited and could visualize. He also discovered, the hard way, that his frequent trips to and from the Lands of Vendome were negatively impacting his health to the point where he'd been falsely diagnosed with leukemia—something else I remembered from years ago. Recalling that the letter warned frequent travel could be fatal, he refrained from going to the Lands of Vendome for a full year until he'd resumed his health. Now, he only traveled two or three times each year, spending months at a time either in Vendome or at his home in Vancouver. His health remained excellent.

During his initial reconnaissance tours, one of the first relationships he'd established in the Lands of Vendome had been with a morally questionable but enterprising young sea captain. The two of them struck a secret bargain that, in the end, made them both rich. My father imported small, inconsequential items from our world—fountain pens, and waterproof matches—in exchange for gemstones. He'd insisted from the beginning—and this was more on instinct than any real strategy at the time—that the sea captain make his trades for these goods in lands well beyond the borders of Vendome.

Finding a market in Vancouver for his otherworldly gemstones had been relatively easy. He'd used an old military contact to connect him with an expert in forgery who, for the right price, asked no questions and created a counterfeit provenance trail for some of the more precious stones. As a result, my father had quickly accumulated a substantial fortune.

"You talk about finding someone to forge documents as if it's as easy as hiring a Maytag repairman," I accused, belatedly remembering that it wouldn't serve me to alienate him.

"For god's sake, Meredee, don't be so self-righteous," he responded in a superior tone. "Or naïve. You know as well as I do that I wouldn't need to falsify anything if anyone in our world would believe the truth. Take issue with that, if you must, but not with me. And don't forget that the money from the sale of those gemstones kept you fed and clothed until you were eighteen. I may not have lived with you, but I provided for you."

I only just stopped myself from rolling my eyes. "So, there were no lucky investments in the stock market?"

"Sure there was. The market remains a legitimate front for my real source of income, which has grown significantly since those days thanks to my partnership with the Grand Duke. He pays me in diamonds, which are far more valuable than the ship captain's inferior gemstones. I market them at home as Canadian Arctic diamonds."

His mention of diamonds rang a distant bell in the back of my mind. "Wait a minute. There was a story on the news a few days before I traveled here," I told him. "It was about a diamond scam. I remember it distinctly because that's when Marilyn phoned to tell me about Curtis." The phone had rung. I had muted the television. And my world had shattered.

"Are you sure? Did they specifically mention Arctic diamonds? Or just diamonds in general?"

"Geez, Dad, I was a little distracted at the time considering my sister was telling me my brother had just been killed."

He seemed unperturbed by my sarcasm.

"Well, I appreciate the heads up. If it is my diamonds that are in question, I'll have to deal with it when I return. I wonder what might have gone wrong?" He stared into the fire as he stroked the lines on each side of his mouth. "Normally, I could depart this world at a moment's notice, but I've a task to perform that must be done sooner rather than later." His pale eyes shifted back to me. "How often have you traveled here?"

"Uh...this is my first time."

187

Clearly, my father now expected me to share the tale of how I'd found the family journals and launched myself into the Lands of Vendome. I was about to tell him that I had to leave—and mislead him into thinking that I'd share my tale later—but before I could speak he asked a question that made me flinch as if he'd reached out and slapped me.

"How long have you known Lord Loxley?"

I remained silent and did my best to show indifference, but I'd never mastered the art of having a poker face. I wished I'd taken the time to think about how much to tell him. I didn't want him to know I had no means to return; I didn't want him to know I was dependent on him.

When I spoke, I kept my eyes on the Stone, pretending total absorption. "Sorry, what? Who are you talking about?"

"Puh-lease, Meredee."

His sarcasm and slang exactly mimicked what I would have said in my youth when he still lived with us.

"Your shameless lies might have fooled your gullible mother, but they never fooled me. I know Lord Loxley brought you to West Scapah."

We were interrupted by a knock on the door. A welcome reprieve that would hopefully give me time to collect my thoughts.

"Don't lie to me, Meredee," my father said in a threatening tone before rising. He moved to the sideboard, took a moment to put on his jeweled turban, then strode to the door and opened it. I could not see who was on the other side or hear what was being said, but in the next moment he turned to me.

"I have to step out. I won't be gone long." He did not wait for my response but left the room, closing the door behind him.

It took a split second for me to act. I jammed the Stone in the pocket of my skirt as I ran silently across the thick rugs toward the door, limping only a little. But then I froze in sudden shock when I heard the unmistakable sound of a key turning in the lock.

I rushed to the door and rattled the handle. It would not budge. Why would he lock me in? I banged a fist on the door and yelled to be let out, but no one responded. I cursed my father and whatever calculating scheme he was involved in that made it necessary to imprison his own daughter, then kicked the door in frustration, which shot a spasm of pain through my still tender ankle. Cursing, I turned to regard the room, looking for an alternate exit.

When my eyes fell on the closed drapes, I limped toward the windows. When I carefully peaked around the curtain, I was astonished to encounter a wall of brick. I checked the other windows, but they were the same. No wonder my father had not bothered to open the drapes. I searched the rest of the room, but even though I ran my hands over every seam of the walls and shelves, I found nothing.

Eventually, I came back to stand in front of the hearth and withdrew the Stone from my pocket. It would only make matters worse if, upon my father's return, I advertised the fact that I'd been intent on stealing it. Still, it took intense willpower to replace it on its bed of satin.

I leaned against the wainscoting shelf, my mind in turmoil as I distractedly nudged the toe of my sore foot against a panel that was clearly in need of repair. I had not examined the walls on either side of the hearth for a secret exit as I assumed the stone was impregnable. But when I looked down at this piece of board, I noticed it was not flush with the wall. I immediately pictured a tunnel connecting this house to the Inner City. I could escape that way, couldn't I? It would undoubtedly present a whole new set of problems, but it would be worth the risk if it meant I would have possession of the Stone. Inspired, I stooped to tug on the loose panel, but my hope died when the only thing it revealed was a narrow alcove. Tucked inside this recess was a rectangular canvas case large enough to hold a baritone saxophone.

As I stared at that bag, I felt the hairs on the back of my neck rise. I gingerly retrieved it, handling it as if it were a ticking bomb.

Moving slowly, somehow knowing I was on the brink of something unpleasant, I laid it across the arms of the wing chair I'd vacated. I tugged on the zipper, the grinding sound as disruptive as a sudden burst of rifle fire. I lifted the cover, which was lined with a layer of foam padding, then stared speechless at the contents.

The case held half-a-dozen pieces of metal in varying shapes and sizes that fit perfectly into foam crevices. Even though I'd never before seen such a thing, I knew this was a top quality sniper's rife. I attempted to process the significance of finding this hidden object in my father's house, but a temporary glitch in the circuits of my brain prevented me from arranging my thoughts into any kind of order. I could not seem to reconcile the tangible presence of this rifle with the reality it signified. My mind had slowed to tortoise-like speed.

I had to force myself to focus, to think methodically as if I were connecting a series of numbered dots. The first dot indicated that in front of me was a sniper's rifle. That was indisputable. The next dot linked this weapon to my world, also indisputable. I already knew from my conversations with Lox that gunpowder was only in the formative stages of development in the Lands of Vendome. The next dot connected this instrument of destruction with my estranged father's Vendome home, while the next dot, the one I had to force my mind to reach for, made it clear that this weapon had to have been brought to the Lands of Vendome by none other than my father. There was one final dot that would complete the picture and reveal the full truth. My heart resisted making the leap as my mind whirled like a spinning kaleidoscope. Then the kaleidoscope stilled. The pieces fell into place. The horrifying picture became perfectly clear.

The man who'd disappeared into the woods after the thunder and lightning of the gods had killed my horse was my father. *My father?* A trained marksman who'd spent a decade in the Canadian military, he now hired himself out as an assassin in this parallel world. He was the man hired by Rodmyrrah to kill Rikka's ambassadors. His well-honed skill had never failed to deliver death until, by a strange stroke of luck, Lox had shifted position at the precise moment that the sniper fired.

I'd earlier been shocked that my father would so casually delve into the criminal element by hiring a counterfeiter to help sell his gemstones, but his actions as a hired assassin went far beyond white-collar crime. This was the kind of crime conducted by people who lacked a moral compass. I heard the echo of the old Diviner in Conraz's lodge saying, *Beware! He is more than he appears.* I now understood that these words referred to my father who was both *the Traveler who shared my path* and the mercenary assassin against whom Hiltha had warned. Not only had my father made an attempt on Lox's life, he'd almost killed his own daughter. I finally and belatedly understood why he'd looked so chagrined upon first identifying me.

With slow and measured movements, I removed the largest item from its foam padding. A scope was permanently mounted on the long, narrow barrel. Had I seen just this piece on its own, my ignorance of firearms would've made me assume the weapon was complete. But there were other pieces still in their foam crevices, one a rectangular object as long as my hand but half as wide that, I assumed, held bullets. I had no clue about the purpose of the remaining items. As I balanced the heavy weight of this weapon in my hands, the implication of my loathsome discovery finally slammed into me.

I had been so dense. Beyond dense. I was blind. Worse than blind, I was stupid. Stupid, stupid, stupid girl! An hour ago when I realized the Traveler was my father, I had been so discombobulated I'd forgotten my theory that the Traveler and the assassin might be one and the same man. Perhaps subconsciously, I'd deliberately blocked out this unwelcome knowledge when his identity had first been revealed.

God, I was stupid! There could not be anyone as dim and

191

slow-witted and dense as me. If Kimberly had still been with me, she would have been smart enough to instantly connect these dots. My niece would have immediately understood that the Traveler—my father—and the assassin were one and the same man.

In that clarifying moment, I acutely felt Kimberly's absence. I wished with all my being that she was here to help me navigate this emotional minefield. As I stood holding that horrifying weapon, I felt a yearning for my beloved niece stronger than I'd ever felt before. I desperately needed her clever, sharp-as-a-tack mind. I'd never missed her as much as in that intensely debilitating moment. God, how I missed her!

The sound of a key in the lock startled me.

My father re-entered the room. Just as he was about to close the door, he realized what I was holding and why I stood staring at him in open-mouthed horror. He froze for a moment as he eyed me, but then he carefully and quietly shut the door. He stood, silently immobile, as if waiting for me to speak.

"You?" I spat in a croaking whisper.

He had to know the gun I held was not assembled or loaded and therefore not a threat, yet he lifted a hand as he slowly moved toward me. He stopped behind the wing chair he'd so recently vacated.

"You could have knocked me over with a feather when I realized *you* were the Cast Away woman being talked about," he said. "If I'd known it was my daughter who rode with Lord Loxley, I would never have taken that shot. Never. I'd be the first to admit my morals are pretty damn loose, but shooting at my own daughter? That was one hell of a shock."

"Shooting at your own daughter? Instead of killing Lox, you mean?"

My father's eyebrows raised in surprise. "Lox? That seems an awfully familiar way to address the most important man in the Eastern Duchy. I take it you have become...friends?"

I sputtered. "Friends? I've been friends with him since I was ten, Dad. You even met him in our world. And Rikka and Jaybex."

Unlike me, my father was not stupid or dim or dense or slow-witted. His sharp-as-a-tack mind could connect dots instantaneously. I watched his face as comprehension dawned. "You mean those odd friends of yours that the boys hated? That last summer?"

"Jesus, Dad, I can't believe you tried to kill him."

I finally realized why he'd locked me in this room, and the knowledge made it feel as if a giant fist was slowly squeezing the air out of my lungs. My father couldn't allow me to leave his house because he still fully intended to kill Lox. He'd said he had a task still to perform. He intended to keep me locked in this room until he achieved success. *God, I was dense.*

"You can't do it, Dad. Not now you know he's my friend. You can't."

In response, my father lifted a shoulder in a mocking shrug as if to say, *and you think you're going to stop me?*

As he made to move around the wing chair, I knew only one thing. Without the rifle, he would not be able to make it look like the thunder and lightning of the gods had killed Lox. Desperate to neutralize this threat, I didn't think but instead reached out with my left hand and scooped the glittering Stone from its satin cushion in the open box.

In a strange kind of slow-motion, I saw my father's expression change as he processed my intentions. He pivoted on his heel like a panther and launched himself over the solid, high-backed chair, one hand thrust against the top and the other extended toward me with fingers curled like claws.

I leaned sideways and down, sticking my entire fist into the flames. I felt the heat sear my skin. I cried out and instinctively jerked my hand away from the pain, feeling the Stone slip from my grasp. But in that split second, my father and the clutter of his room vanished.

PART IV

HOME

CHAPTER 23

or a fleeting moment I felt an odd suspension as if I were hurtling down a skyscraper's high-speed elevator. In the next instance, I stumbled backwards and fell, landing hard on my backside.

I was in a back alley—clearly in my own world—lined with garages, mismatched fences, and garbage cans. A few leaves clung stubbornly to the otherwise bare branches of the deciduous trees that rose above the fences. The air was crisp, dry, and had the distinct chill of autumn.

Moments before, I'd been wishing for Kimberly's superior brain; now, I wished she were here to greet me, but the alley was deserted.

I still had the rifle-shaped object, although I'd dropped it when I landed. I didn't have the Stone, though. It had slipped through my scorched fingers in that split second before I vanished from my father's home.

I rose on shaky legs, taking a moment to steady myself before picking up the weapon. My ankle throbbed, as did my hand where it had been scorched by the flames. My stomach was queasy but, unlike the only other time I'd traveled between worlds, this time I wasn't vomiting.

I would have to get rid of the rifle, though. If someone appeared, I would be hard pressed to explain my old-fashioned clothes let alone the sophisticated weapon I held. I looked around me for a hiding spot and saw a generous pile of fallen leaves on the alley side of a rickety fence under a tall elm tree. I moved to the fence, stooping and wedging the rifle against its base and piling fallen leaves over it until it was concealed.

When I stood and turned, I froze. A young boy of about seven was watching me from his perch on a pint-sized bicycle. He had one rubber-booted foot on a pedal and the other on the pot-holed asphalt.

"If you have to pee," he volunteered in a reproachful tone. "You're supposed to go home. My Mom said."

"Uh, I didn't...?" Why was I attempting to explain myself to a seven-year old, I suddenly thought? Clearly, he hadn't seen the rifle, which was the important thing.

"Are you a Hutterite?" he asked.

This boy had likely seen Hutterites at the farmer's market. Descendants of German protestants who'd fled to Canada for religious freedom, they lived in communes and were common in certain parts of Alberta.

"Yes," I exclaimed, thankful to have an explanation for my long skirt and headscarf, and giving him a friendly smile. "But I'm lost, so maybe you can help me." I didn't recognize my immediate surroundings, but I assumed I was in the small town of Bellecourt near my sister's property, which was situated between the town's outer limits and the golf course. "Which way to the golf course?" I asked, not at all confident that a seven-year old would even know.

"My Mom said not to talk to strangers," the boy announced, then looked alarmed as if he'd just realized he was doing exactly that.

"Well, actually, you shouldn't," I agreed. "So maybe just point me in the direction of..."

My voice trailed off as I watched him peddle furiously away. When he got to the end of the alley he looked over his shoulder at me, but doing so caused him to wobble dangerously and he narrowly missed crashing into an overflowing garbage bin. Then he was gone.

I guessed that, as soon as he got home, he would report to his mother how he'd seen a Hutterite woman peeing behind the trees in the back alley behind neighbour so-and-so's garage. I would have to disappear quick in case his over-zealous mother decided to investigate.

That was when it dawned on me I'd finally made it home. I'd succeeded in attaining the singular goal that had preoccupied me for the past month. This realization should have filled me with relief, but instead I felt only dismay. I'd vanished from Lox's world as abruptly as he'd vanished from mine, without saying any of the things I'd meant to say before leaving. Far worse, my father—*the assassin who intended to kill my lover*—still had the Stone, which meant he could return to this world and replace the rifle I'd taken.

There was only one thing for me to do. I had to book the next flight to Vancouver and somehow steal the Traveler's Stone before he could go back to the Lands of Vendome with a replacement weapon.

I hurried down the alley intent on finding a familiar landmark, but I'd taken only a few steps when I stopped short. On my right was a garage with a concrete pad between the door and the alley. A car—an alpine white Volkswagon Jetta—was parked on the pad. It looked suspiciously like mine, which I'd left at my sister Marilyn's the day of my brother's funeral. I moved behind it to read the license plate. It was my car. *What was my car doing parked behind a stranger's garage?* Then I finally realized where I was.

This wasn't the small town of Bellecourt as I'd first thought. I was in an alley in the city of Red Plains, and I was standing behind

Val and Kimberly's house. I'd never approached their home from the back alley and hadn't recognized it. I wondered fleetingly why I'd arrived in this location, but then recalled, in those last instances before I'd used the Stone, that I'd been desperately longing for Kimberly. Had my vivid thoughts of her been enough to propel me to her home in Red Plains? Was that what my father meant when he'd said he could manipulate his landing location with his thoughts?

I limped up to the tall fence and peaked over the wooden slats into Val's back yard. An abandoned rake and a small heap of leaves showed that someone had made a half-hearted attempt to deal with the litter of autumn foliage.

I was about to let myself through the back gate when a thought occurred to me. Until I knew what story Kimberly had concocted to explain her absence, I did not want to cross paths with anyone in my family. What if Val, who worked shifts at the Red Plains hospital, was home? How would I explain my attire, let alone my extended absence?

As I paused to consider what to do next, the back door of the house opened. My vision blurred momentarily when Kimberly stepped out onto the back verandah. She was wearing a long-sleeved, beige T-shirt, a puffy, black vest, dark jeans, and her signature Doc Martens. Her dyed hair, cut almost pixie short, had bold blond streaks framing her face. She looked lost and alone as she took a seat on the top step and wrapped her arms around her thin legs. She also looked beautiful. She didn't see me peaking over the top of the fence, so I called her name in a whisper. When she didn't respond, I gripped the wooden slats with both hands, wincing as the burns on my left hand brushed against the rough wood. I called her name again.

As Kimberly's head shot up, I put a warning finger to my lips. Her eyes widened, and then she was off the stoop and flying across the yard, through the gate, and into my arms. I felt an all-consuming wave of relief at the tangible realness of finally embracing my niece.

"Aunty Mere, I can't believe it's you! Oh my god! When did you get back?"

We were both crying and laughing.

"Two minutes ago," I said, withdrawing from her embrace so I could get a good look at her. She appeared to have lost weight. "Are you okay? You're so thin," I admonished.

"I'm fine. Oh, I've missed you so much. How's Jazper? How's the baby? How's Aster and Brebin? Does Conraz still think we're dead? Is Lord Loxley with you?"

We both laughed at her string of questions. "I've missed you, too. I haven't seen Jazper or Brebin or the baby since the day you left, and Conraz is so not an issue anymore. Lox is still in Vendome, but because of me, he's in terrible danger. I've done a really stupid thing, but I think I can fix it."

"I'll help you fix it, whatever it is. God, it's so awesome to see you! You look…"

I realized in all the hours we'd spent together in the Lands of Vendome she'd never seen me in anything but my 'Bellecourt' clothes. "Apparently, I look like a Hutterite," I volunteered.

She laughed. "No way! Hutterites don't rock the va-va-voom," she said, waving her hands to imitate my generous curves. "You look great!"

I laughed. I found her weight loss troubling, but her smile was enormous and, although she was thin, she was bubbling with vitality.

"What day is it?" I asked.

"Thursday. Tomorrow is Halloween."

"Thursday? Why aren't you in school?"

Kimberly rolled her eyes. "Long story. Totally boring. Who cares?"

I chuckled at her oh-so-typical teenage response. "Are you home alone?"

"No. Mom worked a night shift." Kimberly glanced over her shoulder at an upstairs window. "She's still sleeping."

"I take it you have my car keys?" My driver's license, I assumed was still in my purse at Marilyn's house. At her nod, I added, "Can you drive us to my place? I need to get out of these clothes."

She nodded emphatically. "Good idea."

"How long have I been gone?"

"Since I returned? Twenty-nine days!" Her tone was accusatory.

I laughed. It felt good to be missed. "What's everyone saying about my absence? What did you say about yours? No, answer that later. First things first. We need to get out of here before I'm seen. I need a change of clothes and a bandage for these burns." I held out my hand. "And then I need you to drive me to the airport."

"Why the airport?" Kimberly asked as she took a closer look at my hand. "Geez-Louise, Aunty Mere. What happened? Mom should look at that."

"Long story. Totally *not* boring. I'll tell you later. And no, let's not involve your Mom just yet."

Kimberly nodded her understanding. "Did you draw an image of that horrible Lord Rodmyrrah? Is he dead? I can't believe Lord Loxley didn't come with you," she added in an injured tone, looking behind me as if expecting him to appear.

"Lox doesn't even know I'm gone. And he's in danger because of me. If he gets killed now, it will be entirely my fault."

At Kimberly's look of dismay, I realized far more than our geographical paths had re-converged. Not that long ago she'd claimed responsibility for her father's death. She'd suffered badly on account of it. I now had a better understanding of her perspective. Wasn't I responsible for the fact that the assassin—*my father*—had tried to kill Lox, and was intent on succeeding? Now, in order to keep Lox safe, I had to find a way to prevent my father from following through with his intention. If I failed, then Lox's death really would be my fault.

"Is Fredryk with Lord Loxley?" Kimberly asked.

I lifted a shoulder and frowned. "Yes, probably."

Her faced cleared. "Then no one will kill him. Fredryk will make sure of that."

"*I'm* not so sure. They don't know what they're dealing with. Get the keys, okay? I'll wait here."

Kimberly turned to leave then whirled back to give me a fierce hug. "Aunty Mere, I'm *so* glad you're home!"

CHAPTER 24

$\mathcal{I}$n the car on the short drive to my townhouse, I gave Kimberly a quick summary of what had happened in the Lands of Vendome, and also shared the shocking news that her own grandfather was not only a diamond-fencing criminal in our world, he was an assassin in the Lands of Vendome whose current target was Lox. She wasn't nearly as shocked as I'd expected. Instead, she told me my father's counterfeiting scheme was all over the news, and the Mounties had put out an all-points-bulletin to apprehend him.

I emerged from the steamy bathroom of my townhouse in Red Plains after indulging in a short, thank-you-Jesus-for-modern-plumbing hot shower, which had regrettably been rather uncomfortable due to my burns. I carefully wrapped my wet hair in a turban, favoring my injured hand, before shrugging into my periwinkle terrycloth robe. I limped only slightly as I made my way into the living room, my feet stuffed into my cozy sheepskin slippers.

"So?" I said, joining Kimberly on the sofa.

"You're in seat 28D on the next flight to Vancouver," Kimberly said. "We'll have to leave from here in forty-five minutes."

I'd written my credit card information on a pad of paper so my niece could book my flight while I showered.

Kimberly moved the heavy phone book onto the floor and placed the first-aid kit she'd retrieved from the kitchen on the cushion between us. "Okay, pretend I'm my mom and let me bandage your hand. Oh, and I made a pot of peppermint tea," she added, nodding toward the ceramic pot on the coffee table.

I let her put salve on my burns while I poured tea into both our mugs with my right hand, leaving one on the table for Kimberly as I settled back against the cushions.

"What about those family journals your father mentioned?" Kimberly asked, retrieving a roll of bandages and a small pair of scissors. "They're the Travelers of Old that Jazper told me about, aren't they? Do you really think they're our ancestors? I bet those books are somewhere in Aunt Marilyn's attic."

I shook my head. "My father tore the house apart years ago when he first went looking for them. I definitely remember the havoc he caused. He didn't find them."

As she wound a bandage around my hand, I revelled in listening to her animated chatter. She told me how relieved Val had been when her teenage daughter had 'changed her mind about running away'. I chuckled as she described the 'coronary' my sister had when Kimberly appeared on Marilyn's doorstep after a two-day absence. Kimberly, it seemed, had returned to the exact spot in the woods where we'd first seen the apparition. Rather than fabricate a story about my whereabouts, Kimberly claimed not to have seen me, instead saying she'd stormed off after I'd tried to comfort her in the woods.

Although it was evident she was still cut up about Curtis's death, I was relieved to find she could now refer to him without hesitation. She also let me know she'd refused to go back to high school and was taking correspondence classes instead.

"Because you've been gone so long, everyone is totally freaking out about you instead of me, which is awesome. But the police aren't willing to look for you because they say there's no evidence of foul play. That annoys Aunt Marilyn to no end." Kimberly rolled her eyes as she secured the final piece of medical tape on my bandages.

"Thanks, Kimberly," I said, looking with admiration at her bandaging job. "I better go pack an overnight bag," I added, placing my empty mug on the table. I didn't immediately move though. We still had another half hour before we needed to leave. I removed the towel from my head and began to fluff my hair with the fingers of my good hand, regarding Kimberly as she lifted her mug.

"How long did it take you to find my old diaries?"

"Whoa!" She almost dropped her mug. "How did you know?" she demanded, her eyes wide.

I smiled. "Long story. *Very* interesting. First, tell me how you found them."

"I told Mom I should come over here and water your plants."

We both looked at my plants. They were all dead except for a lone cactus.

"And a fine job you did," I commented dryly.

She grimaced. "I don't think I'll be going for a career in horti-culture."

"That's probably best."

"Are you mad I read them? How did you know?"

"No, I'm not upset at all," I assured her. And I wasn't. "Remember that old woman at Conraz's lodge who was like a fortune teller? People like her are called 'Diviners'. I met someone much like her except closer to my age. Because I was worried about you after you disappeared, she did this thing—don't ask me how—that let me 'see' you. And I knew it wasn't just some memory of you because you were reading one of my childhood diaries. And you were wearing my watch." I nodded at her wrist. "Is it working yet?"

"No." Kimberly held up her wrist so that I could see the face.

"Still three-thirty. I brought it to a jeweler to resize and fix it, but she couldn't find what was wrong. I wear it anyway."

Kimberly made to remove it, but I shook my head. "Keep it." My only concern right now was to do everything in my power to ensure Lox remained alive.

Kimberly snuggled further into the cushions, holding her mug with both hands even though the tea was no longer hot, then asked, "So, what are you going to tell Mom and Aunt Marilyn now that you're back?"

I shook my head. "They can't know. At least, not until I get back from Vancouver."

My sole focus for the last month had been to find my way back to my world; yet, now the only think I wanted was to go back to the Lands of Vendome. Back to Lox.

I recalled then one of the pronouncements Julitha had made the first day I'd met her. *The heart of the man who loves you is true, and the fineness of his being shines like a beacon through the cracks of his broken soul.* I now knew her words referred to Lox. Last night —*was it really just last night?*—he'd declared his love for me. I'd been too afraid to echo his heartfelt sentiment. Looking back, I felt only self-disgust about my pathetic non-response. The truth was, I did love him. Despite my claim to the contrary, we'd shared far more than a carefree holiday fling.

I looked around at the items in my elegant and well-appointed living room. I'd spent a great deal of time and money hand-picking the textiles for my furniture and rugs and the colors and mediums of my art. Why had I thought it so important to come back to this? It didn't matter if I ever saw these items again, but it did matter if Lox was lost to me. And it mattered even more that he be protected from the assassin who was my father.

I made a decision in that moment, one that felt inarguably right and logical. If I successfully stole the Stone from my father, I would go back to the Lands of Vendome and stay there for always, just like Lox wanted. *Just like I wanted.*

In that decisive and clarifying moment, I felt a jolt of excitement dart through me.

Kimberly's insistent tone interrupted by thoughts. "Aunty Mere! You're not listening."

"Sorry, what were you saying?"

"I was asking about you and Lord Loxley. You and him, you're like an item now. Aren't you? I can tell."

Not for the first time, Kimberly's shrewd perception made me feel much younger than her. She'd always been a wise old soul, which was why her teen rebellion had been so difficult to fathom.

"Yes, but to make sure we continue being an item, I need to steal that Stone. Only I have no idea *how* I'm going to steal it." I knew I was grossly under-qualified for this task, but I couldn't contemplate failure. Failure meant Lox was dead.

When Kimberly didn't speak I looked over at her. She was regarding me with trepidation, chewing on her lower lip, the way she'd done as a child when she knew she was in the wrong.

"What?" I asked with a frown.

Kimberly hunched her shoulders, then confessed, "I'm in seat 28C." When I stared at her in dumbfounded amazement, she continued, speaking in a rush. "Well, you can't do it alone! And I can help you. I can distract him or something, tell him I really want to get to know my grandfather. I don't know, maybe ask him to take me on an adventure?"

I would love to have my clever niece with me for the daunting task I'd assigned myself, but after the dangers we'd encountered, there was no way I could allow her to join me. The risk of something going wrong was too high. "Kimberly, you can't just disappear with me again. What will your mom say? And besides—"

I paused when the telephone rang. The shrill sound felt strange after having lived without it for a month. The cordless phone sat in its cradle on the end table beside Kimberly. "Let the machine pick it up," I said.

My answering machine clicked on and played the tinny sound

of my recorded greeting, When the caller started speaking, I gaped at the phone with eyes as big as saucers. That distinctive voice was the last one I'd heard before 'traveling' back to my world. It was the voice of my father.

CHAPTER 25

"*M*eredee! I know you're there, so pick up the god-damned phone."

I frantically shook my head at Kimberly. I was not prepared to talk to him yet. Clearly, he'd already traveled back to Vancouver. I fleetingly wondered how he'd managed to get my unlisted phone number, but then I had to shift mental gears when my sister's voice came on the line.

"Meredee? It's me, Marilyn," my sister said in her usual no-nonsense tone.

What was *she* doing at my father's house in Vancouver?

"If you're there, pick up the phone," she practically hissed. "Father is here, at my house! He insists you're here too, some-where. Which isn't possible, since if you'd decided to finally come home, you would've at least contacted me. I've been sick with worry."

My father was at Marilyn's? He'd followed me here instead of going to Vancouver? Why?

I leaned in front of Kimberly and grabbed the phone with my good hand. Clicking on the talk button, I brought it to my ear. "Marilyn?"

Kimberly adjusted her position on the sofa so she could listen at my ear.

"Meredee? You're home? How long have you been home? Why didn't you call me?"

Before I had a chance to respond my father took the phone away from Marilyn and came back on the line.

"What you did was insane, Meredee. You could have stranded me for good if you'd managed to hold onto the Stone. Do you realize that?"

My father. Ever the selfish one. "My concern was—is—for Lox. Not for you."

"Yeah, well, you need to tell lover boy here that the Stone belongs to me!"

"What? Tell lover..." My mind was slow to process the meaning behind his words, but Kimberly was squealing and bouncing beside me like an excited three-year old.

"Holy shit!" I said as I met Kimberly's excited gaze. "Are you telling me that Lox is there with you? *At Marilyn's?*"

My heart pounded at the thought of Lox here, in my world. Safe.

"He is. And so is Boy Wonder."

I had to contain a hysterical giggle that threatened to erupt at my father's description of Fredryk.

"They refuse to return the Traveler's Stone to me until they are assured of your well-being," he added acerbically before resuming his commanding tone. "You need to get here ASAP. You hear me?"

"Wait a minute," I said. I knew better than to take my father at his word. "If Lox is really there, then let me talk to him."

"Oh, he's here alright. He won't know what the hell to do with the god-damned phone since he's never seen one before. But what the hell. Let's shake his unflappable composure some."

I heard muffled voices in the background. If I could've squeezed Kimberly's hand in mine without wincing in pain, I would have. And then I heard Lox's voice and I had to choke back the emotion that sought to overwhelm me.

"Meredee?" Lox asked cautiously.

Happy tears coursed down my cheeks at the sound of his voice. I vaguely recalled Julitha's prediction about how the one I despised would unlock the door of my heart. At the time, I'd assumed Lox was the one I despised because I'd been so angry with him. Now I realized Julitha's words referenced my father. I did despise him, but I also recognized that he'd been the catalyst, at least indirectly, for helping me realize how much I loved Lox.

Any remaining doubts about the depth of my feelings for the beautiful man I'd fallen in love with vanished. I loved Lox. I wanted to be with him. I wanted to share a life with him. And I no longer cared in what world that would be. I could not bear the thought of walking away from him ever again.

Never before had I felt such utter clarity. Never before had I absolutely known, without any shred of doubt, the direction my life should take. I suddenly felt a lightness to my being as if I was floating. I had to remind myself to breathe.

"Yes, I'm here," I choked out. "Are you okay? Are you really at Marilyn's?"

"This, your voice, this is really you?"

"Yes, Lox, it's really me. I'm speaking into the telephone, from another location, like I explained to you. And Kimberly is here, too. She's right next to me."

"Hi, Lord Loxley," Kimberly announced jubilantly.

"Kimberly? You are safe and well?"

"Yes, she's safe," I answered. "And so are you. Thank god!" Before we could talk further I heard a commotion in the background.

"Hello?" I demanded. "Lox?" And then my sister-in-law, Val, was on the phone.

"Meredee? You took Kimberly?" she accused. "Let me talk to her."

"Mom! Chill."

"I didn't *kidnap* her, Val," I retorted.

Val ignored me, scolding her daughter instead. "Kimberly, your note said you went to Lindsay's."

"I'm sorry I lied, Mom. But I couldn't tell you that Aunty Mere was back. It's complicated."

And then the phone must have changed hands again and the ever-capable Marilyn was back on the line, except now she was not merely confused, she was royally pissed.

"Meredee, I have no idea what's going on. I have no idea who these men are, or why Father is dressed up like some Turkish lord. I don't know where you've been, or why you chose to disappear. You have a whole lot of explaining to do, dearie, so you better do as Father says. Get here. ASAP!"

She hung up then in true I'm-Marilyn-and-I'm -the-one-in-charge fashion.

At the annoying sound of the dial tone, I moved the phone away from my ear and stared at it in frustration.

"She is off-her-rocker mad, that's for sure. We better do what she says," Kimberly stated, jumping up from the couch. She took the phone from me and clicked off the talk button, then grabbed my good hand and pulled me up as she crowed in unsuppressed delight. "Aunty Mere! Fredryk and Lord Loxley are here."

Lox was here. The blood in my veins seemed to hum in tune with my thoughts. Who cared if Marilyn and Val were mad at me? *Lox was here. Lox was here.*

"It's a good thing Uncle Jim and all the boys are away on their annual hunting trip."

I hadn't even thought of Marilyn's husband and sons. It was indeed a good thing they were away.

"Where are the car keys?" I said, hurrying toward the door. I knew I was limping, but I felt no pain.

"Aunty Mere." Kimberly hadn't moved from where she was standing by the sofa.

"What?" I demanded impatiently.

She had the phone in one hand and jiggled the keys in the other. "I got the keys, but...you might want to change?"

I looked down at my robe and fuzzy slippers. For a fleeting moment and despite the fact that I was wearing nothing underneath, I actually contemplated jumping in the car as is. All I cared about was seeing for myself that Lox was safe. And telling him, now that I had the chance, that I loved him and that I wanted to spend the rest of my life with him. What did it matter what I was wearing?

Kimberly seemed to read my mind.

"Aunt Meredee," she admonished, gesturing at my attire. "Do you really want Fredryk and your delinquent dad to see you like that?"

"Good point," I said, and hurried to my bedroom to change.

$\mathcal{M}$y bandaged hand meant that pulling on and fastening my favorite jeans was a bit of a struggle, but I managed it. I flicked through my wardrobe until I found my favourite cashmere sweater. The Tiffany blue of the cable-knit complimented by skin tone and blond hair. My hands were clumsy as I struggled with my sore hand to get a sock over my tender ankle. I hesitated briefly as I regarded my footwear options, but then chose my sneakers, loosening the laces a little to make room for my still puffy ankle. I fluffed my damp hair with my fingers, waved a can of hairspray at it, and then detoured into the bathroom to put on some lip-gloss and blush.

Four minutes after I'd left her, I rejoined Kimberly. She held my buff-coloured leather jacket in one hand and a half sack of Pepsi in the other. She must've stocked my fridge during her visits to 'water my plants'.

"Oh, you're so smart," I crowed in delight, eyeing the Pepsi.

Kimberly gave me a playful smile. "Let's see if Lord Loxley likes it as much now as he did when you were kids."

During the twenty minutes it took Kimberly to drive us to Marilyn's house, the butterflies in my stomach fluttered and danced with excitement. Everything seemed beautiful to me; the cloudy, overcast sky; the bare trees; the dull grass that was waiting for its winter blanket of snow; the unimaginative new developments with their cookie-cutter houses; even the congested parking lots at the mall. It was beautiful and yet I didn't care if I ever saw any of it again.

"You know," Kimberly said as she sped down the highway. "The Traveler's Stone will be yours now, not grandfather's. You should do what the Travelers of Old did and file some of the 'dust' off so that Lord Loxley can give it to Old Ethwin. It's been tradition for hundreds of years, maybe longer, that the Astromancer to the Grand Duchess is Custodian of Traveler's Dust. Poor Old Ethwin doesn't have any."

I'd always valued Kimberly's thoughtfulness and was so pleased our experiences together in the Lands of Vendome had caused her to shed that horrible attitude she'd adopted these last few months. "That would delight Lox, I think," I said, then heard the echo in my mind, *Lox was here. Lox was here.*

Just as Kimberly pulled into the drive of my childhood home, the skies opened up and a downpour began. We both bolted from the car to the covered verandah with our jackets over our heads. Even with my sore ankle, I got there ahead of Kimberly.

Before I could reach for the front door handle, Marilyn swept it open from the inside and stood blocking our entrance. With her thick bob of fair hair, she looked like an avenging angel.

I knew my sister cared deeply about me, but I also knew she needed to make me suffer for the distress my unexplained absence had caused. Although there was a time when I would have quaked at the thought of being subjected to her wrath, today I was not remotely concerned. *Lox was here.*

In that moment I realized we'd left the Pepsi in the car. "Crap," I said, bouncing the heel of my good hand against my forehead.

Marilyn gave me a laser-piercing look that said I was currently dirt and therefore not worth hugging despite the fact that she hadn't seen me for over a month and hadn't known if I was dead or alive.

"I meant 'crap' because we forgot the Pepsi in the car, not oh-crap-it's-you."

Marilyn's only response was to step onto the verandah and pull the door closed behind her.

"Uh, I'll go get it," Kimberly volunteered, then turned to jog back to the car with her jacket over her head.

It occurred to me finally that my sister, who was usually fastidious about her appearance, was badly rattled. Her hair was mussed, her lipstick faded, and there were blotchy patches of mascara underneath her eyes.

"They're all in the kitchen at the back of the house so they wouldn't have seen you arrive," she said in a frosty tone. "I've been waiting here for you because I want to know what we should do about Father."

It sounded odd, Marilyn referring to our dad as 'Father'. I wondered if the formal address made it easier for her to deal with the fact that he'd been a stranger to us all these years.

"Well, hello to you, too." My words were sarcastic, but my tone was light and airy. *Lox was here.* "What do you mean, what we should do about Dad?"

"There's an all-points-bulletin out for his arrest, don't you know?"

"Yes, Kimberly told me. Marilyn, can I at least come inside?"

She didn't budge from her stance in front of the door. "But what do we do?" she hissed, crossing her arms against her chest. "We can't turn in our own father."

"Oh, yes we can." Realization dawned then. "Damn! I'm an idiot. I should have phoned the police from my house. Having him carted off to jail is the perfect solution."

"How can you say that?" she accused. "We don't even know if he's guilty."

"Oh, he's guilty, alright. And not just for creating a fake provenance trail for those diamonds. Yesterday, he tried to kill Lox. Instead, he shot my horse right out from underneath me. Of course we call the cops."

"Meredith, since when do you have a horse? And while we're on the subject, since when have you been befriending...lunatics brandishing swords?" She gestured behind her in the general direction of the kitchen. "It's positively medieval."

I knew Marilyn did not use the word 'lunatic' lightly given the legacy of our mother's mental illness. "Marilyn, I'll explain everything, I promise. And we will most certainly call the cops, but not until after I make sure we have the Stone."

"Not you, too. After our phone call, Father got into an argument with those...alarming men about a stone. There's been a dreadful altercation. I wanted to call the police, but Father forbade me even though he's the one who's bleeding. Not that he has the right to tell me what to do. This is my house now. But I want an explanation from *you*, Meredith. Who are these people, *and what the bloody hell is going on?*"

Kimberly had just re-joined us, but she froze at Marilyn's uncharacteristic swearing. My sister had always been of the opinion that, since an educated person had access to an expansive vocabulary, they did not have to resort to cursing in order to express their perspective.

"Whoa, Aunt Marilyn. You okay?"

"Of course I'm not okay!" she hissed at Kimberly.

I realized my sister was close to tears. Feeling out of control in her own home was well beyond the boundaries of her comfort zone.

She pointed a manicured finger at me. "You have some serious explaining to do." With that she opened the door and strode inside. "And take off your shoes," she ordered over her shoulder.

I pulled a comical face at Kimberly as I stepped into the house behind Marilyn. I ignored her order, not to piss her off, but because my ankle felt more supported in shoes. Then I practically ran her over in my haste to get to the kitchen.

The first person I saw when I entered the large room was, disappointingly, my father. He was seated in the captain's chair at the head of the breakfast nook. I was taken aback by the fact that his forearms were duct-taped to the arms of the chair. Marilyn had mentioned an altercation, but she hadn't mentioned restraints. A trickle of blood inched down his temple from a cut on his forehead. He did not look up when I entered the room, but continued to glower in the direction of the scissors and the discarded roll of tape that lay like a taunting culprit out of reach on the table in front of him. Fredryk was standing slightly behind my father in front of the lit gas fireplace, holding his sword. Val, who'd been sitting on the padded bench, let out a cry when we entered the room and darted up to enfold her daughter in a protective embrace. She gave me a malevolent glare over Kimberly's head as if I'd been torturing her favorite cat.

This survey of the room and its occupants took only a brief moment. It was Lox I wanted to see and it was Lox I wanted to ensure was safe and well and in one piece. He'd been standing near Val—his sword sheathed, at least—but he immediately approached me when I entered the room.

"Meredee!"

I went to him with my arms out, but then checked my action when I noticed the burgeoning discoloration below his left eye.

"Lox, what happened?" I gave him a quick, fierce hug and then stepped back to inspect his injury.

"Thank the gods you are safe."

"But Lox, what happened to your face?" I turned to scowl at my father as a growing realization came upon me. "You did this to him?"

"I wished I'd shot the bastard when I had the chance," my father snapped without deigning to look at me.

CORINNE AARSEN

"Shot him?" Marilyn demanded from where she hovered just inside the kitchen door.

"See? I told you, Marilyn," I said in a vehement tone. "He shot at Lox but he hit my horse. Our father, who you seem to want to protect, tried to assassinate the man I love. And he almost succeeded."

Everyone began speaking at once. Marilyn re-launched her demands that someone, meaning me, tell her what was going on. Val began reproaching Kimberly for lying about where she'd gone while Kimberly zealously defended her actions. Fredryk, who kept one eye on my father, turned his attention to Kimberly and Val and was employing his ultra-reasonable tone to assure Val that, with everyone now safe, there was no longer cause for concern. On top of that, my father was demanding I make Fredryk return the Stone to its rightful owner and for god's sake, *tell these sons-a-bitches to release me!*

In the midst of all this babble I turned in helpless exasperation to Lox. He was looking at me with an expression of wonder. When he reached for me and pulled me close, it was as if I'd pressed a mute button and the volume of the collective, complaining voices around us faded and disappeared.

"The man you love?" He asked with wonder. "You love me?"

My heart felt wide open. In spite of the chaos in the room, I was basking in the rays of his adoration. The Diviner at the Cast Away ceremony had been right. The frozen pockets of pain had taken up too much space in my heart. As I stood gazing into the golden depths of Lox's magnetic eyes drinking in the true fineness of his being, I wondered what I'd been so afraid of. Of course I loved him. How could I not? Of course I wanted to spend my life with him. What woman of sound mind would voluntarily walk away from such a man when he declared his undying love? My impulsive action of grabbing the Stone in my father's house and disappearing from the Lands of Vendome could've permanently separated us. I would never do anything so risky ever again.

222

Lox brought his hands up to my shoulders and shook me gently, clearly impatient for my answer. "Do you love me?" he repeated.

Over the past month, I'd convinced myself that the emotions founded on that girlhood crush were no more relevant than a fairy tale. And perhaps they weren't. But I no longer felt *those* emotions. They'd been the seed that had grown into my current feelings of certainty, knowing, and joy. An acorn wasn't an ancient oak tree, but it was imbued with the potential of becoming one, just as I now realized my initial crush had seeded the potential for the love that now blossomed.

I moved my hands up to cup his face. "Yes," I stated with conviction. "Yes, I love you, Lox. With all my heart. I don't want us to be apart ever again."

The kiss we shared held more emotion than any words could've expressed. But Lox and I were not alone, as evidenced by the babble of voices I could no longer shut out. But we would be alone soon, I promised myself. And then I would make up for all the words I hadn't yet said.

I dropped my bandaged hand to his shoulder as I leaned back to look into his eyes, lifting my good hand to gently graze the swelling on his cheek. "We should put some ice on that."

"Ah. And your world has a convenient source of ice, yes?"

I nodded.

"You must know how delighted I am to be visiting your world once again."

I chuckled as I reluctantly stepped out of his embrace.

"You burned yourself when you used the Traveler's Stone?" he asked, leaning his sheathed sword against the counter and touching my bandaged hand.

I'd been oblivious to the pain of the burns during the last few minutes, but now my hand renewed its throbbing. Still, it was minor compared to the painful thought of never again seeing Lox.

"Yes, but when I burnt my hand I dropped it. I could kick

myself for that. But I'll be fine." I stepped to the counter where Kimberly had deposited the Pepsi, glancing briefly at the other occupants of the room, but none were paying us any mind. "Kimberly brought a present for you, Lox."

"A present?"

"It looks different than the last time you saw it, but the taste will be the same."

I released a can from the plastic ring and handed it to Lox.

A delighted grin lit his face. "Pepsi!" He studied the can in bewilderment. "But how…?"

I laughed and took the can from him, popped the top, and handed it back. I watched him with a grin as he took his first taste after a hiatus of twenty-two years.

"You like?" I asked.

"Yes, it is as I remember. Cold and very fizzy. Only sweeter I think."

"Probably just your grown-up taste buds getting in the way."

I reluctantly turned to face the others. I saw now that Marilyn, short of dragging me away from Lox, had been trying to get my attention. When the others noticed Lox and me looking at them, one-by-one their voices stilled.

"Marilyn, Valerie." I leaned back into Lox's embrace as he possessively wrapped an arm around me. "You haven't been properly introduced," I added with a grin. "In his world, he's called Lord Loxley of Hawkwood Heath, Chancellor of the Eastern Duchy in the Lands of Vendome and cousin to the Grand Duke and Grand Duchess, rulers of the Twin Duchies." I smiled up at him. "But I think in this world it makes sense just to call him Lox." I gestured at Fredryk. "And his companion is Fredryk, a trusted friend. Fredryk, Lox, this is my sister Marilyn," I gestured toward Marilyn. "Marilyn, you may not remember, but you met Lox when we were kids."

Marilyn seemed unconvinced, and continued to regard the

men with suspicion even though they favored her with perfectly polite and formal greetings.

I gestured at Val. "And this is Kimberly's mother, Valerie."

When Lox and Fredryk greeted Val, they pronounced her name with a soft 'h' sound added, so it came out sounding more like Val-*ha*-rie.

"Kimberly." I turned to my niece. "Can you get an ice-pack for Lox's face?"

"No, she will not." Val laid a hand on Kimberly's arm to prevent her from moving. "We're going home. Immediately."

"Mom," Kimberly said with patience. "We have nothing to fear from these men. They're my friends. I mean, Fredryk and Lord Loxley are."

Lox complimented her new hairstyle then, which made Kimberly flush with pleasure.

"Val, give me a chance to explain, okay?. I know you're both pissed at me," I said, taking in Marilyn's rigid expression. "You want to protect Kimberly and you think I've suddenly become a bad influence. But I haven't." I addressed Marilyn. "Do you have any wine?"

"Meredee, it's two o'clock in the afternoon."

"Marilyn, for what I'm about to tell you, you're going to want some fortification."

Marilyn gave me an exasperated look and then did what she always did. She took over.

"Kimberly, get some ice like Meredith said. And Val, for heaven's sake, stay. For my benefit, if no one else's. You," she pointed first at Fredryk and then to a chair on my father's right. "Sit down. And put away that...that blade. It's making me nervous. And, Father, don't ask to be released again until after I hear Meredee's story. Apparently, she's in love with this man, which means we're going to treat him and his friend like proper guests. Lox, right? You and Meredee can sit there," she added, pointing to two chairs on my father's left.

Marilyn's take-charge manner reminded me of Shulha. Although the Vendome woman had been far less dictatorial than my sister, the end result was the same. People did as they were told. Val took a seat on the bench seat. Kimberly gave me an icepack as Lox and I sat opposite Val. Fredryk was the only one who didn't do as Marilyn ordered. He kept his sword in his hand and remained standing on guard just behind my father's right shoulder. I saw Marilyn frown at him, but she seemed to recognize it would be pointless to argue. Marilyn placed a couple of bottles of wine on the table with a corkscrew and six wine glasses, although not her best ones, I noted.

I slipped out of my jacket and turned in my chair to face Lox, gently dabbing the ice pack against his swollen cheek, which made him wince.

"Do you have the Traveler's Stone, Fredryk?" Kimberly asked. "Can I see it?"

Fredryk removed a handkerchief-wrapped object from his pocket and handed it to Kimberly. We all watched, transfixed, as she folded back the edges of the pale blue square of lawn cloth to reveal the Stone. The veins of ore made it glimmer and twinkle as if it had a life of its own.

"Wow," she said.

Val and Marilyn both seemed to regard the Stone with deep suspicion, but my father scowled darkly at it.

"I'm going to get a file from Uncle Jim's workroom so that you can bring back some Dust for Old Ethwin," Kimberly announced, handing the Stone back to Fredryk. "I'll be right back," she added as she left the room.

Marilyn poured wine for each of us, including a small amount for Kimberly, although she excluded our father. She slid onto the short bench seat and took a generous sip of her wine, clearly no longer concerned with the time. Kimberly returned, file in hand, and sat beside Val with the Stone, and began to file dust onto the handkerchief.

I began my tale on that long ago day when Rikka and Jaybex first disrupted my Ken and Barbie picnic. As expected, Marilyn and Val were skeptical and interrupted me frequently to ask questions, but after a while, they simply listened, engrossed.

With five of the seven people in the room having performed the rather neat trick of traveling between worlds, my sister and sister-in-law had little choice but to accept the reality of my seemingly far-fetched story. By the time I got to the part where I'd made the shocking discovery that my dad was a hired assassin intent on killing the man I loved—Lox and I shared a smile when I made that comment—my throat was hoarse. I got up and filled a glass with water before resuming my seat.

Kimberly's tone was gleeful as she addressed her mother and aunt. "See why I couldn't tell the truth about my absence?"

By now a generous pyramid of dust lay in the center of Fredryk's handkerchief and Kimberly's palms sparkled as if she'd been playing with glitter.

"You would have told me I'd lost my marbles," Kimberly added.

Marilyn and Val shared a look as if to say, *who says you haven't?*

"I know," I said to them. "It seems utter nonsense to hear a sane person talking about being teleported to an alternate world. Or to look at that Stone," I gestured toward Kimberly, "and believe it's the key to all of this. But it's all true. I swear."

"I just can't fathom how it's possible," Val said in a bewildered tone, then held up a hand to stop me from interrupting. "I'm just saying."

CHAPTER 27

*I*n the silence that followed Val's comment, my father finally spoke. His tone was venomous. "Have I heard you correctly? You have not found the family journals? And you do not have a god-damned stone of your own?"

I gave a pointed look at the Traveler's Stone in Kimberly's hands. "I do now."

"That Stone is mine."

"Call it my inheritance." I said dismissively. I turned to Lox. "But how did you get here? I was flabbergasted when I heard your voice on the phone."

Lox then explained how, upon Alberic and Lita's return from the Traveler's house without me, they'd assumed the Traveler had threatened or coerced me into remaining behind. Lox and Fredryk disguised themselves as laborers while Alberic commandeered a brewer's delivery wagon. Upon arriving at my father's home, the two men maneuvered an oversize barrel out of their wagon as if it was extremely heavy. In reality, it held only their swords. Once inside the house, they'd surprised the servants and knocked them senseless. Soon after, they had my father at sword point.

My shawl, which they found on the chair I'd vacated, gave Lox and Fredryk irrefutable evidence that I'd been in that room. Despite the blade pointed at his chest, my father would not divulge where I'd gone. He knew these men would not kill him. If they did, they would never find me. That was when Lox started systematically destroying items in the room hoping to find something that would trigger my father's cooperation. When he opened the copper box and saw the unexpected contents, Lox immediately knew that the Astromancer's Dust had been filed from that very Stone. When Lox confiscated it, my father panicked and finally confirmed that I'd used it to return to my world. Lox, concerned for my well-being, was determined to use the Stone to come after me. At sword point, they forced my father to project them to my world with the threat that if they found themselves anywhere else they would not hesitate to make him bleed. My father had reluctantly instructed Lox to picture my childhood home. He'd told Fredryk, who'd never been to my world, to keep his mind blank.

I had to suppress the urge to make a joke about the blankness of Fredryk's mind. Now was not the time.

The men, Lox continued, linked arms in front of the hearth. My father insisted all three of them had to be touching the Stone as they inserted its tip into the flame. They floated briefly, just as I had, and then found themselves in the grove of trees on the edge of my family's property in Bellecourt. As expected, my father immediately grabbed for the Stone, but Lox and Fredryk quickly subdued him. A few minutes later they were standing on the verandah and knocking on Marilyn's front door.

At this point in the tale, Marilyn interrupted to say that Val had just arrived for tea when they heard the knock. She'd been bowled over to see our father standing on her doorstep wearing an outlandish costume and flanked by two strange men wielding swords. Upon entering the house, my father ordered Marilyn to call me. When the phone call ended, our father used the distraction to once again lunge for the Stone. That's when Lox politely requested Marilyn provide some restraints. He'd never seen duct tape before, but had quickly figured out the use of it.

During Marilyn's account, I noticed Lox giving my dad a look of loathing. This despicable man—the buffoon who was the Traveler and the assassin—was the reason I'd been identified as a Cast Away. Lox found that deed unforgivable.

By that time, dusk had fallen. Marilyn got up and flipped on the kitchen lights. I noticed that the abrupt and sudden glare momentarily stunned Fredryk, but he quickly resumed his panther-like wariness.

"And where's my rifle now?" My father demanded.

With all that had happened I'd entirely forgotten about the rifle. "Still under the pile of leaves in Val's back alley, I guess."

"Don't tell me you left it there," Marilyn admonished. "It's Halloween tomorrow. Kids will be swarming the streets like bees to honey."

"The kids will be on the streets, Marilyn. Not the back alleys."

"Regardless," she said as she resumed her seat. "A rifle can't be left there for a child to stumble upon, even if it's harmless in its present state. It's almost dark. You should go now." Marilyn nodded decisively. "And while you're gone, we can stretch our legs and use the powder room if needed." She pointed an accusing finger at our dad. "No, Father, not you. You can suffer. You belong in jail for what you've done. Living all these years away from your family has made you a heartless, disgraceful man from your core all the way to your ridiculously outlandish surface."

I had been about to rise from my chair, but froze, as did everyone else. Marilyn's tone had started out matter-of-fact, but it was escalating in volume and steeliness.

"How dare you come into my home, *my home,* and create such upheaval. How can you be so selfish as to care more for that rock of yours than for your own children? Have you expressed any sympathy to your daughter-in-law and granddaughter for the loss of their husband and father? Have you expressed your condolences to Meredith and me for losing a brother we loved? Curtis was your eldest son. And you didn't even bother to attend his funeral!"

Earlier, when I'd been telling my tale, Marilyn had stared at me in wide-eyed disbelief. Now I stared at her with the same look as she continued her seething tirade.

"You have not shown the slightest evidence you care that Curtis has passed. Do you think you deserve to freely walk away from your responsibilities in this world—again? I am so ashamed of you, and so relieved my boys are not here to witness what an embarrassment my father has become. You will never again work as a mercenary, not in their world," she declared, pointing at Lox and then Fredryk. "And certainly not in ours. You will stay taped to that chair until a Mountie comes and carts you off to jail. They've already been here looking for you on account of that nefarious diamond scheme of yours. From what I just heard, it looks like they'll be able to pin income tax fraud on you as well. Well I, for one, will take great satisfaction in helping them put you behind bars."

When Marilyn noticed her riveted, silent audience, she raised a hand to pat her hair self-consciously. "Well, I will, you know."

"Tongue like a wasp is a family trait, I see," Fredryk observed dryly, addressing no one in particular.

"Well, yes, thank you." Marilyn flushed in pleasure at Fredryk's remark.

At Fredryk's startled look, I had to force down another overwhelming urge to giggle. "So you believe us?" I asked instead.

Marilyn looked momentarily startled as she shared a glance with Val. "It seems that I do."

My father interrupted then and his tone cut through the air like an invisible blade. "I would think again if I were you, Marilyn."

Had he been able to move, I felt sure he would have flown across the table and curled his hands around Marilyn's neck.

"Oh, no, no, no." Marilyn waved her index finger at him. "You revoked the right years ago to have any kind of say in this house."

He leaned forward in his chair and spoke in a low, menacing tone. "Think, Marilyn. Let's say the Mounties come and haul me off to jail. Maybe I get sentenced. To what? Ten years? Five? Out early on good behavior? And then what do you think will be my first order of business? Weren't you listening to your little sister? I make my living as a mercenary assassin now. If you make that call, who do you think will be first on my list when I get out of jail?"

There was silence in the room as we all gaped at him. Marilyn's face had turned white and one of her hands clutched feebly at her throat.

"No, not you," my father continued in a quiet, threatening tone. "Instead, I will pick off each of your children. One. By. One. That's what I'll do. Oldest to youngest. I will let *you* live. After all, a man shouldn't eliminate his own daughter." He glanced at me before he turned his attention back to Marilyn. "Only you can keep your children safe, Marilyn. So, hear me when I say, *no one calls the cops.*"

After a moment or two of silence, I spoke. "Jesus, Dad! Enough." I reminded myself that my father was a consummate actor. Since I'd seen for myself how chagrined he'd been when he learned he'd almost killed me, I felt certain his threats were empty.

I turned to my sister. "Marilyn, he wouldn't."

"Meredith." My father transferred his electrifying gaze to me, his pale blue eyes like chips of glacial ice. He spoke softly, menacingly. "I may have felt a twinge of remorse when I realized it was your horse I shot and that I could have killed my own daughter. But don't make the mistake of believing I'm the least bit guided by sentiment. Not when my freedom is at stake. Under no circumstances do I intend to relinquish that Stone. And under no circumstances do I intend to go to prison. If either of those events unfold, one way or the other, you and your sister will suffer the consequences. I promise you. If there is one thing you girls need to do, it is to believe me when I say no one, *and I mean no one*, calls the cops."

I looked at the faces around the table. They all reflected a combination of apprehension, terror, concern, and disbelief. Strangely, Kimberly looked far more terrified than Marilyn.

"I want two things. No, three," my father continued. "I want my rifle back. I want my Stone back. And I want a promise that no one is phoning the cops."

"Go get that rifle, Meredee," Marilyn said in a small voice.

"Dad, put a lid on it," I said instead. "Enough with the threats. You're talking about your own grandchildren, for god's sake. Okay, we won't call the cops. At least, not yet. I'll go and get the rifle, and we'll talk more when I get back—"

"I want you to promise that you won't stop at a pay phone and make that call."

"I promise." At my father's look of disbelief, I lost patience. "For Christ's sake, Dad. You've been hanging out with criminals for far too long. I said I won't, and I won't. So chill," I added, using Kimberly's favored expression.

I stood up. "Lox, how do you feel about going for a car ride?"

"I would like that very much," he stated as he rose. "May I be at the controls?"

My laugh sounded overly brittle when nudged up against the tension in the room. "Absolutely not."

Lox lifted my bandaged hand by the wrist and brushed a gentle kiss on my bare fingertips. "How will you manage all the controls with an injured hand? Is it paining you?"

I was not accustomed to anyone being so attentive to my health. I liked it. I wanted more of it. Once again, it was like we were in a world of our own. "It's throbbing, but I'll have Val look at it later. She's a nurse. A medical practitioner," I amended when I saw Lox's blank look. "And I'm not driving a team of horses, you know. It's a car."

I turned to my niece. "Kimberly, can I have the keys?"

My niece's face was ghostly white. It was clear her grandfather's threats had terrified her. "Kimberly, don't pay him any mind." I waved dismissively in the general direction of my father. "He's just trying to scare us."

"I want to go with you," she said.

"Oh, honey," Val protested, laying a hand on Kimberly's arm to stop her from rising. "Please, just stay here with me. Please?"

Kimberly reluctantly dug the keys out of her pocket and tossed them to me.

I shrugged into my leather jacket and asked Marilyn if she still had my purse, which had my wallet and driver's license. She briefly left the room to retrieve it. I slipped the strap over my shoulder then took Lox's hand in mine, leading him out of my sister's home.

CHAPTER 28

*I*t was still raining outside, so I made a jogging-with-a-limp dash for the car, gesturing for Lox to go to the passenger side. I hopped in behind the wheel, but then saw the blurry figure of Lox searching for a doorknob. I chuckled and leaned across the console to unlatch his door. As soon as I started the engine and blasted the air to defrost the windows, I turned to him with a wide grin. He looked gorgeous there beside me even though the shadows from the dashboard lights accentuated his burgeoning bruise.

We simultaneously reached for one another and shared a long, passionate kiss.

"You truly love me?" he asked, when we finally pulled apart.

"I do. I can't imagine not sharing a life with you, Lox."

"A life in…?"

I could see he hardly dared put words to his desire.

"Yes, a life in the Lands of Vendome. With you. If you still want me."

And then we were kissing again. It was a good thing the fan was pumping air from the defrost vents or we would have steamed up the car in seconds flat.

At the sound of an insistent, sharp knocking on my window we startled apart. I looked over my shoulder and saw the indistinct shape of my sister leaning down to look into the car from under the shelter of a red golf umbrella. I fumbled for the power window release.

"Necking in the car, Meredee?" she rasped when my window opened. "You're not seventeen anymore."

The days of allowing my overbearing older sister to dampen my spirits were long gone. "And that's exactly the reason why you can cease and desist with the lectures, Marilyn. Give me a break. If I want to kiss my boyfriend, I'll kiss him."

"But now isn't really the time for that sort of thing, is it?"

"That's what you came out here in the rain to tell me?"

"No. I want to make sure you keep your promise. You won't phone the police, will you?"

"I said I wouldn't and I won't. But Marilyn, you can't take what Dad said seriously. There's no way he would follow through with his threat. It's ludicrous."

"I'm not so sure. And it's *my* kids he's talking about. *You* can't possibly understand. *You're* not a mother. If he were to hurt them because of something I did? And I could have prevented it? Then—"

Marilyn seemed on the verge of hysteria. "Marilyn," I interrupted. "I *won't* call the cops."

"Promise?"

"Yes, I promise. What is this, the Spanish Inquisition? You want me to cross-my-heart-hope-to-die? I'm not seven anymore."

"Okay, okay." Marilyn stood up and backed away.

I pressed the button to roll up the window, but had to reverse it when Marilyn stooped and called my name.

"What?"

"I'm glad you're safe and well, Meredee. Really, I am. And I like your boyfriend. He seems nice." She smiled at Lox and wiggled a few fingers at him before dashing back toward the house.

I shook my head as I closed the window. "Honestly, I don't get her. I never have." I switched on the windshield wipers and reversed out of the drive.

"She cares about you. That much is very evident," Lox said. "You have a special place in her heart."

"Sometimes I'm not so sure," I muttered.

"Meredee, what is a 'boy friend'? Does it carry the same meaning as an intended?"

I laughed as I drove down the narrow, private lane. "In our case, yes."

"I have come to believe that there are a great many words and phrases like 'okay' and 'pick-nick' and 'boy friend' that you use in your world but that are not used in mine."

"Like what?"

Lox ticked a finger to correspond with each word and phrase he recited, "*Lost my marbles, Halloween, put a lid on it, so-chill, sons-a-bitches, cops, Mounties, necking, Spanish Inquisition, cross-my-heart-hope-to-die.*"

"What does that last one mean?" he asked. "Hope-to-die?"

I spent the rest of the drive to the city explaining these phrases and then answering Lox's questions about the purpose of the various indicators and knobs on the dashboard. He expressed surprise that this 'self-propelling carriage' looked so different than the one that had brought us to Sandpiper Lake. Then I made him stop talking so he could listen to the song that was playing on the radio, which happened to be *Hey Jude* by the Beatles. I told him this was what professional singers with accompaniment sounded like, but he claimed my singing was better.

Twice on the highway to Red Plains we passed police cruisers heading in the opposite direction with sirens wailing. I was tempted to break my promise to Marilyn, but knew if I did she would never forgive me even if her kids lived to old age. When we arrived in the dark alley where I'd met the little boy on the bicycle, there was not a soul in sight. When we got out of the car, I realized I should've brought a flashlight—and an umbrella—but it took me only a few second to retrieve the rifle. Lox was childishly delighted when I popped the trunk of the car. He was already impressed that the interior where we sat was entirely waterproof and the windows clear, but that the car had waterproof storage made it all the more impressive.

During the return drive, it stopped raining. In the welcome silence that followed after I turned off the windshield wipers, Lox adopted his customary sober tone and shared his concerns about my father's threats, advising me to take them seriously. We were still debating this topic when the activity at the turn-off to the tree-lined drive that led to my sister's property caught my full attention.

A police van was parked at the entrance, lights flashing. The lane itself was blocked by a wooden barrier and guarded by a policeman in a bright reflective raincoat.

"Holy shit!"

"These flashing lights are your authorities? The ones who want to apprehend your father?"

"Yes, but how did they know he was here?"

I rolled down my window as I approached the barricade. When I slowed, the officer gestured for me to move along.

"But down that lane is my sister's house. Did something happen to them? Are they okay?"

I could pretty much predict what had happened—the police had found my father at Marilyn's—although I was puzzled as to the how.

"Ma'am, I can't answer your questions. It's best you come back later."

"But I need to know if my family is all right."

"And Fredryk," Lox added.

I ignored his comment. Fredryk was well equipped to take care of himself.

"I can't let you through, ma'am. You'll have to come back later."

"If it's all the same to you, I'll just pull over and wait here."

The police officer shrugged. As I parked facing the lane, I wished I had one of those new mobile phones so I could call Marilyn.

Too impatient to sit and wait, I dug out a quarter from the loose change in my console and then told Lox to keep an eye out for any new developments. I got out of the car and limped back up the road to the pay phone on the corner. I suspected Marilyn wouldn't answer, not with the police pounding on her door, but it gave me something to do. However, before I could even dial, an ambulance with sirens blaring wailed past me in the direction of Marilyn's house. I pushed out of the phone booth and followed it at a limping jog. The police officer standing at the end of the drive moved aside the barrier to let the ambulance through, then immediately put it back.

What on Earth? Who'd gotten hurt? Surely not my father. He was fit and strong. Had my sister suffered a heart attack from all the stress?

I hurried as fast as I could back to the car and slid behind the wheel.

"That did not look like a poh-lice cruiser," Lox said.

"It wasn't." I explained what an ambulance was. "I'm worried, Lox. What if something's happened to Marilyn?"

"If we went through the trees behind that house," Lox said, pointing to a neighbouring lot. "Could we make our way to your sister's house?"

"I suppose..." I couldn't decide if we should wait or do as Lox suggested and go on foot through the stand of birch and elm trees. Five long minutes passed as we stared out the windshield. "Damn it!" I finally said, slamming my good hand against the steering wheel. "What's happening? Maybe we *should* sneak through the trees."

Just then the police officer standing guard moved the barricade aside. Moments later, the ambulance, its lights flashing but its siren silent, reappeared and drove past us. I was about to turn the car around and follow it to the hospital to find out which member of my family had been hurt when an official looking vehicle came out of my sister's lane. As I powered my window down to get a better look at the car, I spotted my father in the back seat. For a brief second we made eye contact. His look held a mixture of fury, which I understood, and smugness, which made no sense given he was the one in custody.

Clearly, I could strike my father off the list of potential occupants of the ambulance, which was, frankly, unfortunate. So, who was being rushed to the hospital? Marilyn, Valerie, or Kimberly?

The police officer didn't replace the barricade but instead carried it over to the van.

I hesitated. "Do we follow the ambulance? Or do we go to my sister's house?"

"It is your world and therefore it is your decision," Lox replied.

Marilyn's house was half-a-minute away, the hospital five. I put the car in drive and accelerated down the lane. If need be I could always turn around and head for the hospital.

I parked beside a police car whose lights were still flashing. A second, unmarked police car was parked nearby, half on the grass and half on the drive as if it had stopped abruptly.

Marilyn's front door stood wide open. The light from inside revealed my sister standing just inside talking to a uniformed Mountie.

"Marilyn is obviously okay," I observed. "Which leaves either Val or Kimberly in the ambulance." I leapt out of the car.

As I limped up the steps with Lox beside me, the police officer who'd been talking to my sister gave us a brief glance before nodding at Marilyn and moving farther into the house. The fact that my sister didn't berate him for failing to remove his boots was indicative of her level of distraction. "Marilyn, we saw the ambulance. Who's hurt?"

Physical confrontation had never been Marilyn's style so I was entirely unprepared for the sting of her hand on my cheek. Lox took a step forward as if to protect me, but I stopped him with a hand on his arm, lifting my other bandaged hand to my stinging face.

"I should have known I couldn't trust you!" Marilyn accused. She was not crying, but her mascara was badly streaked as if she had been.

"I didn't call the police!"

"Well if you didn't, then who did?"

"I don't know. But who was hurt?"

"It was awful, Meredee," she wailed. "Father went berserk! You should have seen him. I had no idea he could be so ruthless."

Marilyn's voice shook. I grabbed her flailing hands, wincing as she unwittingly clutched my bandaged hand in her agitated grasp.

"Marilyn, take a breath. *Who was in the ambulance?*"

"Fredryk. Father attacked him and he was knocked unconscious. There's blood everywhere."

"Fredryk?" I stared at her in stunned disbelief. I would never have guessed my duct-taped father could've bested Fredryk.

Lox turned to me. "I must go to him."

"Val went with him," Marilyn stated.

"In the ambulance? Thank god." I laid a reassuring hand on Lox's arm. "Lox? Fredryk is in the best of hands. Val is a trained medical practitioner. I'll take you to him, I promise, but let's first find out what happened." I turned to my sister. "How did Fredryk get hurt? And where's Kimberly?"

"She's inside cleaning up the blood. You shouldn't have called the police, Meredee."

"Marilyn, I told you! I didn't." Horror dawned as I finally realized the significance of the smug look I'd glimpsed on my father's face. "Please tell me Dad is not in possession of the Traveler's Stone."

"Don't you dare say I could have stopped him," Marilyn

ᵃ

retorted. "No one could have stopped him. He was like a crazed animal."

"Okay, okay. No one's blaming you. Just tell me, does he have the Stone?"

"Yes. But wait until you see the state of my kitchen. All because of that stupid Stone."

I looked at Lox, thinking that if we couldn't get the police to give us the Stone, then the three of us were as stranded in my world as I'd been in his. "He'll be handcuffed so he won't be able to use it." I wasn't sure if I was attempting to reassure myself or to reassure Lox. "At the station, the police will take all his belongings. We'll have to figure out how to get the Stone back from the police. I don't suppose they'll release him on bail or anything. Will they?" I asked Marilyn even though I didn't expect her to know.

I noticed then that she was trembling. I put my arm around her shoulders. "Come inside, Marilyn," I said in a far gentler tone than I'd ever needed to use on my formidable sister. "You're shivering. We'll figure something out, don't worry."

"Do you think so?" she asked in an uncharacteristic meek tone. "I'm sorry I slapped you, Meredee."

"It's okay. I understand."

"You still shouldn't have called the cops."

I rolled my eyes, but kept silent.

As we made to enter the house, our way was temporarily blocked by the emergence of three police officers. The one who'd been talking to Marilyn carried an oversized ziplock bag that held two swords.

Lox saw the contents and gave me an inquiring look. I shook my head slightly as the two uniformed officers moved past us. The last one, who wasn't in uniform, stopped beside Marilyn.

"We've got all we need for now, Mrs. Buckner. Here's my contact info." He handed Marilyn a business card then turned to me. "You're the sister? And the boyfriend?"

"Yes, we were out running an errand." I didn't add, *to retrieve my assassin father's sniper rifle, which was now in the trunk of my car.*

The police officer nodded and addressed Marilyn in a kind tone. "Sorry you had to go through this ordeal. Sometimes it's violent when we make an arrest. That can be real rough on the family. I hope your friend is alright. Call if you have any questions."

"Officer," I asked. "I believe our father has something in his possession that doesn't belong to him. How do we go about getting it back?"

The officer's sympathetic look evaporated. "Yeah, I heard. I'm afraid you'll have to sort that out at the station." With that he turned and headed toward the unmarked car.

I ushered Marilyn into the house with Lox on our heels, closing the door behind us. In the kitchen, Kimberly was mopping the floor in front of the stone hearth.

"Aunty Mere!" She let the mop drop and rushed toward me, giving me a fierce hug and then, impulsively, hugging Lox as well.

"I'm sorry about Fredryk, Lord Loxley. Mom says he has a concussion, but that he should be okay."

She looked frightened as she slumped onto a chair.

Marilyn headed straight for the half-empty bottle of wine and poured herself a generous helping with a hand that shook.

I took in the disastrous state of Marilyn's kitchen. Behind where Kimberly had made an attempt to mop up the blood, shards of glass from the broken frontal piece of the gas fireplace littered the floor. "What the hell happened?" I asked.

Marilyn then proceeded to inform us—in a biting, reproachful tone—that, after our departure, 'father' said he wanted to gift his grandfather's garnet ring to Marilyn in apology for the turmoil he'd caused. As he fumbled to remove the ring, he dropped it— deliberately they realized later. Fredryk had naturally stooped to pick it up. That's when my father had used his powerful legs, which weren't duct-taped, to trap Fredryk's neck before slamming Fredryk's face into the edge of the solid oak table. The attack had smashed Fredryk's nose and his face had erupted in blood. In the next second, my father had swiped Fredryk's feet out from beneath him. That's when Fredryk fell backwards and slammed his head against the stone hearth plate. He hadn't moved after that.

When Val instinctively ran to Fredryk's side, her former father-in-law trapped her the same way he'd trapped Fredryk. Then he ordered Marilyn to stay seated and instructed Kimberly to cut him loose.

"How serious are Fredryk's injuries?" Lox asked. "We should go to him," he added, turning to me.

"Broken nose and concussion," Marilyn said tearfully. "At least, that's what Val said."

I put a reassuring hand on Lox's arm. "We'll go to him in a minute, Lox. I promise. There's nothing you can do to help, not right now. Whatever his injuries are, he's getting care from expert medical practitioners."

Marilyn splashed more wine into her glass. "As soon as one arm was free," she continued. "He grabbed a handful of Val's hair while Kimberly cut his other arm free. When she was done, he took the scissors from her, holding them against Val's neck as he pushed her into a chair. With the scissors at Val's throat, he made Kimberly tape my wrists behind me and then she had to do the same with Val. *And* cover our mouths with duct tape." Marilyn's fingers fluttered to her lips where only a trace of smudged lipstick remained.

"He restrained Kimberly himself. Then he pocketed the Stone. And that's when all hell broke loose. I wanted to scream, but with the tape across my mouth..."

When Marilyn didn't notice the wine that spilled onto her shirt when she gulped it, I moved to sit on the vacant chair beside her. I laid my hand on her knee in reassurance, although I'm not sure she was even aware of my gesture. I looked over at the broken fireplace. "How did that happen?"

"Look at the state of my kitchen," Marilyn wailed. I reached for a tissue and pressed it into her hand, then looked to my niece for an explanation. Kimberly looked in worse shape than Marilyn, except without the smeared make-up.

"The police started talking on a loudspeaker saying we were surrounded." Kimberly said in a flat tone. "That's when your dad freaked out. He went totally ballistic!" Kimberly finally met my gaze. "He started pounding the glass of the fireplace with his fist but it wouldn't break so he started kicking it. I knew he intended to use the Stone to vanish and he needed a flame. But the glass wouldn't break."

Lox and I both looked at the fireplace where the glass had most definitely been smashed. Someone had already swept the shards into a pile, but there were still jagged pieces stuck to the edges of the hearth's window.

"He moved to the cupboards then," Kimberly continued, "and frantically started opening doors and yelling at us to tell him where the matches were."

"At least you don't have a gas range," I said to Marilyn.

"Our mouths were covered with tape," Marilyn stated in an injured tone as she carefully dabbed at her tears. She didn't realize her mascara was already hopelessly smudged. "So we couldn't answer. Meanwhile, the voice on the bullhorn kept demanding he come out. It was awful."

"Then he found Aunt Marilyn's cast-iron frying pan," Kimberly interjected. "And he used that to smash the glass of the fireplace. But as soon as he did that, the flame whooshed out. He let out this weird yell like *he* was about to combust. I was closest to him and I thought he was going to hit me with that pan, but then the kitchen door crashed open and he fled down the hall."

I glanced over my shoulder at the door of the back stoop, the one Kimberly and I had used on the day of the funeral, a day that seemed a lifetime ago. I saw the doorknob was hanging by a single, loose bolt.

"It wasn't even locked," Marilyn complained.

"And Fredryk?" Lox asked looking from Kimberly to Marilyn. "He is safe?"

I answered for them. "Yes, Lox. Fredryk is safe. He's with Val. I'll take you to him shortly, I promise. The bigger problem is that the Traveler's Stone is in police custody. I'm not sure how to get it back."

"I would have taken the Stone from him if I could have, Aunty Mere," Kimberly said. "But by the time a cop freed me it was too late. I told them though, as soon as I could talk, that he stole my meteorite stone and I wanted it back. I even lied and told them my dad gave it to me just before he died last month." Kimberly bit down on her lip as if she'd just admitted something shameful.

Impressed with my niece's quick thinking, I moved to stand beside her and gave her shoulder a squeeze. "You're so clever, Kimberly. That was brilliant!"

She shook her head. "But it didn't work. The cops said we had to go to the station to sort it out." She removed Fredryk's knotted handkerchief from the pocket of her puffy vest and handed it to me. "At least I still have Old Ethwin's Dust."

I held the knotted handkerchief in my hands. "Thank god you thought to do this, Kimberly." I wasn't sure if it would get the three of us back to the Lands of Vendome, but it might. I carefully tucked it into my jacket pocket.

Kimberly wiped a tear from her cheek with the back of her hand. "This is all my fault. Again." Kimberly's tone echoed the same dejection as the day we'd first disappeared.

"Are you kidding me? How is it your fault that you had the brilliant foresight to file off the Dust? Or, to plant the seed that the Stone belongs to you?" I pulled her against my side again. "You were magnificent. And not a bit of this is your fault." But my reassurances did nothing to alleviate her dejection. "Kimberly," I insisted, pulling out a chair and sitting beside her. "There's nothing for you to feel bad about."

When she met my gaze I saw misery in her eyes. "Actually...there is."

"Don't be ridiculous," Marilyn interjected dismissively from across the table. "The one person who should be apologizing is in the back seat of a police car. And heaven knows he doesn't have a conscience. And apologies don't matter anyway if my kids are...oh God, Meredee! I wish you hadn't called the Mounties."

"I told you, Marilyn," I snapped. "I didn't. I wish you'd believe me."

"Then how did they know he was here? My boys' lives are at stake, remember?"

"Aunt Marilyn," Kimberly said before I could respond. "Aunty Mere didn't call the cops...I did."

We all stared at her in mute astonishment.

"What? When?" I demanded.

Kimberly shrugged. "From the phone in Uncle Jim's study, after I got his file. I called 9-1-1 and left an anonymous tip." Kimberly's eyes welled with fresh tears. "See? All of this *is* my fault."

I understood then why she'd looked so stricken after my father had made his threat about killing Marilyn's children if anyone called the cops.

"Like hell it's your fault." The last thing I wanted was for her to feel guilty about any of this. It was bad enough she blamed herself for her father's death. I took one of her cold hands in mine as I forced her to look me in the eye. "None of this is your fault."

"Kimberly." Lox approached and rested a gentle hand on her shoulder. "You must review the sequence of events logically. Your grandfather attacked all of you before the authorities arrived. Does that not prove you are not to blame for the subsequent turn of events?"

"But as soon as they release him, he's going to kill my cousins. And *that* will be my fault."

"We will not allow that to happen," Lox stated.

It was impossible not to believe him when he spoke in that tone.

"Lox is right, Kimberly." I said. "We'll tell the police everything. They'll throw the book at him on every count imaginable. He'll be in prison for the rest of his miserable life. And we'll get the police to give us his Stone, too. Trust us on this. Everything will be okay."

When I shared a smile with Lox I had no doubt that, together, we could indeed make everything okay.

CHAPTER 29

$\mathcal{O}$ver the course of the next two days I came to realize I'd been utterly naïve thinking we'd be able to claim the Traveler's Stone.

In the end, it was Marilyn who drove Lox to the hospital while Kimberly and I went to the police station. Kimberly tearfully told a convincing tale of how the Stone had been given to her by her recently deceased father, and that her grandfather believed it was something valuable and had forcibly taken it from her. Despite Kimberly's heartbreaking claim, the officers remained immovable. When they told us my father had warned them his family would make a bogus claim on the unusual object, I silently cursed his ultra-intact sense of self-preservation. The police advised us to hire a lawyer and said the courts would have to decide ownership of the contested object.

Kimberly and I then went to the hospital. Val was already checking Fredryk out. He was awake, but groggy and disoriented, and seemed glad for Lox's steadying presence. Iron-red bruises had already spread across his face, making him look ghoulish. While he'd been unconscious, the doctor had realigned and taped his broken nose and confirmed Val's earlier diagnosis of concussion.

We reconvened at Val's house where she settled Fredryk on the long davenport in her living room so she could keep a close eye on him. Marilyn and I got refreshments for everyone, including providing Lox with Curtis's scotch, which he pronounced an equal to his favorite Veldayshyan evening spirits.

The earlier high Lox and I had shared dissipated. Without the Stone in our possession, we weren't sure if the Dust Kimberly had filed was sufficient to propel the three of us back to the Lands of Vendome. Lox theorized that the quantity of Dust Kimberly had accumulated for Old Ethwin could very well be sufficient to propel us back to the Lands of Vendome as it was more than the amount Rikka had used to bring her brother and cousin to our world on that long ago day. But if the Dust did work, I would then be stranded in the Lands of Vendome, albeit, this time by choice.

When I voiced my suspicion that Lox and Fredryk might simply vanish from my world when the power that held them here faded, just like when we were kids, Lox shook his head. He was convinced they would remain because they'd been brought to my world by the actual Traveler's Stone, whose properties of propulsion would be far more powerful, he claimed, than either the Dust or the projection Old Ethwin had helped him create. He added that, when they'd traveled as kids, they'd not only left a drop of their blood in a thimbleful of Dust to 'call' them back, there had been massive meteor showers that had added to the power of the Dust. As none of us had an expert understanding of either the true properties and powers of the Stone or the Dust, our talk was simply speculation. The truth was, we simply wouldn't know until we attempted to 'travel'. And we couldn't do that until Val felt Fredryk was sufficiently recovered.

We discussed what course of action we should take to get possession of the Stone. Val suggested we consult with her brother Theo, a criminal lawyer in Calgary. He could tell us how long my father might be in prison and how we could initiate a legal claim for ownership of the Stone. Early the next morning, I drove with Lox and Kimberly to Calgary to meet Theo. With his advice and guidance—telling him nothing of the Lands of Vendome—we not only agreed to file a suit to claim the Stone for Kimberly, we met with one of his colleagues who dealt with property law so that I could legally transfer all my earthly possessions into my niece's name with Val as legal guardian until Kimberly's eighteenth birthday. I did not have a great deal of money saved, but my townhouse and car were valuable assets. Upon first meeting Theo, the lawyer tried and failed to place Lox's unusual accent. We told him Lox's parents had been diplomats and he'd grown up in half a dozen different countries, which gave him a global mish-mash of an accent.

We'd gone to Calgary on a Friday, and Val's brother, along with a lawyer who was dealing with my property transfer, rushed our requests and had all the paperwork in place by the following Wednesday. Val and Fredryk accompanied us on our second visit. We needed Val to sign the papers and, as Marilyn couldn't get out of teaching her grade three class and Val wasn't willing to leave her patient at home alone, Fredryk came along. Unlike Lox, he wasn't thrilled to be speeding down the highway for the hour-long drive to Calgary, but his discomfort was, at least according to Val, mostly due to his concussion.

Theo told us my father would not be eligible for bail and that, once the case went to court, he would likely be sentenced to anywhere from five to fifteen years. As far as Kimberly's case for possession of the Stone went, this could take as little as three weeks or as long as six months depending on a whole variety of circumstances that were out of our control and hard to predict.

On the drive back to Red Plains, we devised a plan whereby Kimberly, upon being granted ownership of the Stone, would travel to the Lands of Vendome. By that time, she could let us know the length of my father's sentence and, subsequently, how much time was available to us to devise a plan to neutralize his threat against my nephews. I was surprised when Val did not protest Kimberly's plan to return to the Lands of Vendome, and attributed this to her burgeoning friendship with her patient.

Despite our concerns about whether we could successfully propel ourselves back to the Lands of Vendome with the finite amount of Dust in our possession, there was no end to the thrill of spending a week with Lox in my world. The two of us reveled in every moment we had together, whether we were making love or soaking in a bubble bath or sharing hot, steamy showers. For Lox, one of the highlights of being in my world—aside from repeatedly watching, in complete and utter fascination, the speed at which a mug of water could boil in my microwave oven—was on the Sunday morning when I let him take over the 'controls' of my car. Just before dawn, we'd dumped my father's rifle into the nearby river, after which I'd taken us to a deserted parking lot at an office complex. He got the hang of driving surprisingly fast and announced he was ready to tackle the challenge of navigating on proper roads. As much as I delighted in fulfilling his wishes when it came to experiencing the more fascinating aspects of my world, I laughingly refused to accommodate this particular request.

One of the activities that most puzzled Lox—I think Fredryk was in too much of a daze to take it in—occurred on the evening of our first full day in my world shortly after Kimberly, Lox, and I returned from Calgary. Close to one hundred children came 'trick-or-treating' to Val's front door. Characteristically, Lox asked countless questions and even sampled some of Val's Halloween candy although, unlike the Pepsi, he did not develop a taste for the sticky caramels that stuck to his teeth. Val led Fredryk—who groggily expressed curiosity about the costumed children—to her front door. The children were far more awed by his 'awesome Halloween makeup' than Fredryk was by their costumes.

By the seventh day, with all the papers signed and Fredryk on the road to recovery, it was time for us to attempt to use the Dust. As much as Lox was enjoying every moment of discovery in my world, he was equally impatient to return to West Scapah.

Because the coronation celebrations would have long since passed, Lox thought it unlikely there would be another opportunity for me to observe the foreign lord. I wasn't concerned. For practice, I sketched Rodmyrrah repeatedly in that week until I could duplicate his image with practiced ease. I would not take these with me to the Lands of Vendome in case something went wrong and we didn't 'land' at Alberic's estate. I did wrestle with guilt—after all, my images would cause his death—but I did not waver in my commitment to perform this deed. Lox's safety was paramount. Rodmyrrah may have lost his chief assassin, but he could hire another, even one without a rifle. On top of that was the continued threat of civil war. I was willing to live with guilt in order to prevent these outcomes, not only to protect the people of Vendome, but to protect Lox.

On our last afternoon in my world, the six of us were gathered at Val's dining room table. Fredryk still looked like he'd been run over by a semi, but Val had basically discharged him, with the caveat that it would still take weeks for him to fully recover. Val had removed the bandage from his nose, but had bandaged my left hand one last time, stating that the burn was healing nicely. We were drinking our beverage of choice—coffee for me, Pepsi for Lox, and tea for everyone else—as we waited for darkness to fall. If we were successful in traveling, we didn't want to arrive in Alberic's gardens during daylight hours.

Marilyn and I agreed that explaining the real circumstances of my absence to anyone else in our family—my brothers who lived in Ontario with their wives and children, or her husband and sons —would be pointless, at least for the time being. In the meantime, she would tell them, and my boss, that I'd been in contact with her to apologize for my abrupt disappearance and to say I would be traveling for an extended period of time. I knew Marilyn was more than capable of dealing with this aspect of my self-imposed disappearance.

"I still can't believe you're going so far away," Marilyn lamented as she distractedly tapped her painted fingernail against her mug.

The fact that my sister was expressing her discontent with my decision to live with Lox in his world rather than her disbelief that this other world even existed illustrated how she—and Val—had come to accept the truth of our extraordinary circumstances.

"Once you're gone, there won't be any way to contact you. It will feel like you've fallen off the face of the Earth." Marilyn looked at me in wide-eyed consternation. "Literally. That's exactly what you will be doing."

"But *technically*," interrupted Kimberly. "Since it only takes half a second to get there, it's closer than anywhere in this world. Well, after I get the Traveler's Stone," she added.

"Marilyn, I thought you were okay with my decision," I said, after giving Kimberly a quick smile. "I belong with Lox and he belongs in his world. And I told you Lox owns a textile factory. I'll be the first to admit it's not exactly how I pictured my new career unfolding, but I get to share my life with the man I love and learn about an industry that has always interested me. And aside from you three," I nodded to Val, Kimberly, and Marilyn, "there's nothing to keep me here. Besides, once Kimberly has the Stone, we'll see each other regularly. Be happy for me, Marilyn," I pleaded in a soft tone.

My sister grimaced in half-hearted acceptance. "I am happy for you. Really. I'm glad you found someone as nice as Lox." She gave Lox a tremulous smile.

Over the course of the past week, Marilyn's characteristic testiness had softened around Lox and Fredryk. No surprise given the value she placed on manners. They were both men who knew how and when to be chivalrous, polite, and charming. Far more so than any men from my world. At least the ones I'd met. Marilyn had also willingly put her trust in Lox when he promised to protect her sons from our father.

"Despite what Kimberly says, you still don't have the option of hopping on a plane and coming home," Marilyn complained. "What if something goes wrong and you can't ever come back? What if—"

"Of course she's coming back." Kimberly interrupted before my sister could expand on her litany of what-ifs. My niece was almost as eager to return to the Lands of Vendome as Lox was. "Uncle Theo said the ownership of the Stone should be resolved within six months, tops. I'll use it as soon as I get it."

Val looked apprehensive and Kimberly immediately got defensive. "Mom, chill! Planes crash all the time. This type of travel is way safer."

"Honey, that's not why I'm concerned," Val said in a patient tone. "What if the courts decide in favor of your grandfather?" She waved a hand at the rest of us. "I know you're all assuming we'll win this case, and I hope we do," she added with a special smile for Fredryk. "But Marilyn is right. What if we don't?"

Kimberly shrugged. "Then we'll just have to figure something else out. You're always telling me we'll cross that bridge when we get there. So, let's just cross that bridge when we get there. I'll be on Aunty Mere's doorstep before she knows it. And Uncle Lox," she added, smiling at Lox. "Since you two plan to get married, I can call you Uncle Lox, right?"

Lox gave Kimberly an indulgent smile. "It would honor me greatly if you did so." He looked at Val then. "Val-ha-rie, when the Traveler's Stone is granted to Kimberly, there is no reason you cannot accompany your daughter to our Lands. We would be honored to have you as our guest."

Fredryk immediately reinforced Lox's invitation. "Yes. It would give me the opportunity to properly thank you for how well you've taken care of me."

I watched, a little perplexed, as the two of them exchanged an enigmatic look. I also noted the color that crept into Val's cheeks just before she dropped her gaze.

"My invitation extends to you also, Marilyn."

I noticed that Lox seemed oblivious to whatever was going on between Fredryk and Val.

"Oh, no. No, no! Not me." Marilyn waved a finger in emphatic denial. "Meredee, you and Lox, and Fredryk too, can come here as often as you like. But under no circumstances am I doing anything to launch me off this planet any higher than thirty-five thousand feet. Uh-uh. No way."

"Ah, yes," Lox said in a tone of regret. "I have watched these flying machines. And Meredee drove us to the nearby airplane port to watch them lift from the ground and others land, a feat I cannot fathom. I would dearly love to claim personal experience of this flying one day."

Kimberly, who was sitting next to me, briefly leaned her head on my shoulder. "I wish I were going with you. I'm going to miss you so much, Aunty Mere."

I gave her a one-armed hug. "Not half as much as I'm going to miss you. I'll be on the lookout for you every day. Remember, when you use the Stone, hold thoughts of Brebin's cottage in your mind. We'll let him know to expect you."

Once we had the Stone in our possession, I knew I would have the option of visiting my world as often as I liked—within the frequency parameters of what my father had discovered was safe.

And then it was time for us to say our goodbyes. Marilyn clung to me, weeping a little, and I felt a surge of love for my abrasive, well-intentioned sister. I really would miss her. I embraced Val affectionately, and profusely thanked her again for all she was doing to support Kimberly's efforts to claim the Stone. But when I bid farewell to my niece, I couldn't speak and I could no longer hold back my tears. On impulse, I removed the shell necklace Julitha had made and draped it around Kimberly's neck.

And then Fredryk, Lox, and I were kneeling in front of Val's wood-burning fire in her living room. The logs crackled cheerily as if sharing our anticipation of our other worldly adventure. We wore our Vendome clothes, although Lox and Fredryk were missing their swords, weapons they would never see again. I did not attempt to bring any earthly belongings as we couldn't risk having extra objects along that might jeopardize the power of our limited supply of Dust. I was on Lox's right with the arm of my bandaged hand entwined firmly with his. Fredryk mirrored my position on Lox's left. We intended to mentally picture the largest fountain in the courtyard of Alberic's home in hopes of projecting ourselves to this familiar place that was so fresh in our memories.

I turned to take a last look at the women of my family. They were hovering at the entrance to the living room. As I met Kimberly's tear-filled gaze, she raised a hand and smiled tremulously at me. Then, with blurred vision, I turned toward the flames of the crackling fire.

"Okay, let's do this," I said.

Lox had knotted and folded the handkerchief containing the Dust so that it mirrored the shape of the Traveler's Stone. We each held a portion of it as we inched it toward the fire. When my hand got close to the flames, I had to forcibly resist the impulse to jerk away from the heat.

As soon as the handkerchief made direct contact with the flame there was a white flash and, for a split second, the now familiar sensation of being in a high-speed elevator. In the next heartbeat we found ourselves kneeling in the darkness on flagstones near the large fountain that gurgled in Alberic and Lita's courtyard. Light from the tall windows of the palatial home stretched toward us across the manicured lawn like welcoming homing beacons. I let the scrap of lawn cloth—all that was left of the handkerchief—flutter to the ground and then fell into Lox's arms.

We were both weeping. We'd succeeded! The future was now ours to shape and cherish. The relief and joy I felt in that moment was so strong it was almost tangible. While Lox held me like he would never let me go, I heard a faint echo of a husky-voiced singer float as if on a residual breeze from my world to this one. *At Last.* At last I had opened my heart. At last I had found the person with whom I would share my life. At last I was home.

At last.

EPILOGUE

 ore than five years have passed since the day Fredryk, Lox, and I appeared in Alberic's garden; five long years and still no visit from Kimberly.

Upon our return to the Lands of Vendome, everything went as Lox planned. In the safety and shelter of the cloth merchant's home, I drew multiple sketches of the foreign lord. Lox and Fredryk lacquered each portrait onto thin wooden boards and then had them secretly posted in the dead of night at various prominent locations throughout the city.

While the Priests of the Temple of the Gods were predictably enraged by what they believed was the foreign lord's impudent audacity, the inhabitants of the city—including Rodmyrrah's Vendome sycophants—were horror-struck that the foreign lord would be so foolhardy as to break a sacred taboo and publically declare himself an equal to the gods. Those citizens who'd been supportive of Rodmyrrah, either openly or secretly, scrambled to change their allegiance and convince their colleagues and neighbors they'd never truly aligned him.

Within a day of posting the images, the fierce-looking Warriors who served the Priests rode through the streets of West

Scapah on huge, intimidating black warhorses. Soon after, they had the foreign lord in their custody. Despite his vociferous protests of innocence, Rodmyrrah was publicly beheaded the next morning.

Even all these years later, I still shudder at the thought of my role in the man's execution. I have endured many a sleepless night, not on account of the fear of being apprehended as the image-maker, but on account of my own arrogant audacity of taking the fate of another human being into my hands. Regardless, I have also come to know that my actions served my adopted country well. The intensity of my guilt has faded as peace and prosperity once again bless these Lands. More importantly, I know that because of my actions, founded or unfounded, the man I love is no longer the target of an assassin, whether that role be played by my father or some other hireling.

After condemning Rodmyrrah to death, the Priests of the Temple of the Gods launched a search for the image-maker even though they'd already concluded—correctly—that the perpetrator could not possibly be a native of the Lands of Vendome. Unable to conclusively identify the culprit, they banished the remaining Veil of Mist foreigners, giving them two days to ready their ships for departure.

A handful of Vendome people chose to depart with the banished delegation, likely because they knew their public affiliation with the executed foreign lord now made them pariahs in the Lands of Vendome. I did not go to the riverbank to witness their departure, but I was told every inhabitant of the city lined both sides of the river to observe the spectacle. For weeks after this unprecedented event, people regaled each other with stories of watching the haughty Toriah board one of the ships on the arm of the Earl of Avercorris, with Lord Conraz and the traitorous Chancellor of the Western Duchy, who'd been a toady of Rodmyrrah's since the beginning, trailing behind.

Before dawn on the day following the foreign fleet's departure,

Fredryk, Lox, and I left the city in disguise and rode into the same forest into which I had first seen my father disappear. We emerged at dawn, making it look as if we'd been traveling for weeks and had just now arrived in West Scapah. To make sure I was recognized, I wore the distinctive silk dress and the black wig. Lita's personal maid had spent considerable time camouflaging the fading bruises that still marred Fredryk's face. My two companions, dressed in the finest clothes Alberic could provide, looked imposing, authoritative, and, more importantly, official. As we rode past the spot where my horse had been killed, I tensed, half expecting to hear the resounding echo of a bullet, but this time we made our way without mishap into the city. As expected, I was quickly identified as the rumored companion to Lord Loxley who'd enchanted her audience in Ballindale and who was finally arriving in West Scapah. As such, our passage drew a growing number of enthusiastic followers.

When we finally entered the royal compound in the Inner City, we found it in complete chaos after the hurried exit of the foreign delegation. Lox timed our arrival perfectly, as not one person defied him when he claimed command of the Western Duchy on behalf of the Grand Duke who had fallen into a coma.

Lox chose to publicize what had been done to the Grand Duke. In response, the inhabitants of the Western Duchy rallied for their ailing leader. For a week Jaybex did not stir despite the expert attention of numerous medical practitioners. Then, when he did finally wake, he was weak and confused, and his memory of the last three years vague and sporadic.

Jaybex's convalescence was excruciatingly slow. Six full months passed before he was well enough to resume the lightest of his obligations. Two long-term consequences of the mind-weaver's spell would always remain with Jaybex; his formerly jet-black hair had turned completely white during his coma and, where once he'd been friendly and outgoing, he was now quiet, contemplative, analytical, and slow to laughter. Regardless, we were all relieved he was of sound mind and would, with time, resume all his duties.

On the off-chance my father would one day make his way back to the Lands of Vendome, Lox also made a public proclamation that the man who'd called himself a Traveler had, in fact, been an imposter hired by Lord Rodmyrrah. A warrant was issued for his arrest, although that was entirely for show. We did not expect to see him in these Lands ever again. When Fredryk searched my father's Vendome home, he found the remaining components of the sniper's rifle as well as a pistol and ammunition. Upon our return to Hawkwood Heath, Lox hid these weapons in a secret compartment in our bedchamber.

One of the greatest delights during those first months of living at the Royal Residence in West Scapah was my belated reunion with Rikka. She arrived three weeks after Rodmyrrah's death and was overjoyed to finally visit with her convalescent twin. And although her official duties kept her busy from dawn until dusk, she spared time to visit with me. We quickly and easily renewed the friendship that had begun all those years before. I grew to love and admire her even more than I had as a child. I was also able to laugh about how angry I'd been to learn of her ruthless decision to Call me to these Lands. As often happens with hindsight, I was able to bless past events, recognizing they'd placed me on the path to this, my satisfying life. I also came to greatly admire and love Rikka's consort and husband, a soft-spoken man named Corian. He was loyal and pragmatic, and could not have been a better support for the woman he adored.

Upon her arrival, Rikka's first order of business was to appoint a new Chancellor in the Western Duchy, a position left vacant when the foreign flotilla departed with the traitors loyal to Lord Rodmyrrah. On the recommendation of Lox and her other advisors, she appointed Alberic. After signing over his cloth merchant business to his grown children, he and Lita made their home with Lox and me in the Royal Residence where he took to this difficult and important role with great alacrity. In those first hectic months, I was immeasurably grateful for Lita's close proximity and friendship, for I relied heavily on her to teach me the necessary protocols that came with being the 'intended' of the Chancellor of the Eastern Duchy.

A further delight for me in those first months was taking the time to examine the gifts that had been given to me at the Cast Away ceremony. To this day, I treasure each and every one. I was also elated to discover that Lita's maid had successfully removed the bloodstains from my beautiful peacock shawl. I wear it frequently, as do many Vendome women. It seems they regularly copy my style of dress, whether my peacock-themed shawl or my slim, manly looking trousers that I wear for riding.

During the six months that Lox and I lived in West Scapah awaiting Jaybex's recovery, we exchanged numerous lengthy letters with Brebin. Although he grieved for the wife he'd adored, I was relieved he was playing an active role in raising his four children, including the baby Singer. After hearing Kimberly's account of her last moments in the felter's cottage, I'd been concerned that the grief-stricken man would reject the child whose birth had resulted in Shulha's devastating death. Unfortunately, Lox and I did not have the opportunity to reunite with him until after Jaybex resumed his duties as Grand Duke and we could finally travel back to the Eastern Duchy. Three years later, Kennan took over the operation of the felter's mill, and Brebin and his children finally returned to Hawkwood Heath. They are, as Lox claimed, like family to us.

Six weeks after our return to West Scapah, Jazper joined us. He continues to live with Lox and me as a member of our family. In fact, the boy has become an unexpected and added joy in my life, in large part because he never tires of talking of Kimberly. I dote on him as if he were a favorite nephew. We are all thankful his hands fully healed, and we credit Aster for her proficient medical skills and her exceptional devotion, without which his full recovery would not have been possible.

A week after Jazper's arrival, Lox received a missive from the High Priest of Sherha's Mound on the Isle of Mathe. In it, the High Priest officially granted Lox's request to sever his marriage union with Toriah on account of her public affiliation with the disgraced foreign lord. Not long after and with much public fanfare, Lox and I officially entered our marriage union. Initially, I'd wanted to delay until Kimberly arrived so that she could be a part of our big day, but Lox had looked so forlorn when I suggested postponing that I let it go. Five and a half years have passed since our return to the Lands of Vendome, and there is still no sign of Kimberly, so it was just as well we did not wait.

Fredryk, of course, remains Lox's constant and devoted companion. As such, I see him daily. We have managed to develop a friendship of sorts although, not infrequently, we also manage to grate on each other's nerves. Shortly after settling in at Hawkwood Heath—and after having discovered that Julitha would occasionally use her skill to allow me to see Kimberly—he asked me, with uncharacteristic nervousness, after Kimberly's well-being. I was initially puzzled by his unusual behavior until he rather awkwardly asked if I also saw Kimberly's mother. Until that conversation, I'd forgotten about the friendship Fredryk and Val had forged. It struck me then that he might have been longing for Kimberly's visit in hopes of renewing his acquaintance with my sister-in-law. I regretfully informed him that I had not ever seen Val. I was tempted to ask him about his feelings for her, but I knew he would not welcome this invasion of privacy. Regardless, I have come to truly value Fredryk's continued devotion to my husband, and I hold the man in much higher esteem now than I did during that first month traveling through the Lands of Vendome.

Over the course of my sojourn in these Lands, my dearest friend outside of Lox has become Julitha. She traveled to West

Scapah to join us in celebrating our marriage union. It was then I took her into my confidence, telling her about my years of trying and failing to conceive. She provided a special mix of herbs and assured me motherhood was in my future. I knew I could trust and believe her, so I put my worries on this matter aside. Although I would like her to permanently join us at the court in East Scapah or at our palatial mansion at Hawkwood Heath, Julitha prefers to remain in her cottage by the sea. I make do with regular visits and frequent letters, and am delighted when she finds time to visit in person. Interestingly, Julitha and Lox's relationship mirrors mine and Fredryk's. I value Fredryk for the loyalty and friendship he freely gives to my husband, and Lox feels the same regarding my friendship with Julitha.

About six months after our return to the Lands of Vendome, Julitha learned that Hiltha passed away. I still feel a little sad that I never had a chance to reconnect with that old woman who'd so startled me on my first day in these Lands. Periodically, Julitha will help me to 'see' Kimberly. The last few times I saw my niece she was wearing a police officer's uniform. I would never have guessed Kimberly would choose a career in law enforcement, and this knowledge has left me deeply puzzled. The process of allowing me to see Kimberly is exceptionally taxing for the Diviner. Since I can neither communicate with my niece nor allay the anxiety about these unknowns, I now very rarely ask for Julitha's aid in this manner.

I sometimes wonder if the reason for Kimberly's long absence is because my father has been released from prison and has the Stone in his possession. Lox tells me my fears are unfounded, and that news would come to him if there was any indication a person matching my father's description lives in or journeys through the Lands of Vendome. I can only hope Lox is right and that my nephews are alive and safe, but there are times when I am frustrated beyond measure at Kimberly's continued absence, for I am feverishly impatient for her return.

One of the delights of living in these beautiful Lands with Lox has been involving myself in his textile design and manufacturing enterprise. The overseers and artisans were initially suspicious of my participation, but soon came to appreciate how passionate I am about all aspects of this industry. They have since generously taught me much. I am still learning, and get great satisfaction from my involvement in this endeavor. An unexpected outcome is that any textile or fabric touted as my design always becomes wildly popular. I am thrilled I helped make this endeavour not only more lucrative, but one that provides a good livelihood for many families. I've kept my 'Bellecourt clothes' thinking one day I may need to visit my world, but I also endeavour to manufacture a match to the quality of my beautiful Italian wool-blend skirt. So far, I have not been successful.

In the years since returning to the Lands of Vendome, I have become a figure of fame not only on account of my being the wife of the Chancellor of the Eastern Duchy, but also because of my status as Traveler—despite not having the means to 'travel'. I am alternately referred to as either the Lady Meredith or, more formally, Lady Chancellor. Rather astonishingly—at least to me— I have also become affectionately known as The Enchantress. I dislike this appellation, but it grew from tales of my ability to 'enchant' my audience with my voice. It has become an annual tradition for me to don the black wig—most people here assume I need it to sing—on Cast Away night and perform in the market square of East Scapah. I am told that people travel hundreds of miles just to hear me sing. Each year, the audience grows larger.

During my first months at Hawkwood Heath, I offered to give singing lessons to anyone interested in learning. Although I had many pupils, it was greatly disappointing to discover that, like Lox, not one of them had the capacity or the ability to carry a tune. I have since abandoned my dream of introducing the inhabitants of the Lands of Vendome to the joy of lending one's voice to song. Instead, I satisfy myself with integrating into my performances the limited number of percussion instruments used in these Lands. Although it is always a pleasure to perform once a year for an appreciative audience, my closest friends and family are really the only audience I need. One of my deepest regrets is failing to bring song lyrics with me from my world. But if I cannot remember the lyrics of a favorite melody, I do not hesitate to craft new words.

When Lox and I first arrived at Hawkwood Heath, he showed me the secret compartment in his bedchamber where he kept my sketchbook and where the guns Fredryk confiscated from my father's home were housed. I immediately insisted he burn the book as well as the Polaroid photograph that he still kept tucked away in its leather wallet like a treasured talisman. Although he agreed to burn the sketchbook, he adamantly and vociferously refused to destroy the Polaroid. He argued that if he could successfully keep such a small item secret for the last twenty years, then there was no reason why he could not continue to do so with equal success for the foreseeable future.

I was not willing to take this chance with my husband's life, not after the gruesome death of Rodmyrrah at the hands of the Warriors. As a result, since Lox refused to destroy the Polaroid himself, I took it upon myself to obliterate it from this world. In the dark of night, with Lox sleeping soundly next to me, I crept out of bed and stealthily retrieved the Polaroid from its secret hide-away. I took a last long look at the images captured on film that magical day in another world, and then tiptoed into my dressing room where a fire had been left burning in the hearth. With one last perusal, I tossed the photo into the flames. I suffered only a few minor qualms as I watched it melt.

In the morning I informed my husband, albeit with a significant degree of trepidation, that I'd destroyed the polaroid, stating I hadn't chosen to live in this world with him only to have him killed. My confession sparked a vehement and heated quarrel where both of us hurled hateful words at each other. Lox berated me as if I were a stupid child and I, hurt and indignant, made a comment I'll always regret about how it was no wonder Toriah had found living with him insufferable. In obstinate self-righteousness, we stopped speaking to one another. We were foul-tempered for days to the extent that our household staff tiptoed around us. Fredryk and Jazper even made themselves scarce by concocting a trumped up excuse to visit Brebin and his family. Julitha had not been with us at that time and, for those few days of wounded silence between us, I felt desperately alone and bereft of love and friendship.

By the third day of our prolonged battle of wills, I discovered two things about myself that motivated me to repair my relationship with my husband. The first was my acceptance that, because I might never see Kimberly—or anyone in my family—ever again, I needed my friend and lover to be my comfort during hard times, not someone who contributed to my loneliness. The second thing was the realization that my loss of appetite and nausea were not on account of my depressed emotional state but on account of my first pregnancy, a condition that likely contributed to my irrational behavior. I decided to share my newfound knowledge with my husband in a manner that also relayed my sincere and heartfelt apology, not for burning the Polaroid, but for saying hurtful things in anger. I hoped—expected—that news about my longed-for pregnancy would go a long way in repairing the damage my harsh insults had caused.

Previously, Lox had given me a number of tray-sized slates and a wide variety of colored chalk that I often used to sketch out textile designs and color schemes. Sometimes, and only if I was certain I would not be disturbed, I would sketch Kimberly, and even Marilyn or Val, and then erase the image before anyone could discover my act of heresy. The day I realized I was pregnant, I decided to draw not only a replica of the Polaroid on one slate, but a nude self-portrait showing me heavily pregnant on another.

When Lox came into our bedchamber later that day and I wordlessly showed him what I'd drawn, he dropped to his knees beside me and practically wept. I stroked his hair and, through my tears, apologized profusely. Since then, although Lox and I certainly squabble and argue, we have never again fought so heatedly or hurled hateful words at each other. Nor will we ever, for I could not bear to live in these Lands I now call home without his ever-present love and support.

There are two things I desperately miss from my world. The first, obviously, is music. The second, surprisingly, is air conditioning. The summers in the Lands of Vendome are exceptionally hot and humid. Although Lox owns a lovely holiday cottage on the seaside, a 'machine that makes the air cool' would be a welcome reprieve, especially for those summer months when my pregnancies made the heat intolerable.

Eleven months after establishing our home at Hawkwood Heath and seventeen months after leaving my world, we welcomed our most precious baby girl. I'd been sick with worry remembering Shula's ordeal, but my delivery went very well. We named our daughter Kimberly, but somehow started calling her Kimly as a baby, and that name stuck. Two months ago we rejoiced at the birth of our healthy baby boy. I'd wondered if Lox would want to name him Axel in memory of his first son, but he suggested Curtix, a name I still find utterly delightful.

Since the arrival of our second baby, my thoughts seem to drift more and more often to my niece. Where is she, and why hasn't she come? A week ago, perhaps because of these thoughts, I woke from a dream where Kimberly and I had been sitting on a giant replica of the Traveler's Stone. We seemed to be by a body of water but, as usual with dreams, details were vague. At the time, I dismissed it, although the good feeling of being on an adventure with Kimberly lingered with me for days.

Two days ago, while nursing the baby in our bedchamber and feeling the wash of contentment that so often comes on such occasions, my thoughts drifted to the mysteries of this other worldly travel that had transformed my life. I pictured that small lakeside beach where Kimberly and me had first arrived in the forested lands north of the Avercorris hunting lodge, and I suddenly realized something I should have grasped years ago. I jerked up and shouted for Lox who was dozing on our big bed less than ten feet away from me. After reassuring my startled husband that no catastrophe had occurred and simultaneously calming my crying baby and encouraging him to resume nursing, I described to Lox how the boulder upon which Kimberly had sat seemed to have been cleaved open like an egg, and that it had a dark, pit-like stone embedded deep within it. I also added that, when his hologram had appeared above that boulder, its clarity had been exceptional.

Lox understood immediately that this dark stone could be the remains of a meteorite that had likely slammed into the beach during that summer when the Lands of Vendome had experienced unprecedented meteor showers. Potentially, that small, dark stone could hold the same powers as the Traveler's Stone. He immediately sent Fredryk and Jazper to investigate.

It will take a week, perhaps longer, for them to return. There is only a slim chance that our idea has merit, but I am now filled with hope that, if Kimberly cannot come to us, perhaps we can go to her.

In a few days, Lox and I will be traveling to the Astromancer's estate for the inauguration of the new Astromancer following Old Ethwin's death. Perhaps, by the time we return, Fredryk will have brought good news.

Despite having spent the last five-and-a-half years longing for a visit from Kimberly, I can say with absolute certainty that I am truly delighted with the life Lox and I have carved out in the Lands of Vendome. Lox is a faithful and devoted husband. Moreover, he is an incredible, amazing, patient, and loving father to our two children. I love and respect him more now than I did five years ago when I chose to return to these Lands with him. My children are a joy and a blessing to me, even during those frequent times when my bright and precocious daughter tries my patience. The abiding and overwhelming love that flows forth from within me like a gushing spring when I look upon my children sometimes takes my breath away. They instill within me a kind of love I find impossible to describe, and yet...

And yet I yearn for the company of my niece.

To soothe the ache of her absence, I frequently tell tales of 'the other Kimberly' to my daughter. For Kimly, my niece has become the heroine of her favorite fairy tales.

One day—maybe sooner rather than later if Fredryk's mission is a success—I shall see Kimberly again. When that day comes, when my devoted husband, my delightful children, and my beloved niece surround me, then I will know the fulfillment true happiness brings.

And then, *at last,* my joy will finally be complete.

ACKNOWLEDGMENTS

I owe a debt of appreciation to many family and friends who have, over the years, been supportive and interested in what I was writing. I especially want to thank my wonderful sisters Anita Moes, Grace Berkenbosch, and Gwen Bosch (Gwen, you rock!); my very dear friend Angie Neal who read multiple rough drafts (and delighted me by describing Lox as "yummy"); my niece Esther Moes whose insightful feedback enhanced the story; my friend Renee Hawk Lewis who was refreshingly enthusiastic about the story; to my friend and talented graphic designer Jina Mousseau for delivering wonderful visual art; to my friend and gifted writer A.K. White for her unstinting support; and to my fellow story-teller friend Jeannette Bedard for paving the way to indie-publishing..

Mostly, I appreciate you readers. Thank you for joining Meredith and Kimberly on their adventure!

ALSO BY CORINNE AARSEN

The Travelers' Chronicles series:

The Reluctant Traveler

The Traveler's Stone

The Reluctant Thief (forthcoming autumn 2019)

The Ordinary Immigrant series (forthcoming late 2018):

The Ordinary Immigrant – New Beginnings

The Ordinary Immigrant – Promises Kept

AFTERWORD

Thank you for reading *The Traveler's Stone*. And a special thanks, too, for your reviews and for telling your friends about the book. If you liked the first two books of this series, I hope you'll enjoy Book III, *The Reluctant Thief*, which will be available for purchase in the fall of 2019.

If you want to contact me, you can email me through my website, CorinneAarsenBooks.com.

Thanks for reading!

Made in the USA
Middletown, DE
06 December 2018